B.C. CROW

THE NEPHILIM CONSPIRACY

BLUE HOUSE PUBLISHING

This book is a work of fiction. This book is derived from the imagination of the author. If any parallels to actual people, places, businesses, or institutions is present, it is used fictitiously and or is purely coincidental.

BLUE HOUSE PUBLISHING

11 N. 500 W.
Springville, UT 84663

Picture of Earth: Courtesy of Nasa

For information regarding bulk purchases, send a request to Blue House Publishing, or email us at BCCrow@BlueHPublishing.com

First print run August 2015 by Blue House Publishing

1 2 3 4 5 6 7 8 9 10

ISBN-10: 1-943239-04-5

ISBN-13: 978-1-943239-04-7

Library of Congress Control Number: 2015909480

Books by

B.C. Crow

<u>Nephilim Series</u>

Nephilim Device: Book 1

Nephilim Effect: Book 2

Nephilim Conspiracy: Book 3

To follow B.C. Crow

Visit www.BlueHPublishing.com

To special order bulk shipments for promos, premiums, or fundraisers

Email your requests on the Contacts page of our website.

Special thanks to all my readers who not only have given me, a budding new author, a chance, but who've also shared your excitement for these books with all your friends.

My success is entirely due to you.

Chapter 1

August 5
Present day

1 day after the eco-terrorist attack on the world's oil supply chains.

The political, albeit amiable atmosphere of the congregation was much more hospitable than the raging protestors outside. This was partly due to courtesy and partly due to planning. The President of the United States took the podium. Cameras flashed, and a nation waited for him to begin his statement to the nation. A speech originally had been prepared for today, but was addressing a different political issue. That speech was scrapped last night after news broke about a terror attack, one that crippled the world's oil supply and shocked the world.

"My fellow Americans, I address you tonight not

as Republicans or as Democrats but as fellow Americans"—(applause)—"brothers and sisters, sons and daughters of this great nation." (applause) "Once upon a day, monarchs and leaders depended on their own abilities to provide succor to their citizens. Trade was common among neighboring nations, though a severed relationship would not have destroyed them. As of late, specialization of regions, along with global dependence on trade, has significantly changed the dynamic of world affairs. A shock in one country can produce tremors felt around the planet.

"While one country may hold the market on information, another might be rich in raw materials. Just as one country has an abundance of labor-intensive jobs, another might rely entirely on the distribution of such goods. Regardless of geography or wealth, all nations that aspire to having a thriving economy depend on a few key resources. The one that has come under hot debate in recent years has been the ever-powerful battery, which comes in the form of oil.

"This battery spurs transportation. Both commuting and shipping rely heavily on it. Manufacturing of nearly every good in the world somehow requires the use of this precious resource. If one were to take a look around, one would find it difficult to ignore the influence of oil in nearly every aspect of our lives.

"To this end, we have consigned our fate. Yesterday, a group of unknown eco-terrorists struck not only our nation, but the entire global supply chain for oil. Despite our best efforts to combat terrorism, they managed to elude us all. It is my regrettable position to announce that the state of our great nation is not what we would prefer. However, I say this with the hope that we can all come together to overcome this hurdle that has been placed before us." (weak applause) "The United States of America is built upon something greater than oil. It is built upon the backs of courageous and innovative men and women"—(applause)—"people who came to a wild land and overcame all obstacles"—(applause)—"a people who had a dream, and found a way to make that dream come true"—(applause)—"a people whose descendants we are!" (wild applause)

"Now this crisis is not limited to our great nation; most countries have been affected by it. There will be shortages and rationings that must take place while we develop and expand our own oil resources. I ask you all to not only look after your own affairs with wisdom, but to also look after your neighbor. In a few places, mostly outside of our country, martial law has been enacted. We must prove that we are better than this." (applause) "I strongly encourage all people to behave in an orderly manner while we work our way through this time of difficulty. Riots and hoarding will not help us through this. Only by hard work and rational activities will we move forward." (applause)

"As with all crises that come, this too will pass. When it does, it will leave us all transformed in some way. For some, it will be to their detriment, both in circumstance and, more important, in character. The better part of us will find the strength of character that in some cases we didn't even know we possessed. Those of us who do, will be the ones who benefit most from this situation." (weak applause)

"And though the times look formidable, I want to assure you that I will do everything in my power to get us through. As many of you know, when our strategic oil reserves were hit and most of the supply chains cut us off from imported oil, our financial markets began to crash. Therefore, pending a little more stability and reflection, our stock markets have been temporarily frozen." (silence)

"As for our fiscal house, we will still honor our debt obligations, as we encourage all to honor their personal debt as well. While it is true that foreign investment in our government may shrink as countries focus their financial efforts on repairing their own countries, we still encourage them to handle their finances responsibly." (weak applause)

"This shall be the moment of truth for our generation." (applause) "Our children and their children will look back on us with respect, admiration, and pride." (applause) "We will rise from this, becoming a better nation than we have ever been." (applause) "We must move forward, developing renewable sources of energy. For the first time ever, renewable energy is more attractive an investment than relying on oil. I hope that while we are having a shortage of oil, we will take advantage of this and look at it not as a curse but as an opportunity." (strong applause)

"However, our need for oil will not go away. As our imports of oil have stopped, we must rely solely on our domestic production. Some countries will be less affected, especially those in the Middle East that have traditionally been large exporters of oil. As soon as they are able to overcome their distribution problems, they have assured me that they will strive to find ways of moving the oil abroad again. In the meantime, we will endeavor to fast-track our own domestic production. Permits that had previously been held back will all be reconsidered." (partisan applause)

"Some of our fellow nations have succumbed to violence as a means of protecting their interests.

Some of our allied nations will also struggle without the necessary aide that we have traditionally been able to give them. Our thoughts and prayers go out to them. As we work to strengthen our own country, I have issued an order to recall all of our troops abroad. They will still serve actively, protecting the rights and interests of everyone here at home. I will also be working with Congress to suspend all foreign aid, as we try to reduce our budget deficits." (applause)

The president continued for a little longer, discussing various matters that were being highlighted in the news. Most of these revolved around the oil crisis. He also vowed that those responsible would not go unpunished, even though, as he failed to mention, he didn't have a clue yet as to who he was even looking for.

Then as the applause for his closing remarks died down and he left the stage, he was ushered away with the first lady. "That was a good speech," she commented.

"As good, I suppose, as can be expected, given the circumstances," he responded. "The sad part is, though I talked the good talk, I truly am worried. I'm afraid that a lot of people are going to be hurt pretty badly. It will take a miracle to come out of this in one piece."

She put her hand in his, and the rest of the trip back to the White House was quiet as she left him to his thoughts.

Chapter 2

The room was dark. A hypnotic hum came from the air conditioner below the only window in the motel room. Dusty rolled over in bed, her body still ached. She wanted to turn the air conditioner off, because even while it was somewhat hypnotic, it was just loud enough to keep her from falling back to sleep. But that would require getting out of the rented bed. To get out of bed would be to forfeit the comforting pug her body had created under the quilt. The sacrifice was not desirable. Sleep had been too hard to come by last night.

Instead, Dusty pulled the blanket over her head and tried to ignore the sound. She doubted that she'd slept at all. Last time she looked at the clock, it registered 3:00 am. Before that, she'd been tossing and turning. She'd had a lot of bad days in her life, most of which had been with a man named Marshall Steel. He was an anthropologist like her, well, not like her. He was a grave-robber and murderer. She'd fallen for him at the beginning when, under the employ of a Chinese investor, they'd looked for and eventually exhumed the remains of an ancient Martian spaceship. But as she came to know the criminal, she found herself trapped. That was until the day that Flint had come into her life. Sure, she'd nearly caused his death in the beginning. But now...

Stop thinking! She scolded herself. This was the reason she hadn't slept most of the night. Her mind was racing too much. But the reprimand was futile. Once a mind is racing, it's hard to pit again.

Yes, yesterday had to of been my worst day, she reckoned. Not only had she discovered that Flint was still married, but he still might have feelings for his wife. As she understood it, Flint's wife had run out on him two years ago, never to make contact again. Then on a whim, right when everything was starting to look good for herself and the first decent man she'd met in years, he thinks he saw his wife. So dragging Dusty from the Philippines, away from a paradisiacal vacation with a man of extraordinarily good potential, Flint brought her back to Egypt. But the *magic* just kept going from there.

After arriving, she, Flint, and one other companion, an autistic Bible quoting Mexican named Monk, split up in search for Flint's wife. Not only had Dusty not wanted to find the woman, but she alone did, and what a mess that turned into. She could still feel the bruises. It was a wonder that Lydia, Flint's wife, hadn't killed her.

Rolling back again, Dusty decided to look at the digital clock on the nightstand. If last time she'd checked, it had been 3:00 am, she was sure that it would now be no later than 3:30 am. What she saw however, didn't make sense. 10:30 am. Dusty pulled the blankets over her head. Her head was still a little foggy. *It can't be that late. The clock is off, it has to be. It's still dark. But how could the clock be wrong. The curtains,* she realized. They were thick enough to block all light. She still felt exhausted, but her mouth held the stale taste of morning breath.

"Ugh," she grunted as she threw off the blankets. She lay there for another moment, still in her clothes from the night before. They were clammy from her night sweat, made worse by the tossing and turning. With strained willpower, she clicked on the TV and stepped into the bathroom to freshen up.

The shower helped clear her head. It felt good to be clean again, even if only to don her dirty clothes right after. As she stepped back into the bedroom, using a cheap complimentary toothbrush to scrape away at her morning breath, she caught the breaking news on the TV. She nearly swallowed her toothpaste when the reporter announced the terror attack.

Apparently yesterday, an eco-terrorist organization hit the entire world's oil reserves and supply chains. They'd put some form of bacteria into the oil, solidifying it into a permanent rubber-like substance. Pipelines were completely gummed up, reserves and tanks literally had turned solid over the course of a single night. *This is the oil age. Everything depends on the stuff. Even if we've made strides in other energy sources, that is just a tiny drop in the big black energy bucket that we dip from. This would change everything.*

With eyes glued to the TV and a little toothpaste threatening to drip out of her mouth, Dusty saw something that actually did make her swallow her minty foam. Her eyes popped wide open from the TV, and watered from the burning sensation that was now freshening her throat. On the screen, a video of Flint and Lydia was shown, not fully condemning them as the criminals, but surely hinting at the crime as they were escorted by police into waiting vans. True, Dusty had seen this scene transpire last night with her own eyes, even if from a distance. But the way the camera crew showed it, Flint looked pretty guilty. Dusty could hardly believe that the two incidents were even connected. Not only were the incidents related, but her Flint was being paraded around on international news as one of the perpetrators of the crime. Dusty could care less about Lydia. For all she knew, Lydia might have been the mastermind behind the attack. But Flint!

Dusty dashed back to the bathroom to spit and rinse. In an instant she was back to watching the TV. She hadn't realized the significance of the firefight that Flint had gotten in the middle of last night. They were at ground zero for the attack. Everything had been coordinated and executed from that office building where the news was placing Flint at. She hoped that he could be exonerated. There was only one thing to do. Sure she hadn't known Flint for very long, but he was her man. This Lydia was obviously not worthy of such as he. Dusty had to go to the police and vouch for Flint.

Dusty finished pulling on her shoes, and was about to run over to find a taxi to the police station when the reporter showed some alarming figures. Since the whole world had been targeted, chaos was spreading quickly. She realized how bad the situation was. The whole world seemed to be coming to an end. No taxi would be running. She'd have to walk.

Chapter 3

Despite the gloom of recent events, the sun was shining brightly, and high stratus clouds were whisking gently across the Egyptian sky like bleached sand blowing off the top of a towering dune. The only sound besides the footsteps of this new team was the occasional squawk of some sea bird scavenging near the shore. Flint's heavy breathing seemed to intrude on the afternoon calm as he and the others hiked up the steep ramp leading away from the docks.

Flint and Lydia were no longer at the police station. After one night in police custody, and a visit to a very well connected albeit strange and mysterious man named Fran, who'd brought them onto his sailboat, they were sent on their way to find a new source of energy. This new energy source was meant to restore some hope for surviving the social heart attack that was crippling the world.

"So this girl, Dusty, you like her?" Lydia asked

Flint, trying to sound nonchalant but failing.

Flint thought for a moment and answered carefully, "We just met. She was part of my last adventure, right before I discovered that you were somehow involved in all of this."

"So tell me about this last adventure of yours," Lydia said. Any idiot could tell that she wasn't referring to his capture by the eco-terrorist Amos, or about near death encounters in the Philippines. The only story Lydia wanted to know about concerned his relationship with this woman who'd nearly gotten him killed.

"Huh," he breathed, remembering the helicopter ride he'd had last time he was in Egypt.

"What's so funny?"

"Oh nothing," Flint said. His mouth twisted in a fake smile. There had been nothing funny about that day Lydia had shot him down. Of course she hadn't known at the time that Flint was in the chopper.

Lydia wasn't satisfied. "Does it have to do with this adventure?"

"No, it's just that the only two women in my life, both tried to kill me in one week."

"So Dusty is a *part* of your life?"

"There will be plenty of time for that." Flint diverted the conversation. "Right now we need to focus on actually finding her."

"What about our mission?" Labeeb asked as he broke into the conversation.

To which Flint replied, "I brought Dusty here from the Philippines, and I'm not about to abandon her; at least not like this. Besides, she happens to be one of the foremost experts on Arabian archeology. I can only imagine that would benefit our little endeavor here. She's spent the last several years studying these Martians." To which he added a slight emphasis on *Martians*, making it sound as though he fostered a little contempt for them, which was also partially honest.

"Careful," Lydia teased. "Half of us are part Martian."

Flint didn't bite; he simply remarked, "Ever since I learned about your group of half-breeds, I've been shot at, nearly blown up, I've saved the world from being completely incinerated, my good friend Philip has been tortured, I've been kidnapped, the world has plunged into a massive depression, and now I'm supposed to be on the hunt for some miracle plant brought from Mars that may no longer exist. If I can't help find it, then we're all screwed. On top of that, this stupid club of yours is what was apparently more interesting to you than your marriage to me. Please forgive me if I find little sympathy for Martians and the hell they have given me for not only the past couple of weeks, but the past couple of years, for that matter."

"I can't blame you," Labeeb agreed after a slight hesitation. "It would seem that the allure of power has corrupted the group we had been working for. However, on Lydia's behalf, I have heard her speak of you before. I'm not surprised she left you."

"Labeeb!" Lydia cried. "Flint, what he means is—"

"I know what he meant." Flint cut her off. "It means that you left me, then tried to blame me for it. I really thought you were better than that."

"No! Augh!" Lydia vented, "If you hadn't—"

This time it was Monk's turn to butt in. "'But the day of the Lord will come as a thief in the night; in the which the heavens shall pass away with a great noise, and the elements shall melt with fervent heat, the earth also and the works that are therein shall be burned up. Seeing then that all these things shall be dissolved, what manner of persons ought ye to be in all holy conversation and godliness.' 2 Peter 3:10–11."

"Monk's right," Flint relented. His autistic friend had such a unique way with words. The eccentric Hispanic was great at two things: quoting inspired words, and killing people. "We have work to do, and though we may need to work things out a little further, we better not waste any time or effort arguing."

"That sounds sensible," Labeeb agreed.

Lydia gave a huff of defeat, and began to follow as Flint led the way. Already he was trying to plan a way to find Dusty. A whole day had passed since the final battle against Amos. Dusty hadn't been seen since just before that engagement. Flint wasn't sure where she might be. He doubted Dusty would have gone far, since commercial airline travel had been suspended. His first thought was that she would try to mingle in with some nomadic Bedouins, a not so far-fetched possibility, given that she had already built up some relationships with them when she was searching for the remains of the Martian ship. But at the same time, he doubted that she would leave the city when she hadn't found out what happened to him. She might have been resourceful, if not a little malleable, but Flint knew she was also determined and unafraid. After all, she had accompanied him this far, and he suspected that she wouldn't give up just yet.

Not only was he proven right in this assumption, but she in fact found him. A manic driven pedestrian bumped into Flint, his Egyptian face filled with anxiety. In his arms were two duffle bags. A well dressed woman followed closely behind, carrying a toddler who was screaming in protest. The small well-to-do family was racing a tidal wave of panic gripped people who were trying to secure a home on the few remaining sailboats as if the oil shortages would render the land uninhabitable. Flint's group tried to sidestep the crowd, but as soon as they were away from the bustling foot traffic, the sound of a pistol being cocked stopped him in his tracks. His first instinct was to run and duck for cover, but his stupid curiosity compelled him to look in the direction of the noise. Standing five feet away, half concealed by a tree, he saw Dusty as she stepped into view. Flint's breath caught in his throat until he noticed that her pistol was leveled not at himself, but at Lydia. Wary concern filled him.

A small clink of metal alerted Flint, and he put a hand out to stop Labeeb from tossing one of his razor sharp throwing rings, a weapon Labeeb seemed very fond of carrying. With Dusty's attention on Lydia, Labeeb could easily have killed the anthropologist.

"Dusty," Flint called out, unsure of her intentions. "We were just about to come looking for you." It was then that he noticed a shiner around her eye, and a scab where her lip had apparently been split. "Dusty, what happened to you?"

"Ask your wife," Dusty accused. "I found her the other day, and she immediately attacked me. I didn't even have time to explain myself. She nearly killed me, and now that I've found you all, I want to make sure she is muzzled before I get too comfortable around her."

"You've already met and fought with Dusty?" Flint questioned Lydia.

"I thought she was one of Amos's assassins," she replied in self-defense.

Flint shook his head in disbelief. Quietly he wondered what other surprises lay in wait for him today. "Dusty, it's okay," he said, trying to soothe her.

"Would you please come here, and give me the gun?"

"If it's just the same," she said, "I'll keep the gun." However, she did lower it and carefully tuck it into the front of her pants.

"Where did you even get that thing, anyway?" Flint asked. "And for that matter, how did you find us?"

"That was easy." Dusty smiled. "After my run-in with Lydia here, I followed her for a short distance. I did lose her for a little bit, but as I weaved in and out of buildings searching for her, I heard gunfire. I don't know if I suspected her or not, but I was drawn to it. By the time I got to the building, it was being stormed by police. I stood across the street until I watched them bring you and Lydia out. I knew where to find you after that. So I found a hotel, and tried to catch up on some sleep. Unfortunately, I overslept into the next day, and by the time I got to the police station, I found out that I'd been mistaken. You were being kept somewhere else. I then went to where you were being held, only to find that you had left. The police were so busy, but I found one who thought you were headed to the pier. He didn't have time to talk to me because he was rushed into another room. But wouldn't you know, he left his gun in his office. Given recent events, I thought it a good idea to have a little extra insurance. That's my story, what's yours?"

"I don't know where to begin," Flint said with half of his bottom lip tucked into his mouth. "Apparently Lydia here unknowingly helped turn the oil off around the world, and now we have to find *some* plant to replace *some* of the energy so that the world can have *some* hope of moving on again."

"It's not just some plant," Labeeb broke in. "Many years ago, some soldiers from the French Foreign

Legion found it. They understood its potential, but the Germans eliminated them before they were able to deliver the prize. Their story suggests that the ship they were on was destroyed after all their diesel fuel had been rubberized, most likely by the same sort of thing that Kore and Amos used to solidify the world's oil supplies."

"So where do we look?" Flint asked. "At the bottom of an ocean?"

"No," Lydia finally said. "We've already been there. From our best estimate, they would have found it somewhere in Egypt, very near to where the actual Martian spaceship crashed." She then explained how the plant was more of a moss. "From what I understand, it doesn't photosynthesize the same way most of our plants do. Instead of using direct sunlight, it absorbs gamma radiation. This made it very useful to the Martians for space travel, since natural light would be limited. All around us we find gamma rays, but in space there is an abundance of solar radiation—so much that it can be harmful for people to be exposed for long periods. The moss, therefore, had two purposes. They would let it grow all over the walls, ceilings, and floors of their ship to protect them from the solar radiation, and at the same time, the moss would pass a mild current through the wet metal mesh that made up the sides of the rooms and halls. This current would then be stored and be used as the main power source of the ship."

Labeeb added, "Yes, and because it doesn't need natural light to grow, it might have survived in an environment where other plants would have died."

"So let me get this right," Dusty said. "We are looking for a moss in the desert, one that nobody has seen for decades. It can grow in dark places, so we need to start looking for a dark place with plenty of moisture for moss to survive. It sounds to me like we need to be looking underground."

Labeeb and Lydia looked at each other with the same expression: *Of course, why didn't we think of that?* Lydia then asked, "Are there many caves in Egypt?"

Dusty confirmed that there were. "But just so you know," she said by way of a disclaimer, "when we were excavating the Martian ship, we never found any such caves."

Lydia imparted the other clues she knew. "As the history goes, or at least as it was related to me, the original settlers from Mars had a hard time giving up their electricity dependence. So for many years they cultivated the plant on Earth. But as the original Martians began to die off, their children began to spread across the land, assimilating into the primitive culture. Their reliance on electricity then ended. This would suggest they were able to grow it near the crash site, but that they were either unable or unwilling to move it very far from there. If the Bible is any indication, they might even have been driven away by some small war. Seems that happened quite a bit after the Hebrews left Egypt."

When Monk eyed Flint suspiciously, Flint added, "Not that I've actually read the Old Testament, but I did go to Sunday School as a kid."

"I was all over inside their old ship," Dusty commented. "When we unburied it, I don't remember seeing any signs of water. I'm also pretty sure there was no moss inside it."

"That doesn't matter, anyway," Flint commented. "Even if there was, our good friend Marshal Steel made sure that nothing more could be scavenged from it when he blew it up."

"It really was sad," Dusty lamented. "That ship

should have been in the Smithsonian."

"So where does that leave us now?" Labeeb questioned.

To this, only silence followed. Then like a light turning on, Flint knew. "Of course! I know right where to go. But unless we want to go hiking for several days, I suggest we find some transportation. We're going back to where the ship was—well, close to it, anyway."

Everyone looked at him for explanation, but he was too excited to explain just yet. His focus was now concentrated on finding a car, and the fuel to go with it.

Chapter 4

Flint and Monk had gone off in search of gasoline while Dusty took some cash to buy supplies. Labeeb began work on borrowing a light truck. People hadn't gotten used to living without fuel yet, and they were still hopeful enough for its return, that they weren't ready to abandon their cars. After having been denied several times, Labeeb switched approaches and hot-wired a late-model pickup truck.

Lydia was still mad at Labeeb for having told Flint that she had bad-mouthed him. Sure, she had suspicions that Flint was angry with her over the loss of their child. It had helped fuel her desire to run away two years ago. Even though she may have talked poorly of Flint once or twice, warranted or not, it was just an attempt to justify her actions in front of her crew. There was no denying in her heart that she still loved Flint and yearned for his forgiveness. But despite her humiliation, she had trained her mind to focus on her work.

Lydia decided that until Flint and Monk returned with fuel, she would use the time to call her brother. As far as she knew, he was still oblivious to the deception that Persephone, aka Kore, had created. She knew that Troy was in Hong Kong, working on some special project. Beyond that, she wasn't sure what Kore was having him do, only that it must be something bad.

The phone rang several times, and she imagined the impact of no oil on a large city like Hong Kong. She hoped that if things were turning chaotic over there, he would still be okay, and be able receive her call. Just as she was about to give up, her phone clicked, and she heard the familiar voice on the other end. "Lydia, is that you?"

She sighed a breath of relief. "Troy, it's good to hear your voice again. How is Hong Kong holding up?"

"Obviously not much happened yesterday," he replied. "But it seems that everyone is realizing that there isn't much use staying in the city. Food is already running scarce, and some people have taken to hoarding and looting. Most now have begun their exodus, making for the outer territories in hopes of finding a means of living."

"But are you safe?" she asked, realizing that he was being a typical man, and not catching that Lydia was more interested in his well-being than Hong Kong.

"Yeah, we're holding up pretty good," he replied. "In fact, we were stocking up in case this oil threat actually happened. You know Persephone, she doesn't like to take any chances."

"Actually, Troy, that's what I need to talk with you about," she said, getting back on point. "Our righteous leader is not who we thought she was. In fact, I think GRIP is really a terror organization."

"What are you talking about?" Troy asked, sounding puzzled.

Lydia could understand his consternation. She too had believed that GRIP or Global Representatives for International Progress was just another Non-government organization like Greenpeace. But whatever GRIP had once been, Lydia knew better now.

She went on, "Amos, the one we were trying to stop, was working for her the whole time. She even manipulated my team into helping him. Persephone was behind the whole oil plot, and whatever she has you working on, I'm sure that it's just as evil and dangerous."

"That can't be," Troy defended. "She's always seemed good to me, and the project that I'm working on can't possibly be harmful. It can only be for the betterment of all people. I can't—and I won't—believe this. Someone has to be setting her up. Maybe it was Amos's plan to shift blame to her while he got away clean. He has to be setting her up."

"Listen, Amos is dead, I saw him die with my own eyes. Troy, it's all true!" Lydia exclaimed. "When I saw her at Amos's headquarters, I confronted her on this very thing. Just the fact that you are my brother is going to put you in serious danger. You need to leave Hong Kong now. Get away before she has you killed."

"What are you going to do?" he asked in reply.

"I'm heading up to the crash site of our ancestors' ship. I'm here with Flint, of all people, and he thinks he knows where we can find that solar moss. If we can, we might be able to cultivate it and give the world a cheap alternative to petro energy."

Lydia waited while Troy thought for a minute,

then he asked, "I don't know how much this move on your part will help, but if what you say is true, I might try coming and helping you. About when do you think you'll be reaching the crash site?"

"I think we might need a day or two to get there, and then it sounded like Flint was going to lead us just a little ways from there to where he thinks the moss could be. How he would have any idea where it is, I can't begin to figure. But if we can find it, we'll be back in Suez within two more days. If we aren't there, check with the U.S. Embassy. I don't know where we would go, but I might be able to leave word with somebody there if we do leave."

"Okay. This all sounds outrageous, but let me think about it for a little bit, and then I'll let you know what my plans are."

"Don't think too long," Lydia warned. "The longer you wait . . ."

"Don't worry about me," Troy assured. "I'm a big boy, and I can handle myself. Take care, and I'll be in touch shortly."

"Please be safe," Lydia begged, but the phone went dead, and she wasn't sure if he'd heard her.

Needing something to do, she walked out to inspect Labeeb's truck. Her face must have shown the despair and worry that she had for her brother, because Labeeb expressed, "You don't look too good. I mean, you look good—what I mean is, is Troy okay?"

Lydia laughed, and it felt good. Normally he was a smooth talker; every word was thought out and expressed precisely. "He's okay, but I'm worried. I don't think he wants to believe that GRIP is really a terror organization."

Labeeb agreed. "It is a difficult thing to believe, and I bet that if you had been told this one week ago, you would not have believed it, either."

Not wanting to worry herself into despair, she changed the subject. "How much gas does your *rental* come with?"

Labeeb, ever the honest one, replied with a note of guilt, "They only had about one-quarter of a tank left. We will need at least two full tanks to get to the crash site. Getting back will be another issue entirely."

"Let's hope this old truck has what it takes to make the trip," Lydia murmured.

Twenty minutes later, Labeeb spotted Flint racing their way with a shopping cart. Lydia could hear him shouting something as he approached, though she wasn't able to make out his words. The urgency in his voice required no explanation, as it clearly emphasized that they needed to get moving. Lydia jumped behind the wheel of the truck. With hands fumbling under the steering column, she pressed the bare ignition wires together to start the engine.

By the time she had it running, Flint had let go of the shopping cart and was pulling gas cans from it as the cart coasted closer to the truck. Labeeb grabbed two more gas cans as the cart slammed into the tailgate. After heaving them into the truck, both men went back for the other four cans. In total they had loaded thirty gallons of gasoline.

"Get moving!" Flint shouted to Lydia, and she popped the truck into gear just as two men with clubs reached the truck. One threw his club at Flint; and, though he dodged it in time, it broke through the back window of the truck and startled Lydia. Her natural fighting spirit kicked in, and she was able to keep the truck under control while Labeeb fought the other man, who had managed to jump onto the tailgate. Before long, the attackers were left behind.

Flint then crawled through the broken window.

"Hello, honey, I'm home," he said with a cheesy grin.

"Mind telling me what that was all about?" she asked coldly. "And what about Monk and Dusty?"

"I'm glad you asked," he replied, his smile not fading. "Monk and I couldn't find anybody willing to sell us gasoline, so we went to a small gas station and offered them a trade. We wanted about fifty gallons of gas, and we would give them our nice fuel-efficient hybrid car. At length they agreed, but we got only six gas cans before the actual owner of the car we had pointed out to them decided to leave. Once they realized that we'd tricked them, they came out to stop us. I told Monk to stay behind and grab another couple cans of fuel while I led them away. He fought them just long enough to give me a head start. So we need to go back now and pick him up."

Lydia followed Flint's lead, and found Monk. He was waiting just outside the pump station, looking down the road for Flint to arrive. They loaded the last few gas cans on the truck and then took off, not wanting to be around when the two men got back.

Dusty was just exiting a small hardware store when they found her. She was struggling to juggle two shovels, a pickax, a five-gallon metal bucket, and two grocery bags full of food. To add to her comical appearance, she was half squatting as she walked, trying to keep a long and thick coil of rope from falling. Half the rope was still on her shoulders, but the other half had slumped down and was being supported around her parted legs.

The sight gave Lydia a mirthful grin. Not one to take pleasure in other peoples' struggles, she couldn't help the giddy joy she found in watching Dusty stagger and nearly trip over her load. True, she felt a little guilty, but this was the stray cat who was chasing after her husband. *Sure, he was bound to start dating after having been on his own for the last couple of years*, she tried to explain to herself. But Flint was still her husband, and though she would have been able to justify it had she seen this happen to another couple, the jealousy within prevented her from being settled with the situation.

She had left Flint once, because she felt that he'd blamed her for their son's death. There was more to it than that, but she struggled to make perfect sense of it right now. Now that he was here, she wanted to give their relationship another chance. This new hillbilly girl wasn't going to get in her way.

Once they were loaded, and half the fuel cans were emptied into the truck's tank, Flint crawled up front with Lydia. Monk, not wanting to bounce around in the bed of the truck, decided to sit up front in the cab with them. Lydia was angry but relieved at the same time when Monk chose to sit between herself and her husband. Once Dusty and Labeeb were situated in the back, they gave the word, and Lydia began what she knew would be a long drive.

Chapter 5

Troy hung up the phone, then scratched his chin. *So she found Flint in Egypt*, he mused. *How on earth did he end up there?* The last time they had met, Flint had expressed interest in touring the Philippines.

Troy hadn't wanted Lydia to see her husband previously, since Flint might distract her from her mission. But now that everything was in the past, Troy wondered how things might be changed going forward, especially now that they were together.

Then there was the issue of the moss, and that Flint might know where some of the ancient plant was growing. If they did find it, Troy believed that it really might be able to inspire hope. According to the history he knew, the moss could easily be cultivated in a short amount of time, which is how the ancient Martians could keep the walls, floors, and ceilings of their ship covered with the stuff.

Finally there was now Persephone, and Lydia's concern about GRIP as a whole. This was a complication Troy hadn't anticipated. He started biting a pen while thinking, a habit he hadn't shaken since he was a kid. At length he pulled the partially mutilated plastic from his mouth and set it on the desk. He wanted to check on the progress of the ship they were building, but at the same time he knew it would be pointless. Nobody in their entire organization was more familiar with this project than he was.

There had to be a way to make everything work in light of recent events. With only a matter of days before the ship would be ready, he knew there would be no stopping the project. His only solution seemed to be bringing Lydia here. He didn't believe that Persephone would be a big problem, but he decided that he'd better take a few precautions just in case.

Picking up a telephone, Troy pressed the number three; somewhere else in the underground complex, a man picked up. "I need a jet prepared, and loaded with some extra barrels of fuel," Troy said. "I have to get to Egypt and back ASAP."

The man on the other end confirmed the order, and Troy hung up the phone. He then walked over to a neighboring room and discussed his plan with two others. "Don't worry," one said. "We'll have everything ready for when you get back. As for Persephone, we will just tell her that you're picking up an essential part for the ship, and you'll be back in a day or so."

"Very good," Troy said, feeling confident. He then made for the tunnel that would take him out of the mine, and to the small airport where his jet would be waiting. Though few obstacles were anticipated, he took with him a group of five loyal men, heavily armed. Troy doubted he would need them, but already things weren't going the way he thought they should, and he didn't want to risk anything else going wrong.

Chapter 6

The ride was uncomfortable and it had little to do with the truck itself. Flint was unsure of what to say to Lydia, and she seemed hesitant to talk back. And though Monk was a great friend and could be completely candid, Flint wished his unique pal had chosen to ride in back so that he could talk to Lydia in private. He had so many questions, the least of which was why she blamed him for her running away.

But instead of going into their previous relationship, Flint found it easier to explain what he expected to find near the Martian crash site. He began by telling Lydia that since she'd left, he'd wanted to find an escape, or way of shutting out the whole world. Then he jumped into explaining his backpacking adventure across the Egyptian desert.

Most important was the part where he had run out of water and climbed down an ancient well to replenish his canteen. He described how, once down there, he'd had to dig through some sand until he found the water; and, when he'd touched it, he felt as though it had a mild charge, like touching a nine-volt battery to one's tongue. The charge only lasted a second, and at the time, he'd dismissed the phenomenon as static or his imagination. Now it seemed clear to him that the charge could only have come from this plant that Lydia and Labeeb were so passionate about.

Lydia voiced skepticism about the moss actually being down there. In fact, she experienced a little titillation over the possibility. She'd spent so much time looking for the moss, and up to this point, the whole process had been so hard. To have Flint find it merely by chance was almost too good to be true. Her trepidation served more for her own security, a hedge against possible disappointment. But since she didn't want to totally discount the plan, she voiced her resolution to try, "as they had no better leads." Flint related a few other things that had happened to him in the last week, including his encounters with Marshal Steel and Shen Mao, and how he'd destroyed a device that they were using that could either launch a ship into space or destroy a planet's atmosphere. He didn't forget to point out how somebody in an armed Learjet had shot his helicopter down a few miles from the Sharm El Sheikh airport.

Lydia blushed at the thought that she'd almost killed Flint, but she didn't apologize. She simply stated with a half laugh, "I thought you were Marshal." Flint wasn't bothered by it, though. He could easily understand how she could have mistaken him for Shen Mao's grave robber at the time. But he still found it discomforting that she not only had killed a couple of men when she shot down his chopper, but she didn't appear as affected by it as he had been. Those were innocent men, and you don't just walk away from killing someone, no matter who they are. Truthfully, though, he wasn't sure how she should be reacting, but he did get the vibe that she had killed before that incident, and that she had an attitude toward those deaths as being casualties of war. Either she had changed a great deal in the last two years, or she hid her feelings really well. Then again, she did work for a private military contract company before they were married. She rarely talked about her time there. Maybe this cold disregard for human life was something she learned there. *Did I ever really know my wife?*

Flint remembered back to his first encounter with Marshal's men on the rim of the canyon, where he had shot and killed someone for his first time. He remembered that even with his own life being in peril, the guilt of killing somebody had a significant impact on his conscience. Then the haunting memory of leaving the dead bodies of innocent men behind when their chopper had been shot down by Lydia's jet came back into his mind.

These recollections stirred a brief wave of guilt, followed by anger at Lydia for having been responsible for their deaths and not showing any signs of remorse. But at last he called back the memory he retained of her before she ran away, and his anger was slowly replaced with sorrow and empathy. The Lydia he knew would have felt, and most likely did feel, the pain from every death that she caused, perhaps even more so than his own guilt. He also knew her to be the type of person to bottle up her emotions, so that others would have a hard time seeing her pain. She didn't want others' sympathy, even if she truly needed it. *That has to be who she still is.*

The conversation soon fell flat, and awkwardness crept back into the cab. Flint wanted to ask her why she'd left him, and he felt that she wanted to talk about it, too, but it was still too difficult to bring up. After another hour, he decided it was about time to break the ice, but right as he was about to start, there was a small pop, followed by a hissing sound.

"What was that?" Flint asked.

"I have an idea," Lydia said, "but if I'm right, it can only be bad."

Lydia let off of the gas a little, and then the tell-tale sign of steam rising from under the hood confirmed that they were losing coolant. Coasting to a stop, Lydia turned the truck off. Flint got out and lifted the hood. He paused for a moment as a white cloud of steam billowed out from around the engine. He remembered the first time that he'd met Lydia. She had been stranded on the side of the highway. Flint had pulled over and checked under her hood, though at the time he had no idea what to even look for. He just enjoyed pretending to help the beautiful woman.

This time, however, the problem was clear enough for even the least savvy of gear-heads to diagnose. The old radiator was hissing out steam fast enough to drain all the coolant within a minute or two. A quick examination revealed that the old radiator had been cheaply patched in the past, and it's owners never expected to use it for any long distance traveling. The metal tubing at the bottom where the hoses connect, had shed its soldered patch, causing the brittle hose to dangle, without anything to reconnect it to. Though they had enough gasoline to make the trip, he was well aware that they would not be able to go much farther in this truck.

Dropping the hood, he shook his head in disappointment. The road was barren and traffic was non-existent. "How much food did you pack?" he called to Dusty. "Because I think we're on foot from here."

"How far are we from the ship?" she asked.

"About a day and a half to two days, if we hurry," Flint replied.

Dusty lifted an eyebrow in a sarcastic way then said, "I think we might manage with how much food I've got, but unless you have a better way of carrying it than in two plastic grocery bags, I seriously doubt that we'll be able to bring it all."

Flint realized how despairing the situation seemed, but he refused to let it get the better of them. If the food disappeared before they got back, he could always introduce them to the nearly palatable insect buffet that had sustained him on his first trip across the desert mountains. For now, he considered splitting up the contents of one bag, having everybody carry what they could so they could double-bag the other and take turns toting it. That way the bag might not rip before they got there. With everyone's hands already full of shovels, buckets, and ropes, he knew it would be difficult. If only they had thought to find a hiking backpack to bring along! Labeeb saved the day when he pointed off in the distance and asked, "Does anyone know how to ride a camel?"

Sure enough, on the horizon, three camels headed in their direction, all being led by a single man. After fifteen minutes the man approached them. He didn't speak any English, but luckily Dusty knew Egyptian Arabic. She learned that the camels were to be sold for meat. It wasn't the most honorable means of using camels in the area, but there was still a market for it.

Flint suggested that they buy them off the man,

and Dusty translated. At first, the man seemed hesitant to agree, but when Flint pulled out a stash of cash, his eyes widened with delight. Flint knew he would likely pay double what the animals were worth, but it would make the trek much easier, and be well worth it.

The man agreed, and Flint peeled off half the remaining bills. Lydia watched with wide eyes, then with a hint of suspicion, she asked, "Where did you come into that kind of money?"

Flint winked at her as he tucked the remainder back into his pocket. "I don't know if you know a guy named Troy; he's a part of your secret club. I helped him stop Shen Mao, and I gave him my guns. In return, I held on to this little stash of cash that we found in your plane. At the time, I felt it was a decent compensation for my services."

"You know that was my slush fund, don't you?" Lydia claimed.

"Yeah, I suspected as much," he replied. "And frankly, now that I know more about GRIP, I think I wouldn't have a problem robbing them of every last nickel they have. I've actually spent most of it already. My guess is that there is just enough to get us home when this is all over with."

Then something else about what Flint had just mentioned clicked in Lydia's head. "Wait, did you just say that you met up with Troy?"

"Yep. Why?"

"You do know that he is my brother, don't you?" she asked.

"Brother?" Flint asked, surprised. "I know you have *a* brother named Troy, but I thought he disappeared before we ever met. Besides, he made no mention of you." Flint never met his brother-in-law. He'd seen age old pictures of him, but still found the resemblance hard to connect. When they were still living together, Lydia often bemoaned her prodigal brother. As often as Lydia had denounced her brother's actions, Flint couldn't help but see a parallel personality trait when she too ran away. Both of them finding themselves employed by GRIP was a compounding irony that Flint saw all too clearly.

Monk then called out, "Mark 6:35. 'And when the day was now far spent, his disciples came unto him, and said, This is a desert place, and now the time is far passed.'"

"Again, Monk has a point," Labeeb commented. "We should get going. The sun is about to set, and it will be an ideal time for traveling."

It didn't take long to tie the supplies to one of the camels. Mounting upon the humped backs of the animals was another issue. They didn't come with saddles, and they proved to be very unwilling to be ridden. "I can see why these ones were meant to be butchered," Flint noted. "I don't think we're going to be able to double up."

Dusty proved to be the most skilled at controlling the camels, and she was given one to ride. Flint tried to persuade Lydia to take the other. But whether she refused to ride the obstinate beast or it refused to be ridden by her was debatable. In either case, Monk proved to be the only other one able to ride it. So it was settled: Lydia, Flint, and Labeeb were to hike while Dusty and Monk relaxed on top of their rides. Though they could have easily argued that it was anything but relaxing.

Flint led the pack camel in front, straining to keep a good pace while the others followed. After a few hours, the camels became a little more accustomed to their new masters, though Dusty's did buck her around, and got a little fussy. Lydia walked up next to the camel and laughed. "Easy there, Dusty, I don't think your ride is too fond of you."

Dusty sneered slightly at her, trying to hold her tongue. But when her camel hurled a cud-filled loogie at Lydia's chest, Dusty found herself snorting as she tried to restrain laughing out loud.

Flint found it difficult not to laugh, also. In fact, only Monk seemed to not find the situation humorous. But they all proceeded without further incident. They traveled throughout the night, and once midmorning approached, Flint gave the word to stop.

They found a large rock, big enough to provide shade, and the weary hikers tried to sleep. They were all bunched together, and Flint stretched to keep a safe distance from both women during this down time. Tensions were already dicey enough, and he didn't need to give either women more fuel for their fury. Though they were tired from keeping such a quick pace, few of them slept very soundly. It was easy enough to make a comfortable bed in the sand, but for the first hour as the sun was getting hotter, they found rest to be difficult at best. Luckily, albeit after a couple hours, most of them fell asleep.

Flint was the first to wake up, followed shortly by Lydia. The sun was still high, but he knew it was close to 3:00 in the afternoon. The heat would start dying down in a couple of hours and conditions would be good for traveling again. He could only handle about ten minutes, stretching out in the sun, before he retreated to another shady rock.

Lydia quietly stepped up to him. "I'm sorry," she humbly admitted. "I didn't want for any of this to happen."

"I have a funny feeling that GRIP would have pulled off their little stunt with or without you," Flint replied.

"No, I'm not talking about that," she pressed. "I mean, I'm sorry for leaving you."

Flint paused but didn't know what to say. So Lydia continued, "After they told me that our son was dead, you tried to comfort me, but I wouldn't have any of it. I could see the hurt in your face. It pained me to look at you, knowing that I was responsible. All I could think about was my guilt. Guilt for the loss of our son, and for the loss of your love. Despite everything you said to me back then, I knew the truth. You didn't know it, but somehow Troy found out, and came to visit. I was surprised to say the least. He told me how you had blamed me for it, and suggested that the best thing I could do was to join him for a couple months to clear my head. My deepest fears of your disapproval of me seemed to be realized. It was too easy to believe, so I followed him. Then a couple months turned into a couple years. I'm only now starting to see how hard you took it."

"I didn't know your brother was even in town," Flint remarked, trying to make sense of what he was hearing. "I'd never met him, and I never told anyone that I blamed you. You told me that he ran away when you were both teenagers, and that even you hadn't seen him for years."

"I hadn't until then," she replied. "But he told me that you didn't even want to be around me, so I thought that he had been talking with you or someone close to you."

"No, I've never met him. At least not until I ran into him in the Philippines a week ago."

This time it was Lydia's turn to pause and think things over. "He was there. But why wouldn't he mention you?"

"Did it ever cross your mind that maybe he is just as corrupt as Kore?" Flint offered.

Lydia shook her head. "Not a chance. I may not have known him very well before this all happened, but in the last couple of years, we have grown very close. Troy is a hard one to understand, but he is a good man. What about you? If you cared so much about me, why didn't you try to find me?"

"I did," Flint argued. "But your suicide letter put a bit of a damper on my efforts. We had a funeral for you and everything."

Her eyes widened and her jaw dropped, "I never wrote a suicide letter."

"Troy then?" Flint suggested.

"No, it couldn't be him," Lydia defended. "It had to of been Kore. Troy is my brother. He's a good man. Different, but good. I refuse to believe this was anyone but Kore. After all, he works for her, not the other way around.

She paused, remembering what she'd been talking about before Flint mentioned the suicide letter, "Anyhow, you already know most of the story, but here is the rest of the story that I never told you. When we were young, our father actually did belong to GRIP, although it wasn't called that at the time. In fact, I don't know what it was called. To join, you had to be invited; you couldn't just apply. Troy always dreamed of joining and following in our father's footsteps. When Dad died, Troy expected to be approached by them. It never happened. He didn't even know where to find them. So in a heated rebellion, he left my mother and me when he was twenty-one, and went in search of them himself.

"I was only eighteen at the time, but I took his leaving hard. That's when I went to work in the corporate military world. The distraction was helpful, and I was able to focus my whole life around it. I guess that's why they thought I had good promise.

I gained quite a bit of experience flying everything from helicopters to jets, as you know. When Troy returned, he told me that he'd finally been accepted into part of GRIP's scientific research division, and that they needed someone with my skills for protecting the secrets of the organization. He also mentioned that I would be doing a lot in the way of protecting the world from dangerous people.

"At the time, it seemed like a good way to redeem myself in my own eyes, and hopefully to eventually find forgiveness in yours. So I accepted, and he told me that Persephone was the head of the organization, and that I would be able to work directly under her guidance. He told me that he also reported directly to her, and that it was by his recommendation that I was accepted to join. It seemed like such a big deal at the time.

"You need to understand: Not a day went by that I didn't think of you. I wanted so badly to return, but I didn't know how. They kept finding things that seemed so urgent, and on top of that, I was afraid to face you again—"

Lydia broke down and began sobbing, releasing two years of pent-up sorrow and frustration.

Flint pulled her into his arms and tried to comfort her. He wasn't sure what to say, so he kept quiet. On one hand he felt bad for her; on the other, he was hurt that she had left him. Trusting a brother she hadn't seen in years over the husband who would have done anything for her. Also he was trying to understand why Troy had lied to her about him, and then kept him in the dark when they met in the Philippines. He could understand Troy's desire to have her join him in their organization, but it still seemed odd. He felt as though Troy had taken advantage of her in her weakened state of mind.

Flint wanted to forgive her, but at the moment he was too angry at Troy to think much on it. He soon realized that his right hand was balled into a tight fist, and he began to breathe deeply. At this same time, Dusty came around the corner and found him with his arms around his wet-eyed wife. A hurt look passed across her face and she turned quickly back.

Flint clenched his teeth, his face taking on a frustrated shade of red. He was stuck between his wife who had abandoned him and his first girlfriend since that time, who had actually tried to get him killed when they first met. *How did I get into this mess?* He wondered. *Most women aren't this hard to deal with, are they?* But as it was not in his nature to run away from a challenge, he decided to press forward with their mission. *Qué será, será*, he told himself, quoting the famous song. *Whatever will be, will be.*

When he finally got up, he found that Monk and Labeeb had already repacked the camels. Aside from a small lunch to prepare them for the next leg of their journey, everything was now loaded up and ready to move, so they continued on their way. Flint had originally planned on heading to the crash site first, then backtracking to the well. But as they were hiking, he began to recognize the terrain and eventually found his bearings. Around 3:00 in the morning, they were all standing at the edge of the old abandoned well.

Chapter 7

August 7

They rested for an hour to regain their strength and to have a light breakfast. By 4:00, Labeeb couldn't restrain his excitement any longer. "We should be moving, Flint," he suggested impatiently.

Dusty flitted from here to there, pacing with excitement. She too was ready to begin their work. She had commented several times along the way that this had always been her favorite part of anthropology. Studying the past was fun, but putting a shovel to the test always gave her adrenaline a boost. So with practiced agility, she swung her pick and shovel onto her shoulders and asked, "How do you suggest we go about this?"

"You're the expert here, you tell me," Flint said. "When I first went down that well, I had to dig for about a foot till I found water. That was when I felt the shock. I didn't have a light, but I remember the walls and the floor had been fairly dry. I don't know much about moss, but I think the well is just a starting point. I doubt we'll actually find the moss in it."

Dusty thought for a moment, then hypothesized, "There are several underground caves in this region, but I haven't seen any sign of an opening around here. Granted, it is still dark, but my guess is that if you felt an electrical shock down there, then a cave would have to be very close. I suggest we go down and try to dig sideways."

"Two questions," Labeeb pondered out loud. "Would that be safe? And how would we know which direction to dig in?"

Lydia looked around at everybody. Each shrugged their shoulders.

Monk was the first person to act. Silently he walked over to one of the camels, and pulled off a long strand of wire that had been used to tie the supplies to the pack animal. After straightening it, he bent the wire in half several times until it broke into two equal lengths. One last bend put them each in an *L* shape. He placed the small ends in each of his hands, leaving the two longer ends pointing straight in front of him.

"You got to be kidding me!" Labeeb commented. "Does he really think that water witching is going to work? I heard that stuff was completely bogus."

"I don't know," Dusty defended. "I've seen dowsing work before. Several years ago, I watched a man do it to find some old buried foundations. The way he explained it to me was that there is a natural electromagnetic field that emanates from the ground. If that field becomes distorted by, say, an old excavation, an underground river, or in this case an underground cave, then that electromagnetic change can cause the wires to move toward each other."

"I'll believe it when I see it," Labeeb said skeptically.

For the next few minutes, all eyes were on Monk. He walked several times around the well, broadening his circle each time. After several passes, everyone became aware of a certain pattern. On one side of the well, there seemed to be something. Monk zigzagged across it several times until he was convinced that there was a long tunnel that ran near the well only a few feet away from it.

"I guess that answers our question," Flint decided. And even if he didn't fully believe in witching, Dusty alleviated everyone's concerns by assuring that it was at least a place to start. Flint then began trying to pry the heavy rock off of the well, and asked, "Labeeb, can you give me a hand with this capstone?"

Labeeb, though he had been skeptical about Monk's divining, nevertheless seemed enthusiastic to help. With the stone removed, Lydia secured the rope around the base. Flint hovered closely over her. Lydia wondered why she felt so uncomfortable with him standing there. She couldn't decide if he wanted to ensure the rope was secured well, or if he was trying to warm up to her a little. In either case, it made her feel very self-conscious.

Once the rope was in place, Flint took hold of it and inhaled deeply. "Back into the pit of Hell," he said. Lydia could tell that he was trying to comfort himself before taking the plunge. He was doing a pretty good job of making everyone else feel okay with it, but she thought she noticed a little tension in his eyes. After all, he had been down there before, and by the way he had described it on their trek, going back into that dark hole wasn't very appealing. At least this time he wouldn't be alone.

Lydia then watched as Dusty dropped the short-handled shovel down the well, listening as it clanked against the sides on the way down. She almost sent the metal bucket after it before Flint stopped her. "It's a long way down, and we need that bucket intact if we are to haul up dirt and hopefully some moss with it."

Instead, Monk took one of his wires and tied the bucket to Flint's foot. "'The Lord our God be with us, as he was with our fathers: let him not leave us, nor forsake us.' 1 Kings 8:57."

"Amen to that," Flint replied, as he took another big breath and rappelled down. The rope went taut as his weight rested on it.

Lydia looked down and watched him slide out of sight. After a minute or two, the rope went slack, and she called down, "Are you all right?"

They heard nothing. This time Dusty called, clearly shaken by the absence of his reply. Again nothing.

"I'm going down after him," Labeeb said as he reached for the rope. He was just about to start down when a distorted echo bounced up the well. Labeeb stopped, and asked, "Did you guys catch that?"

Lydia pushed him aside and called back down, "Flint, are you okay?"

"Yes," came the reverberating reply. He then called up instructions to have the best climber sent down. Apparently the rope was not long enough, and he needed help hauling the bucket up ten feet to where the rope ended.

Monk was the first to volunteer, and nobody was in a hurry to object. Within another few minutes, Labeeb, Lydia, and Dusty were taking turns hauling up buckets of sand, dirt, and rock. The process was tedious and boring, and after an hour, they seemed no closer to finding the cave than before. Even some of Dusty's excitement was disappearing.

Soon the sun started to rise, and the heat flowed over them all in punishing waves. Lydia and Dusty had been enduring a degree of enmity for the whole trip, and as time went by, their irritability with each other worsened. They were both relieved when Flint sent up a bucket of water instead of dirt, and they all took a moment to refresh themselves, and collect their nerves.

In the distance, Lydia heard something out of place. It sounded very much like the thwumping of a helicopter; but given recent events, that seemed unlikely. The sound died down a bit, and she dismissed it from her mind.

When it was her turn to pull up the bucket, she got it halfway up before she saw the wide calculating eyes of Labeeb. Dusty was shaking, and Lydia realized that the noise had returned. She looked behind her to see that a helicopter was indeed almost upon them. It looked more military than civilian, and she became a little uncomfortable.

"Dusty, can you take this for a minute," she almost ordered. Dusty obliged, but right as Dusty took the rope, Lydia stole her pistol from her waist.

"Hey, what's the idea?" Dusty began, but Lydia immediately shushed her.

"Something doesn't feel right about this," Lydia said, "and I actually know how to use one of these." Lydia knew that Dusty couldn't argue. Dusty's black eye and split lip were evidence enough that Lydia knew how to fight better.

The chopper landed a couple hundred feet away, and much to Lydia's disappointment, several armed men jumped out with weapons at the ready.

Chapter 8

Monk was resting at the floor of the well, ten feet below Flint. Flint had his upper back pressed against one wall and his legs spread apart, bracing himself from falling on top of Monk. He was waiting for the bucket to be lowered again. His throbbing and shaking legs told him that the group up top was being much slower in returning the last bucket of dirt, and he wondered what could be taking them so long.

Finally the bucket came rushing toward him. It fell so quickly that it caught Flint by surprise. He slipped about a foot when the bucket snapped to a bouncing stop, inches from his head. "Hey, easy up there!" he shouted.

He didn't hear any reply. There were voices, then a couple of pops. It didn't take long for him to surmise that they were gunshots, and he hoped that Lydia and Dusty weren't having it out with each other. But since he believed that neither of them would resort to that degree of violence over a matter of jealousy, he tried to picture what else could bring them to shooting.

Suddenly the rope jerked and was dancing again. Flint realized that someone was sliding down into the well with him. It must be one of the women, since he doubted that Labeeb would have given the high-pitched shriek this person let out in her descent. Flint quickly unfastened the bucket, and began to shimmy his way back down. Soon Dusty was in sight, only she didn't take into account the drop between the end of the rope and the well's floor.

Flint was still five feet from the bottom when Dusty hit him. He softened her fall, but that made his descent a little more painful. Luckily for him Monk softened both of their falls, though he was certain that Monk wasn't very happy to have the privilege, either.

Their one flashlight was dropped and covered in mud, darkening the whole pit. After fighting to untangle themselves, they all stood up but were stuffed so tightly that they could hardly move.

Dusty began to hyperventilate and panic because of the dark, tight quarters. "It's okay, we're all okay," Flint whispered, trying to settle her nerves. "Calm down now and tell me what just happened."

Dusty, still breathing hard, tried to collect herself. "It was Troy, Troy from the Philippines. He showed up and asked Lydia to go with him. She tried to tell him that you were down here, and that we were so close to finding the moss. He told her that it wasn't important anymore, and that they should leave together immediately. Lydia refused, pointing out again that you two were still down here."

She calmed her breathing then continued, "Troy

didn't seem to care, though. He told her that he wasn't suggesting they leave you here, but that he was ordering it. From there it kind of happened fast, and I don't know who shot first, but we all took cover behind the well. A few shots were exchanged. I think Lydia killed one of Troy's men. But then Labeeb tackled Lydia and wrestled the gun away from her. He turned her over to Troy. Why would he do that?"

"How many men did Troy have with him?" Flint asked.

Dusty sniffed. "I don't know, maybe four or five. They looked pretty militant."

Flint then guessed, "I could be wrong, but there might not have been any way you all would have survived. I think Labeeb was saving your lives by doing what he did."

"But he ended up asking to go with them, mentioning that he still believed in GRIP, and that whatever they were planning, he wanted to be a part of it." Dusty added. "He's a traitor!"

"I don't think so," Flint replied. "He saved your life, and now he's going to have an inside track on what they're planning. I have to believe he is still well intentioned."

Just then they heard a voice from above. Flint knew that it had to be Troy, even though the echo distorted the tone of his voice. "Is it getting a little tight down there, Flint? I wanted to thank you again for your help in the Philippines, and this is nothing personal, but I have to leave you here now. Good luck."

Flint was about to respond, but he was distracted as the rope came rushing down on their heads. Troy had cut it, and was now pushing the heavy stone back over the opening. Flint hadn't thought it possible to get any darker, but with the opening completely covered now, the blackness of the well seemed to swallow them.

Dusty started screaming, but Monk would have none of it. He grabbed her throat tightly with one hand, and put the palm of his other hand over her mouth. "Job 2:10. 'But he said unto her, Thou speakest as one of the foolish women speaketh.'" Then he added, "'Let your women keep silence in the churches.' 1 Corinthians 14:34," only when she stopped squirming, did Monk remove his hands.

Flint was still recovering from her loud shriek when he blew a relieved sigh and said, "Thanks, Monk."

"Please tell me that we can still climb up and get out," Dusty whimpered.

Flint knew that it was unlikely. He recalled the last time he had climbed up the well without a rope. By the time he had gotten to the top, his energy was completely drained, and his limbs were like putty. While he or Monk might be able to make it up, neither of them would have the strength to keep from falling while moving the stone. Besides, between the three of them, he wasn't sure that they would have enough air to make the climb.

It was next to impossible to bend over in the tight shaft, so Flint found the flashlight with his foot. He kicked it loose from the mud where it was embedded, into the tunnel that they had been digging at, revealing the four-foot-long extension that they had dug out so far. To everyone's relief, it also bled enough light back up to return some sight to the three confined spelunkers. The new tunnel was wet and muddy, but the roof of it seemed to be stable enough.

"Monk," Flint said softly, "can you shimmy up the shaft a few feet so that I can get into our tunnel?"

Monk immediately obeyed, and with practiced

agility was soon holding himself a few feet above their heads. Questioning his motive, Dusty asked, "What's the plan?"

"Well," Flint said as he strained to bend over and finally started into his short tunnel, "climbing up and out is not likely going to be an option. The only thing I can think to do right now is to keep going sideways. With any luck, we'll run into that cave."

"How can that possibly help us?" Dusty whined. "Either way we're trapped down here, and we'll die."

"Would you rather die trapped uncomfortably between two stinky men, or more comfortably in an open cave with a soft, mossy mattress?" Flint asked as he started scraping and pushing dirt behind him onto her feet. "Besides, you're the anthropologist; just think about it, how would the ancient Martians ever cultivate the moss in an underground cave such as the one we're trying to find? Don't you think they would have needed an opening to it somewhere?"

Defeated, Dusty replied, "You say that as if you know for sure that there's a cave, and that it does have this miracle moss. How can you possibly even know it's here?"

Monk answered from above, "'Let us draw near with a true heart in full assurance of faith, having our hearts sprinkled from an evil conscience, and our bodies washed with pure water.' Hebrews 10:22."

"What's that supposed to mean?" Dusty complained. "Am I supposed to rely on faith alone?"

"Faith isn't bad," Flint replied as he shoved another pile of dirt around her feet. "But to put your mind at ease, bend down here for a second."

Dusty obeyed and stretched out her hand when Flint prompted her to touch the muddy floor. At first she paused, not understanding what he was getting at, but then relented and pressed her fingertips into the soft earth, mumbling as she proceeded. Though Flint wasn't shining the light directly on her face, he could see by the way she reacted that she was surprised.

"What was that?" she exclaimed. "It wasn't . . ."

"It was—and that, my dear Dusty, is proof that we're getting close," Flint offered. Once they had started digging sideways, the electrical current in the water seemed to have gotten stronger. It wasn't anything uncomfortable, but it did provide a slight tingling feeling when first touched.

The only thing that worried him now, aside from the ever-possible collapse of his ceiling, was that the farther he dug, the higher the water level in his tunnel rose. And with no place to put the extra clay, he was likely to start filling in the hole behind him.

But since going up was not a viable option, he continued using the stubby shovel to dig deeper toward where he hoped a cave might be. Having gone another three and a half feet, and with no other place to put the dirt, his three-foot-round tunnel shrank to about two and a half feet wide and two feet tall. It was becoming increasingly difficult to maneuver. His body was stretched out with his arms in front of him. Since it was now impossible to pull his elbows back against his body, he had to rely on thrusting the shovel against the dirt with his wrists, then scooting back and forth until he could work the muddy dirt toward his legs, and kick it behind him.

The water was getting too high, though, and Flint's head wavered with a small discomforting dizzy spell. He knew that if he passed out here, then he would drown. Yet there was no sense in trying to go back. So he took his shovel and, using his toes to give him a little extra traction, he tried slamming the spade into the end of the tunnel one last time.

However, as the spade went forward, it ricocheted off of a large rock, and angled downward. As it sank deep into the mud, Flint's heart was quickly filled with dread. No sooner had the shovel sunk into the soft mud than a gush of water started to rise even more quickly.

His first instinct was to use the shovel and push himself back, but since the water had risen so fast, it would force him to turn his strained neck back down into the water, fully submerging himself.

He took two big breaths then plunged his face, concentrating his whole efforts on pushing against the shovel. To his dismay the shovel only sank deeper. He was running out of time and needed the shovel to push himself backward out of the tunnel, so he attempted to draw the spade back to him. Again he was surprised to find the shovel only sank deeper, dragging him with it as he struggled. It was as if he were stuck in quicksand.

With his hands tightly gripping the end of the shovel, he tried to avoid wiggling it much more, and instead decided to give it one more good jerk back. At first it seemed that the shovel was coming up, but he quickly realized that he was instead pulling himself deeper into the muddy trap. The more he struggled against it, the deeper he felt himself sink. To give up would certainly mean death, but since doing nothing also meant death, he struggled on. Thus he continued sinking deeper into the slimy grave.

He was probably only submerged for a minute, even if it seemed more like five, when his lungs began to burn. Several thoughts coursed through his mind as he slowed his struggle. Was this what it was like to die by quicksand? How badly would it hurt when his body finally forced him to take a breath of the sticky slime? The thought of being petrified underground like a dinosaur gave some humor to the fate he was now ready to accept.

As he waited for the moment to come, he became aware of a floating sensation. He didn't feel what was often referred to as that bitter sting of death, and his lungs still seemed to burn. His body hadn't forced the killing breath yet. The change in texture around him could only mean that he had fallen through the floor of his tunnel into a large underground pool of water.

At first he attempted to swim, but luckily saw through the futility, knowing that in this circumstance he would likely experience vertigo. So relaxing his body, he fought the urge to struggle, and allowed the searing air in his lungs to carry him upward.

It didn't take long to hit the ceiling, and though his body was protesting the lack of air with every second, he pressed himself to swim along it. At long last he could control his body no longer, and he accidently allowed a small sip of water to enter his lungs.

He caught himself from bringing in any more, but the burning and retching within nearly caused him to fully inhale and drown. If his hand hadn't at that moment pushed through the surface of the water, he would have expired right then.

Using every last bit of strength, he kicked his legs enough to push his head out of the water. Coughing and gasping several times, he was able to bring in the most refreshing air he'd ever breathed. Barely conscious, and completely drained of energy, he tried to find a ledge or something to hold on to while he recovered from his unnatural rebirth.

Chapter 9

Lydia was quiet most of the way back to the airport where Troy's jet was waiting. He had informed her that the chopper they were riding in was complimentary of the missing, presumed dead, Marshal Steel. Troy also seemed excited to show Lydia what he'd been working on back in Hong Kong.

Lydia found it difficult to share her brother's enthusiasm. He must have spent a great deal of effort in getting to Egypt, stealing a dead man's chopper, and finding her in the middle of a desert mountain. Not only that, but to have brought a few armed men with him.

He had apologized for using force earlier, but stated that the soldiers were merely meant to be there for his protection. They had only started firing because Lydia had expelled a shot into the air and startled them. He did thank Labeeb fairly heavily for bringing some sense to the situation, and expressed his apologies for leaving the others in the well.

"Flint is a resourceful man, and he'll easily get back out of that well. I just couldn't have him clambering out and stopping you from coming with me. We are already pushing for time, and I really want you with me on this." Troy said. He also added, "I wish that I had recognized Flint for who he was while we were in the Philippines, but it had been so long since I'd seen him, and even then, only through an old wedding picture. Besides, I would never have suspected him there. I could have brought him in, and we wouldn't be where we are now. But don't worry, it won't be long and I'll make sure that you're reunited with him again."

"You said you really want me, not need me. That implies that I have a say in the matter. If that were really the case, I think I'd rather be trapped in that well with Flint."

Troy leaned forward, opened his mouth halfway, then sat back again. He remained silent for the remainder of the flight.

Once they made it back to the Sharm El Sheikh airport, they switched over to one of GRIP's private jets. Lydia passed several empty barrels that smelled of jet fuel before placing a foot on the first step going into the plane. She had to retreat a few paces as two more armed men emerged and descended the few steps in front of her, one of them addressed Troy. "Sir, we are refueled and ready to go."

"So," Lydia sneered. "It's 'sir,' now, is it?"

They sat down and prepared for takeoff. Troy seated Lydia right across from him. "Lydia, please, I need you to understand there is more here at stake than you know. We have a chance to change the world."

"I understand," Lydia replied coldly. "Persephone

has you in her GRIP, pun intended. Did you know about what she was having me do this whole time?”

Troy thought for a moment on how to respond, then began, “I think you deserve an explanation, and I hope you will try to see things from my point of view for a minute.”

When she did not respond, he continued, “When we were young, as you know, we were destined to follow in our father’s path and be guardians of the secrets which that society held so close. But after his death, they completely snubbed us. I went looking for them. For a couple of years I kept getting close, but they would push me away. Finally I was confronted by one of them, and he told me that I would not be allowed in. But that didn’t stop me.

“I followed him, and found access to some of their secrets. They were crooked, selfish, and corrupt as could be. It was then that I realized that something else needed to be done. They were trying to bury and keep secret everything about our past. But this world is heading in the same direction that our Martian ancestors were. Already we are polluting our air, and slowly choking our planet to death. I knew that if I did nothing, we would repeat their same mistakes. That’s when I decided to start GRIP.”

Lydia began to tremble as the realization began to fully sink in. “So you’re telling me that it was you who manipulated me this whole time, not Persephone?”

“I knew that you would never join me because of my rebellious childhood,” Troy confessed. “That’s why I set her up to be my mouthpiece to you. I only did what I had to. I needed you, and I wanted you with me. We’re going to save the world from itself.”

Lydia was turning more angry than shaken. “How many people are going to die and suffer because of this?"

"That is the unfortunate part of any big change," Troy relented. "But in the end it will be better all around for everyone. Just imagine peace throughout the world, with a single technologically responsible central government. There would be an end to nuclear threats, pollution, and war. Even the rivalries in the Middle East would finally be subdued.

"Some death and suffering will be natural as events unfold, but in the long run, lives will be saved, and the world will be on a more sustainable and responsible path than it otherwise would be."

"You make this sound as though there is much more to your plan than simply cutting off the world's oil supply," Lydia pried.

"Oh yes, much more." Troy beamed. "The plan has been put in motion, and granted, it happened a few weeks earlier than I was ready for, but it cannot be stopped now. Change is coming, and you can be a part of it."

"I was already a part of it. I don't want anything more to do with it," Lydia snapped. "You may be my brother, but you are also an insane sociopath. If Dad were here, he would turn you over his knee, then die of heartache for what you are doing. I can't believe I ever trusted you. I'm betting that you made up everything about Flint when you had me leave him after my accident, didn't you? Was it you or your pet dog, Kore, who faked my suicide note?"

"Lydia, we all have had to make sacrifices, and some of us will continue to need to do things that are difficult for us." He then turned to Labeeb, who had been sitting silently, listening the whole time. "Labeeb, you have been all around the world and seen the suicidal path that humanity has taken. Surely you must see the logic and importance in this, don't you?"

Lydia stared hard at her companion, knowing that he couldn't possibly be buying into this. But to her surprise, he replied, "You know, Troy, at first I was a little hurt that I had been kept in the dark. I never have supported the idea of eco-terrorism, even though I am concerned about the environment. But after hearing that this wasn't just some terrorist attack, but the beginning of something more meaningful, I have to admit that I'm actually pretty excited about it."

Troy gave him a satisfied smile and turned back to Lydia, his smile changed to a pleading look of concern. "See, you have to take a step forward and look beyond what has happened. Was it wrong to deceive you? Yes. Don't you think it hurt me to cause you that kind of pain?"

Lydia didn't know how to answer so she simply turned her head to the side and pressed it into the seat cushion. Tears of sadness and anger wanted to gush their way out, but she felt it would show too much weakness, further empowering her brother.

"I can tell that you need time to think this over," Troy soothed, putting a hand on her shoulder. She twisted away. He pulled his hand back and continued, "I'll leave you for a while to think about this. I know you'll come around soon enough. And even if you have a hard time forgiving me, think instead of the better world that we can make. I really want you to be a part of it."

He got up to walk to the back of the plane, pausing only long enough to shake Labeeb's hand. "I think we can find a good place for a man of your talent and understanding."

Chapter 10

Flint's soaking shirt and jeans fought every effort to crawl onto the stone shelf that sloped into the underground reservoir. By and by, he hoisted his body up until he was laying prone on dry ground. The threat of drowning gone, Flint lifted his head in surprise. It hadn't dawned on him till just now, but he could see! Though he'd lost his flashlight, the cave maintained a soft blue luminescence. It reminded him of the ambiance created by LED Christmas lights.

Between fits of coughing, Flint took in his surroundings. The sloped shore that extended into the underground body of water, also reached another fifteen feet into the relatively dry cave. The rough diameter of the open cave was only about thirty feet. The gentle echo of water droplets suggested that the cave extended quite far in both directions. The appearance was that of a slow river with a walking path.

Tempering the desire to explore his new surroundings, he knew that Dusty and Monk only had a short amount of time before they either ran out of good air or the tunnel collapsed from the water that was filling it. They still might die in here, but at least the air was fresh. Far more refreshing in fact than any air he could remember. Maybe it was just his half drowned lungs savoring what they almost traded for water.

Flint pressed his eyes shut, shuddering away the fear of going back. The return trip into the hand-dug tunnel would be just as perilous, if not more so. After a couple of minutes, he felt that he was as prepared as could be. The water was warm, but still a little colder than the air in the cave. If he wasn't so worried about the task at hand, he might have even enjoyed the dip as he waded back into the calm shimmering pool. Wading out as deep as he could to save his energy, he then swam the rest of the way to where the ceiling sloped into the pond. After releasing two chest-heaving gulps of air, he drew one last reservoir of oxygen and dived beneath the rock.

With a clear mind, and his lungs full of new air, it didn't take long to find the hole from which he'd come. He would have missed it had his feet not kicked the shovel sticking up from the floor of the pool. He started to test the hole above him, and found that his body had plowed a clean hole through the less stable earth that he originally passed through.

Since he wasted too much time finding the opening, Flint quickly swam back to the cave to refresh his breath. Though he didn't want to dwell on it long, he did pause for a moment to reminisce about his good fortune to have found the only soft spot between the well and the hardened rock cave.

After a couple of deep practice breaths, he dipped back below the water and swam as quickly as he could to his tunnel. As he went through, he made sure that his body was positioned so that his head would be faced upward upon arriving into the dugout portion of the tunnel. There would be no room to roll onto his back once inside. This last-second move proved to save his life, as it took considerably more exertion than he had expected to push his way through the slimy hole and back into the tunnel.

Once in the tunnel, he again had that burning sensation in his chest, warning of an automatic reflex that could drown him. He took a gamble, since it was his only option, and prayed that there was still a pocket of air left at the top of the tunnel.

Then, pressing his face up until it touched the ceiling of the tunnel, he allowed his body to suck in a couple short bursts of air. Some water got into his mouth, but he drew in enough air to sustain himself as he pushed his way through the narrow passage back into the well. All the while he did his best not to touch the increasingly fragile ceiling.

Once he made it into the well shaft, his hands gripped Dusty's ankles. Even though his head was submerged, he could hear her shriek. It took a moment before they realized that they needed to help him. But finally a strong hand gripped his wrists and pulled him up and out of the man-made wormhole.

Flint stood light-headed next to Monk. Dusty, on the other hand, had climbed up the shaft like a scared cat would run up a tree. Monk, having guessed what had startled her, had taken her place below to help Flint up.

"I found it," Flint gasped, only now realizing how bitter and stale the air had become inside the well.

"It's not easy, though, and I doubt we'll all make it unless I take the rope with me and use it to pull you through."

"I'm not crawling through there!" Dusty protested.

"I don't really care," Flint replied. "I'd prefer to all stay together. And I doubt the air will remain breathable here for another ten minutes. But if you want to die here alone, I won't stop you."

She slipped down a foot or so and whimpered, "You wouldn't leave me here alone, would you?"

"Frankly, I want to live, and the cave is our best bet. I'll go first, and take the rope with me. Give me a few minutes and feed me as much rope as I need. When I get to the other side, I'll need a few minutes to catch my breath, then I'll give three hard jerks on the rope. When I do, I want you, Dusty, to come first. All you have to do is take a good deep breath, and hold on tight. I'll pull you all the way through. You'll end up in a large pool of water, but just keep holding on until I pull you to safety.

"Monk, make sure I have enough slack to get her and you both through. Once she is through, I may need another minute to rest, then I'll give another three hard tugs on the rope, and it will be your turn. It will be a long and muddy trip, but don't let go, and don't panic. Just let the rope guide you through."

There was a silent tension, and Flint knew that they would follow. To stay was pointless. As he was about to dive back under, Dusty slid down and asked, "Wait." Flint held off until she was standing between him and Monk. "Please be careful," she whispered, and then she pressed her clean, soft lips to his, which were wet and muddy.

Flint smiled, but didn't return the kiss. He simply stated, "This will be scary, but hold tight to the rope,

I'll bring you through." With that, Monk and Dusty climbed up the shaft a few feet so that Flint could grab the rope and get back through the tunnel.

In preparation for what he hoped would be the last time he risked his life in the tunnel, he took a deep breath and pushed through, his one hand holding tightly to an end of the rope while stretching the other hand ahead to feel his way through the mud.

Since he hadn't gone in with his back to the floor, Flint's mouth wasn't in any position to catch another breath at the end of the tunnel. Instead he continued straight down. The path was easier this time around, and he found himself in the underground pool after only a minute and a half.

Out of breath, he began to exhale as he swam in the direction of the cave. Just as his breath finished, he popped back up into the open and inhaled. Then, dragging the rope up onto the sloped shore of the cave, he began to look for a good place to brace himself for pulling the others through.

His strength returned quickly, and by the time he had found a place to anchor himself and keep the rope from binding, he felt ready to bring the others in. So with three good tugs on the rope, he waited.

He didn't know how long it would take before they were ready, but he braced himself for when they were. After two minutes, he felt two substantial tugs on the rope, and he began pulling.

It was easy at first, but became increasingly difficult. He decided that Dusty was hesitant, and freezing up inside the cave. Flint scolded himself. He shouldn't of counted on Dusty being able to hold on the whole time. He should have made her wrap the rope around her body. Now he played a careful game of tug-a-war with her. While he didn't want to pull the rope through her fingers, he also knew that every second counted. So he kept firm pressure and pulled about one foot for every five seconds.

He figured that from the well shaft to the pool of water it was about fourteen or fifteen feet. From there, it would be another fifteen feet until she could pop up into the cave. He did a quick calculation in his mind and figured that by the time she hit the pool, she would have been holding her breath for over a minute. He believed that he could pull her into the air pretty quickly from there, but she would still need to hold her breath for at least a full minute and a half.

Guessing that he had already been pulling for about thirty seconds, he started counting from there. He counted to eighty by the time he felt a little more slack on the line and he knew she was in the pool. Then, as quickly as he could, he pulled her through the water.

However, by the time she was close to the edge, the tension completely fell off of the rope. Flint didn't hesitate; he dived right into the water and found her body slowly sinking.

He grabbed one of her arms and pulled it over his shoulder as he did a side stroke back to the shore. With her legs still in the water, he began mouth-to-mouth resuscitation. It only took a few breaths before she coughed and vomited the water.

Flint turned her on her left side as she recovered from the ordeal. "Just relax for a minute," he comforted. "You're all right, you made it."

She sobbed a little, but choked a smile at the same time. "My hero," she joked.

Flint laughed at the cliché. "Yeah, you'll be all right. I need to pull Monk through now, so hang tight and try to rest for a minute."

She put her head down and curled into a fetal position, trying to recover from her painful ordeal. Flint got ready and gave another three tugs on the rope. Monk had apparently already gotten ready, since he immediately felt two sharp tugs in reply.

This time he began counting out loud, "One-alligator, two-alligator . . ."

Dusty, still slightly dazed, cried out, "Alligator, where?"

"Sorry, just counting," Flint informed. He then switched to, "Five-Mississippi, six-Mississippi . . ."

Monk came through relatively easy. When he popped his head out of the water, he didn't even appear to be out of breath. Monk gingerly got out of the water, took the rope from Flint, and he began pulling it again.

"Good idea," Flint told him. "The rope might still come in handy."

However, it wasn't the rope that Monk was after. As soon as the end of it came out of the pool, Flint saw that Monk had tied the metal bucket onto it before he'd come through.

"Why didn't I think of that?" Flint stated. "I guess as long as we're bringing everything with us, I might as well go grab the shovel, too." He then dived into the water and came out a little later with the shovel that had sunk to the bottom.

By this time, Dusty was up and moving about. The soft bluish light that filled the whole cave had apparently been emanating from dozens, if not hundreds, of small glass stones. Monk picked one up to observe it. However, no sooner had he lifted it from the edge of the water than the light in that particular one went dim.

Thinking that he had broken it somehow, he threw it back into the water, whereupon it immediately lit back up to its full intensity.

"Interesting," Dusty remarked as she examined the glass stones along with the rest of the cave's surfaces. "The whole cave is covered in moss. It has to be the moss we're looking for."

Flint hadn't noticed it before, because it wasn't very slippery to walk on. He scraped some of the plant off of the wall and noticed that the wall wasn't just rock. "Come look at this!" he called out. "It looks like the rock is embedded with quite a bit of iron."

Dusty looked at it, and confirmed that it did in fact have a large concentration of some natural metals. "I bet this cave could play havoc with a person's compass," she observed.

Monk, who'd been examining another one of the lighted stones, came up, and Flint took a minute to examine it as well. He pressed it up against the wall, and it lit up. When he took it off of the wall, its light faded, but didn't go completely out. It still held a faint glow.

It wasn't heavy, so Flint guessed it to be hollow. "It's kind of like a fluorescent bulb," he pointed out. "I bet these are what they used in the spaceship to light it up."

"The electrical current must be passing from the roots of the moss, onto the surfaces of the cave, and through the water. This whole cave is a giant battery," Dusty said.

"Why aren't we getting shocked now?" Flint asked.

"I don't know much about electricity," Dusty hypothesized, "but I think that once we were past the initial shock back in the tunnel, we became part of the electrical field here. I imagine that when we leave the cave, we'll find a similar shock awaiting us."

"I bet this moss is why there is so much fresh air

in here, also," Flint added.

Monk took another approach and quoted, "'But as for the cities that stood still in their strength, Israel burned none of them.. ..And all the spoils of these cities, and the cattle, the children of Israel took for a prey unto themselves.. ..until they had destroyed them, neither left they any to breathe.' Joshua 11:13-14."

Flint thought for a minute, trying to interpret. "Are you talking about the air?" he asked.

Monk nodded, and Flint thought he understood. "Yeah, I think you might have a point."

"How can he have a point?" Dusty accused. "He never makes any sense."

"You just have to get used to him," Flint coaxed. "I think what he's pointing out is that plants turn carbon dioxide into oxygen. That means that there must be a source of CO_2 coming in, and oxygen going out, or else the moss would starve itself."

"How did you get that from--ah never mind! Why is that significant?" Dusty asked.

"Well, it means that there has to be a vent or opening to this cave." Flint looked at Monk to confirm his interpretation. Monk gave an affirming nod.

Dusty's eyes also lit up with understanding. "And if there is a vent, there is likely a way out," she finished.

"Which means," Flint added, "we have work to do. Let's start by getting some samples, and then we can find our way out of here."

Chapter 11

Two hours into the flight, Labeeb took the opportunity to use the onboard restrooms. Once in, he locked the door and sat down on the toilet. He had no need to actually relieve himself; instead he needed the privacy. It was the same excuse that he had practiced on many occasions while flying around with Lydia. Still he needed to be quick. In a plane this small, to do anything more than urinate in the lavatory would be doing the rest of the passengers a real discourtesy. If he stayed too long in the confined room without offending anybody's nostrils, they might become suspicious. Pulling out his satellite phone, he wrote out an e-mail to Fran.

Troy, Lydia's brother, has found us. He is running GRIP. He has something else big planned. Lydia and I are with him, and on our way to Hong Kong. Flint is trapped in a well near the old shipwreck. Will update you when I know more. I have a bad feeling about this.

Once finished, he sent the message. And though he doubted it would send in the airplane, he knew that the moment his phone found a satellite, the message would be off. Standing up, he flushed the toilet and turned the sink on.

He was also aware that if his phone was found and searched, he would be dead as soon as they landed. He started slipping it back into his front pants pocket then changed his mind and tucked it into his calf-high socks, letting his pants conceal the bulge. For now he would have to rely on Troy's self-righteous confidence in the logic of his plan. Without it, Troy might immediately suspect Labeeb's deception.

In all of this, his biggest worry went out to Flint. Though Flint seemed to be fairly resourceful and in good physical shape, Labeeb knew that it would not be an easy task getting the lid off that well. Aside from being with him only a short couple of days, all else he knew of Flint was that women seemed to gravitate to him. In their little party, there had been three men and two girls, and they had both been fighting over him.

Their attraction to Flint didn't bother Labeeb in the least. Sure, Lydia was amazingly beautiful and perfectly capable in many regards, but he had spent enough time with her to know that he wanted a less militant woman for himself. Someday he hoped to settle down with a nice wife who would teach his children something other than the best way to kill another person.

Besides, he'd seen how she conducted herself around Dusty. Unsure of whether most women would have behaved as hostilely, he held out hope that there was a woman with more sense for himself. But even though he didn't find himself romantically attracted to Lydia, he couldn't help but respect her. She had given so much of herself to doing what she thought was right, and she often exercised good judgment in every mission he'd participated in. He really hoped that they would all come through this alive in the end.

He laughed at the prospect of all surviving. Then he would be able to enjoy watching Flint as he would have to choose between two women. Flint seemed to be the type of man who would rather take on a whole band of armed mercenaries than be responsible for sorting through the labyrinth of a woman's heart.

Stepping out of the restroom, he idled back down the narrow isle to his seat. Lydia, however, stole his attention, and signaled him to sit next to her. He knew that she wanted to confront him about taking Troy's side. So to avoid accidentally giving himself away, he took a seat across from her so that they could speak without as much eavesdropping.

As soon as he sat down, Lydia began to quietly grill him. "What did you mean by saying that Troy's ideas sounded good? I thought you were smarter than that."

Labeeb knew that anything he said might be overheard, so he gave her a discreet wink and answered, "I'm sorry, Lydia, it's not that I'm betraying you, but the world was heading in a self-destructive path long before you or I. It was only a matter of time. If Troy really has a plan to bring more unity and stability to Earth's destiny, then who am I to argue against it? Don't you think it's at least worth thinking about?"

Lydia did take note of his wink. In fact he became worried for a moment, and he looked around to see if anybody had seen the look of understanding that she betrayed in her expression. She was quick to change it back to a disapproving scowl, and he doubted that anyone else had noticed. But it did cause him a degree of unease. *Maybe I should have kept her in the dark,* Labeeb thought.

Lydia continued her accusations, for which he was thankful. It would help keep up his ruse. "What about Flint, Monk, and Dusty? Do you also approve of how Troy trapped them in the well?"

Labeeb knew that he could evoke a real emotional response out of her with this question, and not just an act, since she really did feel deeply about leaving Flint behind. "I don't want to argue about it." Labeeb pretended to act diplomatic. But then he went in for the emotional response. "But Troy does have a point. Flint and Monk are very capable. It may not be easy for them, but I'm sure they'll get out. As for Dusty, I doubt very much that you would mind if she didn't make it out of the well."

"What's that supposed to mean?" she asked. "Are you saying that I'm heartless, or that I hate her—that much?"

"Well, you don't deny that you hate her?" he probed, happy to have diverted the conversation, but still keeping her on edge.

"I can't believe I'm hearing this from you!" she cried. "How long have you been working with me? You should know that I'd never wish that on anyone."

"You are right, Lydia, and I apologize." Labeeb then wondered where if anywhere the conversation should move. He was sure that he had set an eavesdropping Troy at ease, but since he could not be sure, he decided to say a few more words regarding Troy's plan.

"Lydia," he continued, "I really don't want to end up at odds with you. If you do eventually come around to seeing the greater good in GRIP's mission, I want to still be your friend. And I do believe you'll see things more our way. Just try not to worry so much about Flint. He'll be just fine, you'll see. I don't know if it was entirely necessary to cover the well back up like Troy did, but I'm sure that he wouldn't have done it if he thought that Flint would truly be stuck down there. I think that Troy is sincere in his goal to help save our world, and you can't do that without having a good heart and a sound conscience."

Labeeb could see that Lydia was disgusted by what he was saying, but they both knew there was nothing they could do about it right then. The best thing for each of them was for Labeeb to continue playing up to Troy, and for Lydia not to push the tyrannical leader of GRIP too far.

Troy clearly wanted his sister to become a part of whatever empire he was trying to create. But until they both knew and fully understood his plan, it would be difficult to stop him. He had, after all, amassed several resources, and already struck a crippling blow to the world economy. If that was just the beginning, Labeeb feared what the ending was going to look like.

Lydia was relieved to find that Labeeb was still on her side. In all of their time together, she had never realized how talented he really was. Not only had he seen beyond the futility of fighting Troy, but he had even convinced her of his change in loyalties.

She still found it difficult not to be angry with him. Those cheap shots at her feelings, she knew to be necessary. Even so, it didn't mean he should have said them about Flint and Dusty. But if she were honest with herself, she knew that he was justified in saying those things. She had nearly given him away when he winked at her, and she knew that she was to blame for the slip in her demeanor. She could see the stress in his accusingly worried expression.

With that out of the way, she tried to focus on Troy, and how exactly his plans might shape out. She was constantly distracted from this by the fact that she didn't know all the facts yet, and because she had serious concerns about Flint. Troy had sealed him in the well, trying to convince her that he'd find a way out. Labeeb had tried to alleviate her concerns in the matter also, but Lydia was practical enough to know that it was likely hopeless. Troy probably couldn't care less about Flint, and Labeeb was just trying to lighten her mind.

Chapter 12

The task of collecting moss samples was easy. The strange plant seemed to grow well on soil or rock face. So they simply put a little dirt in the bottom of the bucket, stuck a little water in, and threw in a couple of moss-covered rocks. Then, for good measure, Flint threw in a couple of the hollow glass stones. He then took off his dripping shirt and covered the top of the bucket with it.

Dusty, upon seeing him without a shirt, took great notice of his powerfully built chest. Flint knew that he didn't have the same muscular physique of a bodybuilder. He was far too lean for that shape. He was, however, aware that he was well defined. A life of being physically active had given him a toned appearance that rivaled that of many men his age.

Dusty stepped close to him, and must have hoped he'd forgotten how whiny she had been earlier. She placed her palm on his chest and let it slide down across his abdomen. "Wow," she stated. "I think you should have made the whole trip without your shirt on. You look amazing."

"It's just the lighting," Flint replied, not only trying to be humble, but also trying to regain focus.

Dusty didn't seem to catch his subtleness. "If I had a man like you, no adventure could have been able to pull me away," she persisted, obviously referring to Lydia's running away.

Flint didn't want to hurt her feelings, but at the same time, his mind was far from thinking of romance. Dusty was highly attractive, and her wet, muddy clothes seemed only to add to her allure. But he was still having a hard time getting past the petty bickering that had so easily beset both her and Lydia.

He was relieved when he found that Monk seemed to be getting annoyed with it, also. Monk stepped so close that he was almost between them, so as to intrude on her personal bubble. He then gave her an icy stare, which only Monk could do with his distinct absence of outward emotion.

Having achieved his desired effect by causing her to step back, Monk motioned for them to get moving. At first they weren't sure which way to go. It seemed to Flint that the cave stretched on quite far in both directions. He did, however, see a small neck in the cave at one end, and it gave him an idea.

He reached the narrow portion of the cave with Dusty right behind. At first he couldn't find what he was looking for, so when Dusty came close he moved in and asked, "I need a favor from you."

"Anything," Dusty said, hoping to rekindle Flint's attraction to her.

But as soon as she neared him, Flint put his hand up to her head and pulled one of her long hairs out. "There we go, thank you."

Dusty flinched, not at all expecting what he had done. "What did you do that for?" she accused.

Flint didn't answer right away. He simply straightened out the hair and let it dangle upside down for a moment. After slightly twisting it in his fingers so that he could make sure that what he was seeing was accurate, he announced, "There is a very slight breeze coming from that direction." He pointed from where they had just come. "My guess is that there is a vent that way, and an opening this way."

Stealing the hair from Dusty to test the air current served two main purposes in Flint's mind. Though it was no firm indicator of the direction of the cave's opening, it was enough to settle Dusty's nerves, and to give her the confidence in him that was needed to keep her from complaining any further. His other reason for using one of her hairs to test the airflow was he wanted her to be just angry enough with him that she would stop flirting for a little while.

Without any objections from either Dusty or Monk, he decided to proceed. He figured that the worst that could happen, aside from not finding an exit at all, was they would have to turn around and go the other way instead. He refused to believe that there was no way out.

They didn't go more than fifty feet before they found their first obstacle. A portion of the cave had collapsed over the walkable area. They were forced to swim underneath the large boulder that blocked their path. There was just enough space above the boulder and the water to pass the bucket across without filling it with water.

Once back on dry ground, they continued for what Flint guessed must have been over a mile. All along the way, they found moss covering the cave, and the ancient glass stones lighting the way. Then they went around one corner, only to find that the lights ended. Not wanting to grope around in the darkness, Flint backed up and took up a couple of the glass stones from the lit portion of the cave and then continued back into the darkened portion. The stones dimmed noticeably, but they were still better than pitch blackness.

They stayed close together as they journeyed through this part. The faint luminescence provided by the stones was enough to navigate by. Only when they needed a little more light would Flint touch the two stones to a surface of the cave to increase the brilliance, allowing them to find their way around any obstacles that presented themselves. The cave was becoming more rugged with every step. It seemed as though this portion had been mined out a long time ago, leaving behind a jagged bed of broken shale. At one point they had to climb up a slide of these sharp rocks and boulders.

After what Flint estimated to be another fifty feet, they came to a dead end. Dusty was again the first to show signs of despair. "Oh great! I thought you said the opening to the cave would be right here!"

Monk shushed her and put his finger to his ear, signifying that they needed to listen carefully.

After a few seconds, a smile crossed Flint's face. "What is it?" Dusty asked. "I don't hear anything."

"That's because you're too frustrated to listen," Flint replied casually. He hadn't meant to sound rude, but she nonetheless took offense. Flint realized his mistake but didn't apologize. He had forgotten how sensitive some women could be. But he justified his mistake by not having lived with a woman for the last two years.

"There is a slight whistling of air going into this

wall," Flint explained as he and Monk began to examine the wall. But the moss had become so thick over this area that he had a hard time seeing behind the organic plaster.

Taking up a flat stone, he scraped off the moss until he found something that clearly was man-made. It was a thick metallic rod. He followed it up to a piece of old machinery. "What do you think of this?" he asked Monk.

Monk studied it for a few seconds before Dusty chimed in, "That looks like something I saw on the Martian ship."

"Do elaborate," Flint encouraged.

Dusty stood closer to examine the device and then explained, "Inside the ship there was a large room that I suspected to be a cargo hold. There had been a place for two mechanical devices, one of which was missing. The one we saw looked just like this. I think it operated the cargo door."

"Now, that's what I like to hear," Flint said as he began to scrape more gently at the moss that had accumulated on the device.

"Why, what are you thinking?" she asked.

Monk responded, "'But I shall shew you plainly of the Father.' John 16:25."

Dusty looked confused, but Flint knew that in his own way Monk was saying, "If it isn't obvious, then just wait and see."

Flint looked closer at the machine and found what he was looking for: a couple of crude metallic rods extending from the wall. This was where the air was escaping from the cave. The small slotted penetration, though overgrown with moss, appeared to be mechanical in nature. With a little strained effort, he was able to slide one of the bars about an inch and a half. As soon as the bar could move no farther, he became aware of a dull groaning. The sound was accompanied by a low tremble beneath their feet, as if a giant millstone was grinding along.

"Look!" Dusty pointed. "The wall is moving."

Indeed it was. Flint guessed correctly that the rod was some sort of switch. The power for the massive device was feeding off the electricity generated by the moss to open a door to the outside. The motor moved slowly, opening the door inward. As the passageway opened, a cool breeze picked up, bathing them in warm humid air as the cave inhaled through the four-foot-wide doorway. The way beyond was still part of the cave, but the air was different. Smelling less fresh, more normal.

"Ladies first," Flint offered. As soon as they were through, Flint found the matching end to the metallic rod he had manipulated. Sliding this rod again caused the grinding to restart. The stone doorway from whence they came began to close behind him. He wasn't sure why he closed the door, but he figured that if he ever needed to get back in, then at least he knew how to do so. Besides, there was just something inside him that wanted to preserve the cave in its original splendor. To leave it open might invite uncourteous visitors.

Once the door was closed, Flint examined it, and found that it was perfectly camouflaged to look just like a regular rock wall. The moss had ended, but his glass stones were still emanating a glow, though fainter than before. They walked a few feet away with Dusty in front—then she shrieked again.

Monk shook his head, as one would do who is fed up with a child. "What is it this time?" Flint asked.

But Dusty smiled and said, "Oh, nothing." She continued on a few more feet and waited.

Flint sighed as he walked next to Monk. Once

they got to the spot where she had shrieked, they too let out a cry of surprise from the zing that let them know that they had left the electric field created from the mossy portion of the cave.

Dusty laughed. "Oh, what's wrong?" she said, relishing in her moment.

Flint couldn't blame her and laughed a little. "Yeah, laugh it up, Dusty."

He then pressed a glass stone to the wall nearest him, but as he expected the stones had stopped working altogether. Even the moss samples in the metal bucket were too weak to illuminate the stones. "I think we're going to have to feel our way through the remainder of this cave," he informed. Then, putting the stones in his pocket, he started moving along the cave wall.

Monk added, "'We grope for the wall like the blind, and we grope as if we had no eyes: we stumble at noonday as in the night; we are in desolate places as dead men.' Isaiah 59:10."

They didn't have far to go before they began to see some light in the cave. As they got closer, they found a small opening, only big enough to squeeze through. It looked as though it had been much larger at one time, but the cave had since collapsed at this point.

Once out, Flint and Dusty surveyed their position. They were surrounded by tall rocky cliffs, and though the whole place looked different now, it wasn't difficult to realize where they were. Ahead of them was a charred depression in the ground. Bits of metal were scattered across the entire valley. They were looking at the littered valley where Marshal Steel had blown up the ancient Martian spaceship. Dusty wore a look of sadness, and Flint sympathized. He may not feel the degree of regret that burdened the anthropologist, but he too would have loved the chance to explore the ancient relic from another world.

With only a minute or two of reminiscing over the site, Dusty collected herself and was first to point out how late in the day it really was. The sun had already begun its descent, and Flint knew that they only had a couple of hours of daylight remaining. They had spent much more time in the cave than he had realized. "I guess it's true," he told her. "Time really does fly when you're having fun."

Dusty simply grunted as if to say, *Only a lunatic would call that fun.*

They rested for the next hour or two before going in search of their camels and supplies. Sleep quickly overcame the fatigued group. Flint woke with a start, surprised that he'd drifted to sleep. He was disoriented for a minute, but quickly came to. The trip back to Fran might be a long restless journey, but he couldn't afford to drag his feet. For every minute he wasted, the likelihood of saving Lydia shrunk. He jumped up, cramped muscles pained his every move, making him walk like an old arthritic man as he woke up the others. Dusty complained, Monk didn't. Flint was hungry and a little worried about their trip back to civilization. But with no food or transportation, all they could do was hike back and look for the well.

It took only an hour. The camels were still where they had left them, though they were as ornery as ever. But, fully exhausted, the party decided to eat what they could of their supplies, and to leave the rest. Then, with some difficulty, they mounted the camels, and began their trip back. They traveled all night and most of the following day before they arrived at the road. Their truck was still there, but the remaining fuel had been taken. With bottoms too sore for riding, they walked, letting the camels carry all their supplies. After an hour of walking they managed to pick up a ride from a small tanker truck that was transporting a load of untainted oil. The camels were released to roam, the lucky beasts having traded one good day of work for the chance to escape some Egyptian's stew pot.

They made Suez by nightfall, and were moving down the piers when they saw Fran's sailboat nearing in the moonlight. "I hope he has a nice shower and bed on that thing," Dusty commented. "Because I'm so exhausted."

"Amen," Monk simply replied.

Flint just kept quiet and looked down at his bucket of moss. He hoped that it would be worth all the trouble. And though he had almost endured enough of Dusty and Lydia's bickering, he felt obligated to find and help his wife. He didn't know why Troy had taken her, but he now believed that Kore wasn't the only corrupt person within the GRIP organization.

He wasn't sure what game Troy was up to, but he doubted that it was admirable.

Chapter 13

Lydia tried to close her eyes, but sleep wouldn't come. It wasn't as if she'd never slept on the seat of a jet before. She'd done that quite often. No, this was different. There are times when her mind just kept thinking too much to settle down. Half way through their flight, Troy changed his plans and landed in India. His jet had enough fuel to make the trip to Hong Kong, but there was another plane that didn't. That other plane was Lydia's modified Leer jet. As it turned out, when Lydia's partner, Grisha, betrayed her and flew away from Amos' headquarters in Egypt, he and Kore landed their chopper at Cairo and confiscated her Leer Jet.

They had money enough, but what they didn't count on was the speed at which India would react to their oil plot. When they landed in India to refuel, they discovered that the Indian government had already shut down all unnecessary fuel sales. Grisha and Kore were trapped in the Indira Gandhi International Airport near New Delhi.

Troy seemed adamant on having Grisha and Kore join him in Hong Kong, hence the reason everybody was camping for the night in Troy's jet on the tarmac. Troy had told Lydia that Kore, though he still called her Persephone, would join them in the morning, at which time they would complete their last leg to Troy's base in Hong Kong. Lydia had never personally been there, but from the excitement in Troy's description, she doubted that it would just be a business building like the one Amos operated from. No, Troy was much more of a secret lair sort of fanatic. But it wasn't the anticipation of seeing his base of operations that kept her awake. It was the looming confrontation with Grisha and Kore that she couldn't stop thinking about. How did Troy expect her to get along with those two after all that had happened?

Lydia knew her brother well enough. He was certifiably nuts. But he apparently didn't know his own sister. Sure he understood her enough to successfully manipulate her for two years, but somehow he expected her to catch his lunatic vision of world terror. He was so self-absorbed that he couldn't reason beyond his own ambitions. Not only could that be annoying to anybody who didn't share his vision, but Lydia suspected it to be a blind spot of his also. Somebody under Troy could easily use that self-important trust to accomplish their own agenda. Labeeb was one such that was succeeding so far in doing just that. How long he could keep the show up, she didn't know. But to work for Troy meant that a person had to have a low moral conscience. Lydia wondered if any of Troy's men were following him, but also plotting behind his back. To what end she couldn't know. Maybe once she learned all of Troy's plan, a clear picture would present itself. If there was anyone plotting against him for control of GRIP, she might be able to use that to escape, or shut GRIP down entirely.

Lydia jumped in her seat, startled as one of Troy's men stepped into the jet. She hadn't thought that she'd slept at all during the night, but she couldn't remember this man leaving, so apparently she had drifted at one point. In one bag, he had something that smelled spicy. In another was some fruit. It was breakfast.

Grisha and Kore showed up later that morning, and by noon, they were back in the air, on their way to Hong Kong. Not a word was spoken by Lydia to her former co-pilot, and an especially cold stare was reserved for Kore. Kore didn't seem bothered, but Grisha and Lydia had a good friendship before this. He at least seemed uncomfortable by Lydia's silence. *Good. Let him feel sorry*, Lydia thought. *He manipulated me just as much as anyone else.*

Unfortunately there was nobody left to talk to now. She couldn't very well chat it up with Labeeb. He was busy schmoozing up to everyone else. To attempt conversing with him would risk giving him away. Troy was the only person she might find herself talking to. But he didn't want to hear what she had to say. Not right now at least. He figured that, given enough time, Lydia would come around. *He could give me all the time in the world and it wouldn't be enough for that.*

Chapter 14

Having come to the docks and picked up Flint, Monk, and Dusty, Fran immediately cast off again. His paranoia did not permit him to stay within such close reach of anybody on shore. Flint then learned how Fran had received a message from Labeeb, through which Fran had learned that Flint was trapped in a well. And though Fran himself was not excited about the prospect of searching for them, he had imagined that they wouldn't be in a well if they hadn't known something about the moss. Fran was about to risk a trip ashore to look for them, when they showed up. He couldn't have been more relieved.

Despite being on the relaxing luxury yacht, Flint was unable to set his mind at ease. Before they retired for the night, Fran had shown him a few news clips from around the world, which only served to increase his anxiety. There were some positive signs, and a lot more propaganda meant to look like good signs, but for the most part people were starting to use up food storages, and they were becoming desperate. His thoughts went out for a moment to Philip, wondering how his boss and mentor might be doing.

Then, in an attempt to refocus his efforts, he asked, "So, in this message that Labeeb sent you, did he mention where they were going?"

"Hong Kong," Fran answered. "I tracked his phone to this point." He then pulled up a map on his computer."

The map showed the Chek Lap Kok airport in Hong Kong, the main international airport, which was built atop a partially man-made island on the northwest portion of Lantau Island. Using the cursor, Fran pointed to the airport and explained. "When I received Labeeb's message, he was just coming in to this airport. I followed him only a short distance, about one mile up Yu Tung Road before they took off onto one of these smaller mountain roads that heads toward Lantau North Country Park. I then lost his signal after only half a mile. Either his phone was disabled at that point, or he went underground. Other than that, I know very little of what is happening."

"That's where we'll start, then," Flint said decisively. "May I place our moss bucket in your hands?"

Fran accepted. "I'll make sure that it gets to where it needs to be. But how are you going to get to Hong Kong?"

"There's always a way. I'll figure that out."

"Might I make a suggestion?" Fran asked.

Flint was open to anything that would make his plans easier, so he readily listened as Fran explained. "Later tonight, there is a diplomatic jet carrying some UN representatives. It will make a quick stop in Cairo to refuel before it extends its next leg to Hong Kong. It will be the only jet in or out of Egypt for the foreseeable future. I might be able to arrange a seat for you and maybe one other, but three would be pushing it."

"So much for a good night's rest. Get me a seat for two, I'll take Monk with me," Flint said. Since Dusty had retired to bed already, and Flint felt no shame in confiding to Fran, he added, "Dusty has been fun and helpful at times, but now she would be more of a liability than anything else. Can you take care of her and let her share in the discovery of the moss?"

"I'd be happy to," Fran said. "But as for you, if you are to make Cairo on time, you'll need to get a start right away. There are only a couple of buses that Egypt can afford to run, and they tend to be full. I'll bring us back close to shore, long enough for you and Monk to get off."

Flint agreed, and was about to find Monk when he remembered one other thing. "Fran, could I ask you one more favor?"

"I'll do my best to accommodate," the man answered.

With his shirt still being used to cover the bucket full of moss, Flint looked down at his sunburned chest. "Could I borrow a shirt?"

Fran not only provided him with a two shirts, but also a satellite phone. It was already programmed with Fran's contact information. "I'm sorry I can't provide you with anything for your personal defense. I tend to avoid conflicts where a gun might be needed."

"Let's just hope I won't need one," Flint replied.

Then, being careful not to wake Dusty, Flint

found Monk and instructed him to prepare for their little voyage. Fran then brought the sailboat back up to the docks for one last time, and allowed the two to disembark. Just before he swung back onto the open water, he gave Flint some last instructions. "Labeeb mentioned in his message that Troy was up to something big. He was very concerned, and I believe that it may have large global repercussions, worse than this oil crisis. Let me know when you find them, and if I can, I'll send the cavalry in. Good luck."

Flint extended his hand for a parting shake. "Take care of Dusty for me."

"Don't worry about her," Fran smiled. "Just try not to bloody up those shirts I gave you."

Fran's light-hearted comment was meant to put Flint at ease, and he knew it. But it had the opposite effect, reminding him of the danger he was getting into. "Trust me, if ever there was a shirt I wanted to keep clean, it would be the ones I'm wearing."

Flint and Monk headed up the pier again. Flint marveled as he reminisced about the last couple of weeks. So much had happened, and now it felt almost second nature to play a part in stopping another global threat.

Once in the streets, they didn't take long to find out where the only bus line would likely stop. An almost spooky quiet permeated the whole area. Without street lights working, the only illumination was from the moon that played peek-a-boo through the overcast skies. Not a soul moved anywhere, yet the line where the bus would stop was already growing with silent sleepy bodies. There would be no more buses after this until the morning, and Flint hoped that this last bus of the night would be quick enough in coming. Tired as he was, Flint didn't dare sit down. If he did, sleep would surely overpower him, and he'd miss his ride.

Flint was awakened by the hissing of brakes and movement of the crowd. He'd drifted to sleep while standing. Some people had taken advantage of his inattention, and cut in front of him, and filled the bus almost immediately. Flint and Monk had to resort to riding on top with about two dozen others. The bus was slow, and it took three hours instead of the normal two to get where it was going. Luckily the bus stopped not too far from the airport, and they needed only to walk for about thirty minutes to reach it.

Once there they found the security to be on high alert. There weren't nearly as many guards as he would have expected, but the ones who were there were heavily armed.

"I'm sorry, sir," one of them said as Flint approached. "But nobody is allowed into the airport at this time."

Flint hoped that Fran had gotten everything done on his end as he ordered the guard, "Check with your superior—Flint and Monk are here to take transport on the UN flight to Hong Kong."

The guard, still keeping Flint at bay, checked in on his radio. After a few instructions, which Flint couldn't hear, the guard's eyes went wide in surprise. "I'm sorry, sir, please forgive me, I had not been informed that you were coming. I will escort you personally to the jet, it is refueling now, and will be ready to leave anytime."

Flint was almost surprised at the reception that they gained. Apparently Fran had some deep and powerful connections. Upon boarding the jet, he and Monk were greeted by each of the dignitaries with respect, and even a little hint of fear. Once they were seated, a Chinese gentleman came up to them and began to speak. "So you awe the two twouble-shootews from the U.S.," he said, with emphasis on *trouble*. "Yowr code names are Flint and Monk. Well, Flint and Monk, I do not know why you awe come to China, but I have been told to assist you in any way possible." He then gave Flint his contact information, which Flint programmed into Fran's phone.

The man continued, "I do not genwally twust Amewican spies, but I have been infowmed that you awe on a mission that is vewy important fow you and fow us. As things awe wight now, I have little choice but to twust you."

Flint thought his speech sounded like more of a warning than a reception. He respectfully replied, "I assure you that our being here is in no way damaging to the Chinese people. I am on the trail of the men who started the oil crisis. They are believed to be hiding in Hong Kong. We also believe that they are planning something much bigger and more destructive. Don't be surprised if I do call you and ask for some support in the very near future."

The man gave a slight bow, but with a straight face he added, "Being on Chinese soil, I would expect that you include us in anything you find. I wish you success, and my sewvices will be at yow disposal." With that, he retired again to his seat, and the jet finished it's taxi and takeoff.

Chapter 15

Upon landing, Lydia and Labeeb were shuttled out of the airport in a large van owned by GRIP. Instead of following the primary road to the mainland, they took a small side road that led into the more mountainous part of the island. Having gone only half a mile, they pulled off and were told to exit the van.

Troy and his guards escorted them a few hundred feet off the road away from the vehicle. Once they were out of sight, he paused and waited for everyone to gather around. "What you're about to see is going to blow your mind," he declared. He then reached down at what looked like an ordinary fallen branch on the ground, and gave it a pull up. It revealed a door, almost perfectly camouflaged with the ground.

Lydia mumbled loud enough to be heard by all, "A hidden door." She followed up her terse comment by lifting her hands to her head and pulling them away, fingers spreading, as if to express that her mind was blowing. After her fingers were fully stretched out, she faked a quiet explosion sound through her lips.

Troy paid her no mind. The secret door wasn't the mind blowing vision he was panning. He didn't much care about Lydia's adult tantrum. He fully expected her to be genuinely wowed in no time. Behind the door a staircase led down into the mountain. Two of the guards went in first, followed by Troy, Lydia, and Labeeb. Then, with the other three guards following close behind, the hidden door was closed. At the bottom of the staircase was a thick metal door. One of the guards spun the wheel that sealed it, and then with great effort pulled it open.

After they went through the door, the narrow confines of the staircase continued in the form of a tight hallway. In no time, Lydia was staring into a huge underground cavern. The facility appeared to have been hollowed out, the roof being reinforced with concrete and steel into an almost perfect dome shape. It was at least two hundred meters wide and one thousand meters long.

The immense underground architecture was in fact the least impressive part of the whole view. Right down the middle of it sat what Lydia knew could only be a spaceship. All around the ship, people were busy working at little stations and cubicles. Some were loading things onto the ship while others were welding finishing touches inside small exposed compartments of the hull.

Troy must have sensed her awe and stepped up to her saying, "Lydia, I would like to introduce you to the future. In these troubled times, the Global Representatives for International Progress is about to launch a ship that will unite the governments of the world into one single body. With our ship we will be able to create and maintain peace throughout the world by having complete air, or rather space, superiority. We will be hailed as heroes. We will save the world from itself."

Lydia couldn't speak, and even if she could, she didn't know what she would want to say. When words finally did come, all she could utter was, "You made a spaceship?"

Troy relished in the opportunity to show her his creation. "It's like I told you on the trip over. I realized that the group our father belonged to was nothing more than a bunch of old cronies who were never really going to take any real action. That is why I knew I must do this. I started designing this ship several years ago.

"When Mom gave us our early inheritance after Dad died, I used it, along with that of a few wealthy supporters, to build this organization. This ship was supposed to be finished as soon as the oil supplies dried up. I was only a week off. We are now completing the final stages and will be ready to launch tomorrow morning. We've still got several hours before it's time to turn in. I'll show you around. Then, later tonight, you both must get some good rest, because tomorrow a new era begins."

Lydia kept silent, still trying to take it all in. Labeeb piped up, though, saying, "It's magnificent—I'd love a tour." While Lydia was disgusted by her brother's feat, she was nonetheless astounded. Her brother had been right after all. This truly was mind blowing. Like before, she pantomimed her head exploding, except this time there was no hint of sarcasm. Just sullen defeat. As if to say, *You called it. You win this round.*

Troy slapped Labeeb on the back, and then looked

piercingly into Lydia's eyes. "What about you, sis?"

Despite her outer protest, Lydia desperately wanted to see everything. So she just nodded in agreement, which seemed to satisfy Troy. "Well, then, where to start?" he asked himself.

The tour lasted a full hour. Troy clearly prided himself in all his accomplishments, which were not a few. During this time, Lydia learned how he had carved the deep cavern out of a relatively small cave. The spoil was carefully spread out on the surface above or hauled away, so as not to draw attention to their efforts.

"Making the ship was easy," Troy explained. "A while back I acquired a couple of Chinese manufacturing plants. Nobody asked any question as long as their paychecks were regular. Smuggling the parts into this place was the more difficult part. The major constraint was making the parts small enough to transport through the narrow openings of this subterranean vault, and doing it without drawing any attention to ourselves."

Lydia gaped in awe at the scope of Troy's accomplishments. GRIP's main headquarters was a feat of both science and ingenuity. Tucked into the sides of the cavern were several makeshift rooms. These housed everything from offices and scientific laboratories to mess halls and dorms. In one of the labs, Lydia learned that Troy's men had successfully created a device similar to what Flint had destroyed in the Philippines. Apparently after Flint had destroyed the original engine component that made the space travel possible, Troy had the pieces collected. Then with those, and other information gathered at Shen Mao's complex, his teams of researchers were able to reverse engineer it.

It was also in these small laboratories where they

came up with their own version of the solar moss that Lydia and Labeeb had been searching for. Seeing this, Lydia was filled first with excitement, followed quickly by the reminder of her betrayal. If GRIP had this plant, why did she waste so much time on her own wild goose chase? Still, she couldn't harbor ill thoughts for very long on the idea. Troy's scientists had in fact been very resourceful and brilliant. They started with a simple Earth moss, then manipulated the genetic structure by replacing portions with DNA from other organisms.

The ability to photosynthesize gamma radiation instead of sunlight came from a form of bacteria called *Rhodopseudomonas capsulata*, and from alga designated as *Anacystis nidulans*. These organisms, found near deep-sea volcanic vents, were able to thrive without sunlight. They made a similar photo reaction, similar to the way a maple leaf photosynthesizes sunlight except instead of using sunlight, these plants are able to use the deadly radiation that is found so abundantly in space.

Troy then had his people splice DNA from a variety of knifefish, more commonly known as the electric eel. Since the eels had the ability to produce a regular stream of electricity up to five hundred watts or more, they were the perfect candidate for the genetic manipulations.

When Lydia could stand it no longer she asked, "So why did you have me searching the world over for the moss brought over from Mars if you were able to make it here?"

"Yes," Labeeb agreed. "If you already had this technology, why bother letting us search for it?"

Troy didn't even skip a beat, "It took two years to get the moss perfected, which is why she had been allowed from time to time to search for the original moss. But she was never allowed to let the search take full priority over her other duties; namely, Finding the Martian journal, and dealing with Amos and his oil-solidifying bacteria."

This last mention made Lydia boil with anger again. GRIP had used her, causing her to distribute the bacteria that crippled the world's oil supply, instead of the antidote for the bacteria that she thought Amos was planting. The whole time Amos was working for GRIP and Lydia was the butt of the joke.

But Troy ignored her steaming head and continued, "We were confident that we could design a suitable replacement. Once we perfected the new substitute moss, which really only happened just two months ago, your team was encouraged to find the original for comparative purposes. We may have a great specimen now, but we aren't opposed to improving it if possible."

The tour inside the spacecraft revealed that this new moss covered the ceilings, floors, and walls. It grew on a perforated metallic surface to collect and transport the energy. The humidity inside the ship was incredibly high, as Lydia expected it might be, owing to the watering mechanism. The treated graywater and blackwater from the ship's sewer system was sent through a humidifier. Condensation would then form and flow along the metal surfaces where the moss grew. The moss would in turn be fully fed and watered, expelling clean air throughout the ship. The water in the air and on the walls, would be collected on condenser pads before being transferred again to the freshwater holding tanks. It was a unique and self-sustaining water purification system as well as a power source and a shield from harmful radiation. It created a very muggy, and slightly smelly atmosphere, but if you could get used to that, it was rather ingenious.

Lydia was impressed by the resourcefulness of her brother. Once portions of the moss died, they could be composted and placed in a large garden on the ship. This garden could grow several kinds of fruits and vegetables, allowing Troy to have a near self-sustaining environment that could easily and comfortably house dozens of people for extended periods in space.

Onboard the ship were various laboratories, exercise rooms, and living quarters. It looked clean and luxurious, so much so, in fact, that Lydia nearly forgot that Troy had a more sinister plan in mind. The reality of his imposing ambitions returned when he showed them the weapons room. Here they found hundreds of metal spheres and several dozen larger canisters.

Lydia dropped the edge of her lip as she glared between Troy and each of the knee high spheres that were held to the floor with nets. These were small bomb packages. Inside each sphere was the same device that allowed the ship to slide in and out of normal space as it traveled. The smaller bombs could be used for assassination of any target that Troy found to be a threat. No bunker on Earth could prevent one of these bomblets from penetrating its walls.

As for the larger canisters, Troy simply stated that they were for demonstration purposes only. Lydia cringed in understanding. They were meant to be larger bombs, possibly even nuclear. The thought made her shudder. She wondered how she could be related to such a man. Even when he did show emotions, they were far too smooth and refined. She wondered if he felt anything for anyone but himself.

Then she thought back to Flint, and how she had selfishly run away from him, just like Troy had run away from her family. The thought that she might be more like Troy than she had thought filled her with dread. *No,* she told herself. *I am not like him.* To prove it to herself, she refueled the burning anger of her commitment to finding a way of stopping Troy, accepting the expense of her own life if necessary.

Lydia knew that reasoning would not stop him, so she determined to find another way. Labeeb was already on her side, and she knew that she must secure some time alone with him to confide, and form a plan.

Chapter 16

After dinner, Troy showed Lydia and Labeeb to their rooms. He specifically chose two rooms for them in the dorms outside the ship. He said that a little work was needed before both of their places would be ready on the ship. This was not true, considering that the ship was practically ready for launch. Troy just didn't want them snooping around the ship during the night until he had a better feel for their loyalties.

Troy had always been skeptical of anyone he brought into his inner circle. For this reason, at the onset of his project, he'd installed hidden listening and video surveillance equipment into the walls of the sleeping quarters. It was the one place where everybody seemed to let their guard down the most. This case was no exception.

As soon as Troy left Labeeb and Lydia to their rooms, he went to his private office onboard the ship and turned on his computer. In seconds he had every noise from their rooms sounding through his speakers.

At first he heard the general rustling around and toilet flushes that accompany one when about to go to bed. He then heard the distinct click of the light switch, and he pulled up his infrared cameras. Labeeb made his room look as though he had gone to bed. Lydia was only a few minutes behind.

Both of them didn't even touch their mattresses. Instead they moved close to their adjoining wall. "Naïve," Troy said to himself. The two obviously expected some kind of hidden camera, but never assumed it could see in the dark, let alone hear them. Troy waited with impatience as the two sat biding their time. Lydia was the first to break the silence when she tapped gently on the wall. "Labeeb, can you hear me?" she whispered.

"Yes, I'm here," he quietly called back.

"What do you think of all this?" she asked.

"I'm of the same mind I was before," he replied. "You?"

"I'm a little blown away, and, honestly, I'm a little scared," Lydia admitted.

"The great Lydia, scared?" Labeeb joked.

"Did you see that weapons room? Troy could kill thousands if not millions of people!" she replied.

"He's going to start tomorrow, you know," he stated. "We can be with him, or against him. With him will probably be the safest place to be."

"And against him will likely get us both killed," Lydia added.

"You know where I stand. What about you?" he asked.

"I think you already know, or else you wouldn't confess that to me," she replied.

"You might need to let him at least think that you are turning to his side of thinking," he suggested. "If not, I doubt he'll give you access to anything that could jeopardize his plans."

"We'll find a way to stop him," Lydia concluded.

"Good night, Lydia," Labeeb finished. He then went to his bed.

Lydia stayed sitting next to the wall for almost an hour before she made her way to her bed. Troy kept monitoring her in case she called back to Labeeb with a plan. But for his purposes, he found out what he needed. Labeeb had nearly fooled him into believing that he would remain loyal to GRIP; and, as he'd assumed, Lydia would still require a little persuasion. Troy didn't like being played, and he made plans to take care of Labeeb before daybreak. Lydia, on the other hand, would just need to be watched carefully. He didn't doubt that his little sister would soon come around, but until then he needed to be careful with how much freedom she was allowed. Whatever the case turned out to be, he wasn't ready to give up on her yet.

Troy logged off of his surveillance system and pulled up the progress reports from the ship. The last of the supplies were being loaded, and all finishing touches would be completed within one hour. His crew could then get a little rest before the big day. He didn't expect to get any sleep, but he still set an alarm to wake him up at 3:00 A.M.

Chapter 17

August 9

The jet touched down, and by this point, Flint felt every eye onboard piercing into him with curiosity and speculation. By now all the passengers on the plane believed him and Monk to be American spies, the type depicted in movies and books. It showed in their small conversations with them and one another. The Chinese delegates especially betrayed a sense of agitation for being on the same flight with the Americans. Monk's emotionless expression seemed only to fuel their imaginations.

Flint wasn't sure if this was good or bad, but it was kind of fun. Besides, Fran had given him the assumed clout of being able to ask favors from the Chinese. This he had learned upon takeoff through his brief conversation with Lum Fu-han. Flint wasn't very familiar with Chinese hierarchy, but he got the impression that Lum Fu-han commanded a great deal of influence in the Chinese military.

Instead of taxing up to the main terminal, the jet parked on the tarmac and a large metal staircase was rolled up to the door. The diamond plated treads had a familiar bleacher clang as Flint climbed down the stairs. He pulled out a small sheet of paper with an aerial printout depicting Labeeb's last known position in relation to the airport, only a mile or so to walk. So when Fu-han asked him if he would need a ride anywhere, Flint told him that it wouldn't be necessary. He did, however, ask that Fu-han keep that phone of his handy in case Flint needed him in a pinch. This, Flint knew, would only fuel Fu-han's suspicions, but having enjoyed hunting much of his life, Flint knew a thing or two about tracking. If Troy was near, he could sneak up on him more effectively on foot, and with as few companions as possible.

Once outside the airport, Flint and Monk took leave of their Chinese companions and began to walk toward the mountain the map indicated. It felt good to stretch his legs again, and after twenty minutes, upon reaching the smaller road, he felt limber and alert. Before walking up the road, he paused and tried to remember his conversations with Troy in the Philippines to give himself an idea of what to expect. All he could remember, though, was some insinuation that Troy did in fact have a secret base here.

Flint decided to attack the problem differently. Thinking aloud, he asked, "If I had a secret base in the mountains, and I was determined to protect it, I think I would keep some surveillance on the roads coming in and out. Maybe some perimeter sensors, also."

Monk added his own thoughts. "'To secure ourselves against defeat lies in our own hands, but the opportunity of defeating the enemy is provided by the enemy himself. Thus the good fighter is able to secure himself against defeat, but cannot make certain of defeating the enemy. Hence the saying: One may *know* how to conquer without being able to *do* it.' Sun Tzu."

"So how do we let them show us their weakness?" Flint asked.

Monk shrugged. Flint thought for a minute longer, then made up his mind. "Well, I don't feel comfortable about walking right up the road, so I'd say let's hang off the road a few hundred feet, and slowly make our way up. Why don't you take this side of the road, and I'll take the opposite. Look for anything that doesn't seem right. I'd hate to alert them of our presence."

Once agreed, they began their gentle hike. After what Flint guessed to be half a mile, he began moving even more cautiously. This was near the spot where Labeeb's phone had stopped transmitting. So far Flint hadn't seen any signs of cameras or microphones, but he didn't doubt that they were here. The night was clear, and his eyes were as used to the dark as they could get. But this only kept him from tripping on every plant and rock. It didn't give him the vision to see every tiny detail. He crept closer to the road. A faint red glow jerked his attention to a man sucking on a cigarette. If it weren't for the man's vice, Flint might have missed the large van that was parked behind a small hill. Looking beyond it, he saw Monk crouching down and watching.

The van had its hood up, but no emergency lights were flashing. Flint didn't believe this to be a coincidence. He was in fact very sure that the van was fully operational. In his mind the men with the van were doubtless to be anything but sentries. Flint could see them on the other side of the van, and he used the opportunity to creep closer. Finding a spot to conceal himself, he stopped and listened.

Their voices were too muffled until one of them moved around to the front of the van to empty his bladder. As he was doing so, Flint overheard him say, "The night shift should be coming to relieve us soon."

The man on the other side said something in reply, but Flint couldn't make it out. However, as the one who'd just finished urinating was zipping up his pants, he said, "I don't know. Maybe after this maiden voyage, once they know if it really works, then I might be willing to go up there with them."

Their radios squawked for a few seconds, and he added, "Looks like they're on their way out. Great timing—I was starting to get hungry."

Well, Monk, it looks like you were right, Flint thought. *The opportunity to defeat the enemy might just be provided by them.*

Flint was surprised to find that two more men seemed to appear out of nowhere. They were in casual clothing, but Flint could see the faint sign of a machine pistol as it momentarily bulged out the front of one of their jackets. That man quickly zipped up his jacket, concealing the weapon nicely. He now just looked like the stranded citizen he was playing the part of.

Flint watched carefully as the two who were being relieved made their way in the same direction the fresh guards had come from. They walked over a small hill, and were soon out of sight. A few large clouds were edging close, threatening to blanket the only natural light from the stars and moon. Flint knew he had little time before it was too dark to walk without stumbling and making a scene. He wasn't sure of how late the evening was. For all he knew, morning might already be here. He did travel east, so he would have lost a couple hours at least. It had to be around two or three in the morning. His curiosity wasn't strong enough to pull out Fran's satellite phone and check. The glow from the screen would be a dead give-a-way.

With a quick motion for Monk to stay put, he sneaked farther away from the van. Once he was clear of it, he backtracked to the main road, and began to follow in the direction Monk had taken. Within minutes he was next to his companion, and they began to carefully sneak across the grassy terrain to where the guards had come.

The only sign they found was a small dirt path, well worn, but otherwise inconspicuous. They followed it to its end, whereupon they found nothing. There was a small dirt clearing, but the trail had dead ended.

Carefully moving back to the main portion of the trail, Flint looked for their footprints in the hardened dirt. The light was getting dimmer, and he had little time to waste. The prints of their shoes were not visible, but someone had come along the trail with a slight drag in their step. Though the small portions of loosened dust would have not signaled anything many others, Flint knew that where footprints were not to be found, any soil out of place was the next best sign for tracking. Since the trail was packed hard, all he had to do was look for a few spots where the dirt wasn't matching. But even that, too, came to an end at a vegetated patch of ground.

Flint examined all around, looking for more signs of where someone could have walked, but found none. The trail had effectively dried up. He wondered if he had misjudged his tracking abilities, but couldn't see how somebody could have gone anywhere but to here. Monk was the first to notice something out of place. He got Flint's attention, then pointed at the small overgrowth of plants where the trail ended.

It took Flint a moment to see what Monk was pointing at, but then the realization hit him. He had been looking for tracks to an eventual destination, but what he didn't realize was that he had already made that destination. The weed-covered spot at the end of the trail was a carefully disguised trapdoor of some form.

Giving some heed to caution, Flint pulled on a branch that seemed to be connected to the ground. It lifted more easily than he would have expected. What lay before him was a downward staircase. With a look of concern, he glanced at Monk. Monk, conversely, didn't hesitate. He started down the staircase with little more caution than to make sure he didn't hit his head on the trapdoor that Flint was holding up. With a shrug of his shoulders, Flint followed, whispering under his breath, "I'm sure getting tired of going underground."

After what seemed to be a three-story descent, he found a large metal door, similar in appearance to a bank vault. "I'll bet you anything they'll know we're here as soon as we open this door," Flint told Monk.

Monk replied, "'Behold, the Lord thy God hath set the land before thee: go up and possess it, as the Lord God of thy fathers hath said unto thee; fear not, neither be discouraged.' Deuteronomy 1:21."

"All right, here goes nothing," Flint said as he gripped the locking wheel and began to spin it.

The door unlatched and he pulled it toward him, just enough to look inside. When he felt that nobody was the wiser to his presence, he slipped in with Monk at his heels. He immediately recognized what he was looking at when he saw the large ship. He also understood enough of how it worked now that he knew why the door he had just gone through was built of such thick steel. This wasn't just a cave, but a giant vacuum chamber. Somehow Troy had managed to replicate the Martian device destroyed at Shen Mao's home in the Philippines.

Flint now understood that though Troy didn't want the device to fall into anyone else's hands back then, he also wanted to secure it for himself. Flint also had a disgusted feeling that Troy's ship might not be for simple scientific or genealogical research. Why else would he throw the world into chaos right before launching it?

"Monk," he whispered. "I overheard one of the guards earlier. It sounds like they aren't far away from launching this ship. We need to find Lydia and Labeeb, and be on that ship before it happens. We won't last long if we're anywhere inside this base when it depressurizes."

Monk understood, and the two split up. Flint didn't know how long they had, but he knew that they needed to move quickly.

Chapter 18

The night had been long and restless. Labeeb was unable to sleep, and he guessed that Lydia was experiencing a similar agitation. Countless times he replayed the day's events in his mind. He wondered if he'd made all the right decisions, and then tried telling himself that, regardless of the past, future decisions would now be most important.

Troy had not yet told him if he would be joining them on the ship in the morning. He hoped that he would, but he also knew from their tour that Troy was going to keep a ground crew inside this base. Troy had shown him a very sturdy room at one end of the cavern, and had mentioned that the room had been built especially for launching and would protect his ground crews while all the air in the cave was sucked out.

There was also the possibility that he could make an escape that night while most of Troy's men were resting for the big day. But even if he did make it out alive, he knew that he wouldn't have enough time to find the help he needed to stop the launch. Instead he tried to relax in order to get some sleep. An alert mind would be crucial in the morning, and rest had been a rare commodity that threatened to muck his clarity of thought.

Labeeb was just reaching the point where daydreams lulled away into what felt like real dreams, that imminent fog that still bordered sensory awareness. He opened his eyes suddenly. A faint sound had triggered a primal warning, but now everything was quiet again. He dismissed it and wondered how long he'd been asleep, or if he'd even made it that far yet. Looking at a small clock next to his bed, he noticed that it was 3:15 in the morning. He had slept for only a few minutes. Knowing that he would need more sleep, he tried to relax again. As soon as he closed his eyes, he recognized the faint disturbance again.

This time Labeeb understood his instinctive fear. The sound was faint, but near—very near. Somebody was in his room, he was now sure. Their proximity was confirmed when a silent shadow tipped the small glowing clock down, hiding the dim luminescence from the display. Labeeb tried to ignore the disappointment he felt for not having looked up when he had his chance. They would have surely seen him awake, but now he didn't have any way of knowing how many people were in his room. His only defense lay on the end table, one of his throwing rings. He tried to discreetly reach for it, but before his hand made contact with it, he was aware of somebody on both sides of his bed. Changing strategy, he brought his hands in close to his face as if to rub them. Whoever was here, they didn't want to make a noise, perhaps out of fear that Lydia might awaken and hear. Their intentions, though, were undeniably clear.

There was no light in the little room, and he wondered if they were just feeling their way along, or if they had night-vision equipment. The answer wasn't long in coming, as a third man flipped the light on. Labeeb was half a second quicker than the men at his sides, and when their hands came down to restrain and silence him, he caught one off guard, and flung him onto the bed.

The other man reacted by bringing a heavy object down on Labeeb's face. Had Labeeb not been in such an awkward position, the bludgeoning might have knocked him unconscious. As it was, he managed to block a second hit by throwing his pillow in the man's face. The one on top of him was regaining his senses and about to pin Labeeb down. Labeeb grasped his razor-sharp ring and with a quick swipe managed to slice open the neck of the man who crouched above him on the bed. Hot blood splashed across Labeeb's face, the acrid smell filled his nostrils as if the thick liquid itself was forcing its way into Labeeb's lungs.

The attacker made little sound as he grabbed his throat in a futile attempt to stave off the hand of death. Then everything went dark again as the other man brought his heavy object down on Labeeb's head. When Labeeb regained consciousness, he found that his hands were bound behind his back with zip ties, and his mouth was covered with two layers of duct tape.

"There he is," Labeeb heard someone whisper as he came to. He blinked a few times, and noticed two men standing over him. One said, "We were going to kill you here, painlessly and quickly, but since you felt the need to end the life of our friend, we decided that we would rather take you outside and do this painfully and slow."

"Plus, that will save us from carrying your heavy dead body all the way out," the other man quietly added.

They stood him up and began escorting him out. Once outside of the room, Labeeb noticed Grisha waiting. "What are you doing? You are supposed to kill him!" Grisha told the men.

"He killed Jacob, so we're taking him outside and—"

Grisha cut the man off sternly yet quietly. "We launch in two hours, there is no time for nonsense. Give me syringe, I finish job now."

The men had clearly set their mind to taking him outside, but as Labeeb knew, Grisha was not one to argue with. So they didn't protest as one of the men handed Grisha a syringe then both held Labeeb tightly to prevent him from struggling. Grisha took the cap off the needle, and prepared to push it into Labeeb's neck. Labeeb knew that this was the end for him, but even still, every muscle in his body argued against the strain of the men who were holding him.

Chapter 19

Flint had spent more time searching for Lydia and Labeeb than he originally thought would be necessary. Upon splitting up from Monk, he skirted around the edges of the cave. Monk, on the other hand, had worked toward the ship. Several times they were each compelled to stop and hide. Eventually Flint watched as Monk made a dash for the inside of the ship.

As he made his way around, Flint kept finding different labs and dorms. He carefully checked each room to make sure that Lydia or Labeeb was not in any of them. He noticed that most people had their attention directed toward the ship. From what he could tell, it looked ready to go. It was a little crude in design but nonetheless a very impressive vessel. It almost seemed to float, and it might even be capable of it, just like Shen Mao's ship. The several thin posts that extended from the ground supporting it were likely just to stabilize the ship. He guessed they would retract before launching.

As Flint was sneaking along, he realized how hungry he was when the aroma of some culinary delight caught his nose. Several trays of food, which had been prepared in a nearby kitchen, were being taken to the ship. Bacon and sausage were the two most powerful smells. If they were getting breakfast ready this early, they must have major plans for today. Flint's stomach growled as it tortured him. He was half tempted to follow them onto the ship, as he suspected that such a feast was likely to be enjoyed by Troy himself. He thought that where Troy was, there he might also find Lydia. He only stopped himself because he knew that Monk was already up there.

So in order to cover all their bases, Flint continued to sweep his way around the cave. All of GRIP's members were so busy that Flint occasionally walked right past some of them without their noticing. There were plenty of security cameras about also, and when he couldn't avoid being seen by one, he moved as if he belonged there, careful not to give the camera a good angle of his face. Being a regular sized man among a whole group of almost giants was unnerving. The few people that gave him a second look, soon dismissed him though. After all, there were still a few people of average height in GRIP's organization. Flint hoped that Monk was doing all right. His autistic friend would stand out even more than himself. After a while of carefully moving from room to room, he had cleared most areas outside the ship. He hadn't seen any sign of Monk since the moment his short Hispanic friend went into the ship. But he knew that if Monk were found, they would come looking for him also. So far everything was quiet, save for the sounds of the men moving to and back from the ship.

Flint kept glancing at the craft to see if Monk would come down. Hard soled boots rattled the ramp to the ship. Flint checked again. He didn't see Monk, but to his delight, there were three men walking out, muttering something about visiting Labeeb. Flint tried his best to see where they were going, but lost them as they went around to the other side of the ship.

Either these men were just coming away from Labeeb, or they were headed towards the Frenchman. If Labeeb was in the ship, then Monk couldn't of helped before, but now might have the chance. If these men were heading towards Labeeb now, then it was up to Flint instead. The one thing he knew was working for him, was that with the morning being so early, most of GRIP's people were still asleep. Flint had little trouble following these men now.

Catlike, Flint quietly sneaked past one of the rooms, and was immediately hit by the faintest remnants of that old familiar perfume. A sense of triumph pulsed through him. The men had gone into the next room down, but this one would do just fine also. The door didn't make any sound as he slowly opened it and stepped inside. Unwilling to abandon all caution, he continued with as much stealth as possible. Though Lydia hadn't perfumed herself since the morning, and given the day's ordeal, her sweeter smells were overpowered by the more pungent odors, Flint felt convinced that he had found the room where his wife was sleeping. Not wanting to disturb her until he was sure, he noiselessly crept up to her bed. The thumping of his heart as he neared, threatened to wake the sleeping beauty. Of course the pounding was inaudible to anyone but himself, and her beauty was just a memory of happier days. Still, there was something familiar about this. He remembered times when he would come to bed late, and try not to wake her as he crawled into the sheets next to her. *Focus*, he told himself as he shoved the dreamy images from his mind.

Once he was close enough to her bed to start seeing the outline of her face in the dark, he noticed that the head of the sleeper was severely disfigured. He reached down and touched it, suddenly realizing his mistake.

The disfigured head was only a pillow, and there was nobody sleeping in this bed. He was suddenly aware of something falling around his neck. Before he was able to spin around, the thin cord tightened around his neck, and somebody jumped against his back, pushing him facedown onto the bed.

His first urge was to stick his hands up and try to free has throat from the strangling cord. He quickly abandoned this idea, assuming that it was a common reflex, and that a garrote would likely kill him, even if he did get his fingers between it and the cord. Instead he reached behind his head and found the wrists of his attacker. Then with all the strength he had, he pulled her over his head.

With his neck free of the cord, he wheezed more than whispered, "Lydia it's me, Flint."

"Flint?" she whispered back. "How did—?"

"Shhh," he coughed, cutting her off, relieved that it was in fact her. "Nobody knows we're here yet--*cough*--and I'd like to keep it that way. Your friend--*weeze*--Labeeb--"

"He's in the room next to us," she replied.

"Yeah, he's got company right this minute. You wait here," Flint said. "I'll go get him."

Flint rubbed his sore throat as he snuck back out

117

of her room. He was about to the other room when he heard people talking behind the wall. Ducking into a shadow, he waited and listened as the men in Labeeb's room came out. Flint also heard heavy footsteps approaching.

The first voice was very familiar, and he recognized it immediately. The distinctively Russian accent chilled Flint's blood and made his joints stiff. Maybe all of GRIP's men were as tough as this guy, but Flint had actually fought the man before, and nearly died. In this instance, fighting an opponent he didn't know seemed smarter than confronting this guy again.

Since he couldn't win in a fair fight with Grisha, Flint knew he would be little help to Labeeb. As much as it pained him to wait, he remembered what Monk had said earlier from Sun Tzu's *Art of War.* "To secure ourselves against defeat lies in our own hands, but the opportunity of defeating the enemy is provided by the enemy himself." *Good advice Mr. Tzu, but I don't know how long I can wait.*

"What are you doing? You are supposed to kill him!" Grisha's reproach, quiet as it was, carried a severe threat of discipline that scared his men, almost as much as it scared Flint.

Flint understood that they weren't just trying to remove Labeeb, but they were going to kill him. Before he had time to talk himself out of it, instincts took over. The rim of a large metal garbage can that was near his hiding spot, was now clutched in vice-like fingers. With a single lifting and swinging move, he brought the heavy object into the open and let its momentum carry it into the back of Grisha's skull.

The Russian went down, and Labeeb did not miss a beat. Although Grisha had stuck the needle into Labeeb's neck, he hadn't managed to inject the poison before getting knocked down by Flint. Labeeb struggled free from the men holding him and shook his body violently, causing the syringe to fall from his neck. Then, in a magnificent display of agility, he rolled to the ground and grabbed, palming the syringe as he passed over it. With his hands still tied behind his back, he continued his barrel roll, stopping less than a foot away from one of men. In what could have only been a carefully calculated move, Labeeb stretched his bound arms as far backwards as his shoulders would let him, and injected the calf of his assailant with the lethal fluid.

The injected man first looked down in surprise, and then sank to the ground. He seemed to be giving up before the drug even took effect. Flint tackled the last man standing, and with his legs, Labeeb assisted by breaking the man's neck.

Pulling out a pocketknife, Flint cut the plastic zip ties that held Labeeb's wrists together. Labeeb then carefully pulled the tape from his mouth.

"Three men down, and in less than thirty seconds. Not bad," Flint said.

"Lydia?" Labeeb suddenly called out.

"She's fine," Flint said. "She's waiting for us in her room."

"No," Labeeb said as he stared somberly behind Flint.

Flint turned around to see that Grisha had gotten up. He had wasted no time in retrieving Lydia, and was now holding her throat with his terrible bear-paw-sized hands.

"One step closer, and I crush her," he warned in that same quiet, terrible voice that meant he was serious.

Flint took a step back, not doubting the threat. "Whatever you guys have planned, it's not going to work," he said. He didn't fully believe it, since he didn't know what they were planning. But he wanted to get Grisha talking so he would be less inclined to hurt Lydia.

"It is too late for you," Grisha sneered. "And though I might have killed you myself, I will take great pleasure in knowing that you suffered here before you die."

He then picked up Lydia like she was a rag doll, and threw her over his shoulders as he began to run toward the ship's entrance. Flint leapt forward to give chase, but Labeeb restrained him. "You'll be shot the minute anyone sees you," he warned.

"He's taking Lydia—I have to stop him," Flint argued.

Labeeb, however, didn't let go. "There is another way," he said.

Flint calmed down. He knew that Labeeb was right. Besides, by now Grisha was already racing into the ship. "So what do we do?"

"They know you are here now," Labeeb stated. "They will either send men out to kill you, or more likely they will speed up their launch. This cave will lose its air when they launch."

"We don't want to be in here, we have to—" Flint realized.

"No." Labeeb took back the conversation. "We can still stop it. If they can't depressurize, they can't launch."

"But how?" Flint asked as a red light and sirens began to go off.

A few speakers sounded, carrying Troy's voice. "Attention all flight crew, report to the ship, launch will take place in ten minutes. Ground crew, prepare for launch. Also we have an intruder. He is with Labeeb. If you see them, shoot them on sight."

"Oh great, we have less time than I thought. We'll have to get to the control room," Labeeb informed. "It's the only place that will be protected from the decompression."

Flint remembered the room. "You do know that everyone not going on the ship will be there?"

"Do you have a better idea?" Labeeb asked.

Flint reached down to one of the men Labeeb had killed and found a small pistol. "So what are we up against?"

Labeeb answered as he ran into his room to collect his throwing rings. "They are mostly mad scientists with large egos, and no morals. Yet they are fiercely loyal to Troy, and some of them have good military training."

"So you're saying it won't be easy?" Flint said.

"I'm saying that you might want to check the other body for another gun before we start," Labeeb replied.

They ran as quickly as they could. Few people noticed them for being the intruders, as everyone was running frantically about, trying to get in place for the earlier than anticipated launch. By the time Flint and Labeeb reached the control center, they found it heavily guarded and filling by the minute with even more men, some still in their underwear.

The opening to the ship also faced the control center, and guards had been placed there to stop Flint from getting onto the ship. "What do you think?" he asked, knowing that Labeeb had actual tactical training.

"Scoot under the ship," he suggested. "Make your way to the other side, then I'll attack. When I draw their fire, you attack them from the other side. If you see a chance to make for the control room without getting shot, then take it."

"Then let me guess," Flint added. "Fight like crazy until either I die or I kill everyone in there before dying?"

Labeeb looked seriously at Flint and said, as though they wouldn't see each other ever again, "You're a good man, and it's been good knowing you."

"Sorry, Labeeb," Flint said. "But I've got a better idea."

Chapter 20

Before being snatched out of her room, Lydia was still trying to make sense of Flint's finding her. Over the last couple of weeks, he had proven that there was nothing he wasn't capable of doing. Now that he was here, it seemed to change everything. She had first felt a new surge of hope in their attempt to thwart Troy. But when her old comrade Grisha had reentered her room instead of Flint, she remembered that she was still on Troy's turf, and he still held all the cards.

She had struggled against Grisha, but he was too massive and strong for her to escape. Then when he had thrown her over his shoulder, she realized how powerless she was to prevent him from having his way.

It wasn't so much that she was afraid of being taken, because during the night she had consigned herself to her fate in taking down Troy in his ship.

But she was now worried that Flint wouldn't make it out alive. As she was being carried away, she saw Flint struggling against Labeeb to rescue her, and desperately she willed Labeeb to not let go. If Flint did break free, he would be gunned down before even reaching her.

Once inside the ship, Grisha had called for Troy.

Troy quickly responded, "What is it, Grisha?"

"It's Flint, he is here in the cave."

Troy craned his neck forward in confusion. "Flint? Here? Are you sure?"

"I have a bump on my head to prove it," Grisha replied, rubbing the back of his scalp.

Troy pursed his lips and exhaled through his nose like a grumpy ape. This was the point when Troy had bumped the schedule by grabbing a radio and calling the control center. "This is Troy, sound the alarms, we are going to speed up our launch to ten minutes from now."

He then looked at Grisha. "Secure her, and post guards at the ship's entrance. Flint is not to get on-board. I'm going to go make an announcement. If we launch now, they will be trapped in the cave, and that will be the last I have to worry about them." He began to walk away, then paused. "One other thing. I doubt Flint would have come down here alone—he has a friend he calls Monk. This Monk is very dangerous, so make sure he isn't already onboard this ship."

"If he is, I'll crush him," Grisha responded.

Grisha dragged Lydia to another room onboard the ship. "I am sorry I have to be like this with you, Lydia. We had good times together. But if you don't see things our way, you are nothing more than baggage. You know how I dislike baggage." His disliking baggage was a reference that Lydia understood from his stories about how his ambitions had tugged him away from a sheltering mother years ago.

Grisha was big and strong, but even he knew better than to try and bind Lydia alone. Instead he threw her in a corner and pulled up his own radio. "Kore, Grisha here, come to room 113, bring zip ties." He put the radio away and barred the doorway so Lydia couldn't escape.

"I can't believe you were in on this the whole time," she accused her old copilot.

Grisha just smiled. "Somebody had to keep eye on you."

"Let me guess. Were Vincent, Sam, and Jay all in on this with you?" she inquired.

"No, even Amos didn't know who he was really working for," Grisha replied.

"Is anything I even thought I knew about you true?" Lydia asked as she labored to her feet and paced at the far end of the room. "And why would you need me? You could easily have done this all without me."

"Yes, we could have," he confessed. "But you see, Troy wants his sister to share his glory. I not mind too much, either; it was more fun this way. Besides, I've grown to like your company."

Lydia had nothing further to ask and fought back tears of frustration. She didn't want him to see her in any moment of weakness, even if it already was showing slightly. Then a woman appeared in the doorway.

"Ah, Lydia," sighed Lydia's former commander and manipulator. "I'm really sorry things happened the way they did. You weren't supposed to know that we had anything to do with the oil plot. I had hoped to bring you in on all of this, but Amos found his way to my helicopter before I had time to take off.

You would have been such an asset to our future here. Troy still thinks that you may be. I'm afraid, however, that our slight mistake has soured you from our organization."

Lydia thought she saw an opportunity as Kore was binding her hands. "I was angry, and I still am," she began. "I was foolish enough to follow you once, but I'm not so stupid as to be blind to the fact that you guys hold all the cards. If you really think this is the only way, I won't fuss. And since I'm here now, and you can use my skills, if you'll just let Flint and Labeeb go, I'll cooperate in any way I can. Please just don't hurt them."

"I'm sorry," Kore said sympathetically as she cinched the zip tie up a little tighter than was necessary. "It's not that easy anymore. You see, nobody trusts you here right now, and that trust will have to be earned. You dragged your husband into this, and now he will have to be dealt with. As for you, we'll keep you here, under Troy's orders, until we finish the job at hand. Then once we have finished, we'll see if there isn't a part for you in our new world, considering that you come fully back to your good senses."

Grisha left the room and Kore was about to also when Lydia called out, "The world isn't full of sheep," Her head boiled with anger. She then spit in Kore's face. "Whatever you're planning, people will fight back. They won't allow themselves to be pushed around."

With a calmness too practiced to be real, Kore stretched out two fingers and first wiped her cheek clean of the saliva, then methodically transferred it to Lydia's cheek. "You are right Lydia, but that's exactly what we are counting on," Kore then turned and gracefully strolled out of the room.

The door shut behind her, leaving Lydia by herself. Once she was alone, she found it impossible to hold back tears any longer. After a few minutes, with deliberate and painful effort, she managed to push Flint and Labeeb to the back of her mind. Instead of focusing on their fate, which she knew she had no control over at this point, she needed to focus on how to stop Troy, and whatever his plan might be.

Chapter 21

"I'm all ears," Labeeb said with relieved anticipation. "Believe me, if I knew of any other way, I would gladly take it."

"If the air can't be sucked out of this cave completely, then the ship's launch would destroy the whole world, right?" Flint started.

"Sounds right," Labeeb agreed.

Flint continued, "So what if we just keep the cave from being airtight? There might be less people guarding the exits, and I could swear I saw a couple of vent shafts that we could block from shutting."

Labeeb smiled. "And keep them from launching, good man. But that'll only buy us a little time. They'll catch on pretty quickly. So how about, while you're doing that, let me see what I can do about a more long-term delay."

"It's a plan," Flint said. "I'll meet you back here as soon as I'm done on my end."

With nothing else needing to be said, Flint and Labeeb parted ways. Flint didn't worry about Labeeb, since he knew the man could handle himself. Monk was a wild card. Since splitting up, there was no telling how Monk could help, or if he was even in a position to help. Flint needed to focus on finding a way of keeping the vents open.

The cave included five large vents. Four were on ground level, but each had massive turbine engines hooked up to them. The bulk of the equipment defied any effort Flint could imagine to disrupt them. This left the front door, which was a little too close to the control room for his comfort, and one single vent in the ceiling on the far end of the cave.

It only took him a couple minutes to reach the ceiling vent. It appeared to be a shaft, about two and a half feet in diameter. He guessed that it went straight up to the surface of the mountain. On the bottom was a thick gasket, clearly meant to create a good seal. The giant plug was made of thick steel, a one-and-a-half-foot-thick Frisbee held by hydraulic arms. It hung next to the open vent, resting on a shiny steel track.

Flint was sure this plate would slide over the vent, creating a perfect seal when the turbines on the lower vents started. For now it was simply keeping fresh air moving into the cave. Flint guessed that once they begin pumping, it wouldn't take long before the air was too thin to breathe. He wondered if he had enough time to get up there and block it from sealing.

Since he was already committed, it was useless to debate whether or not he had time. He just needed to act, and hope that he could move fast enough. Besides, if they began the launch sequence while he was still in the open portion of the cave, then he would run out of air before he could even try to lay any siege upon the control center. And as the only exit door that he was aware of was built to swing outward, he knew that under the pressure of the vacuum, he wouldn't be able to open it and escape.

Ignoring the commotion around him, Flint focused his mind on this single vent. His first and biggest obstacle was that it was a good thirty feet above his head. There had to be a way to reach it. The ship itself was twenty feet tall, and they had been working that high on it when Flint had first found the base. Looking around for anything to get him up there, his eyes rested on a large propane fueled man-lift parked against the wall.

The key to start it was still in the ignition, and Flint fired it up at once. With only a few minutes to get up there before the launch sequence began, he knew the timing would be close. Only one idea made any sense to him, and even that came with substantial risk. As urgently as he could, Flint grabbed a hefty safety rope that was near the machine and hopped into the basket.

The man-lift was more sluggish than he had hoped for, and even though the propane engine was very quiet, it began to draw too much attention from the ground crews that were rushing toward the control center. Of those who were armed, most only had small pistols, which they shot at Flint who was now extending the arm toward the vent. Bullets ricocheted off the basket, and Flint clumsily returned fire.

His return fire bought him enough time to finish maneuvering the basket into the path of the metal plug, and partially into the vent. He then tied his rope around one of the lower railings on the basket, and threw it over the edge. The rope was only twenty feet long, and it dangled almost nine feet above the ground.

Flint was about to shoot a few more rounds at the men below him when they all turned their attention away and ran toward the control center. Flint took the opportunity to climb out of the basket, and let himself down with the rope. When he got to the end of the rope, he dropped harmlessly the rest of the way to the floor.

Then, for an added measure of security, he turned the engine off on the man-lift, and with a swift kick, he broke the key into the ignition so that nobody could turn the machine back on and move it. He then started back to where he was to meet Labeeb; only he hadn't taken more than a few steps when he heard a mechanical hissing noise above his head. He looked up to see the large steel plate sliding along its track to plug the vent.

Curiosity stopped him from moving any farther. He wanted to see if the bucket on the man-lift would stop the plate. It closed slower than he would have expected. After about ten seconds, it bumped the bucket, but, much to Flint's displeasure, it started pushing the bucket out of the vent. He held his breath, and gained a little hope right as one of the metal railing pieces bent and jammed itself inside the vent.

Flint's relief lasted for only a few seconds, because while the plug momentarily jammed, the powerful hydraulics pushing it caused the railing to shear, just as if the plug had been a large pair of metal scissors. Once the vent closed, an almost deafening roar began, growing louder throughout the cave as the turbines began to spin to life.

Already, Flint knew that escape was impossible. His only hope was that Labeeb had found another way to stall the launch. With ears popping, he raced back to the spot where they were supposed to meet. Already the lack of air was beginning to take a heavy toll on him.

He looked around; his eyes were getting fuzzy with fatigue, but he couldn't find Labeeb. He collapsed to the floor, half on purpose, half from exhaustion, and began to look for any sign of his friend. Then he thought of Lydia. *I hope you have better luck than me*, he said to himself as if she could read his thoughts.

Chapter 22

Troy sat anxiously at the luxurious helm of the ship, which appeared more like a gentleman's club than the command center of a vessel. He felt that if he was to design a ship himself, then he might as well make it feel comfortable, too. *After all, shouldn't the ruler of the new world order enjoy a few comforts?*

At a console somebody was calling out the pressure of the atmosphere inside the cave as the air was pumped from it. Once he got down to forty percent air, however, the vacuum process stalled. It even started repressurizing slightly.

Troy had tested the vacuum system several times before, and knew that this shouldn't be happening. He clicked his communication switch over and called the ground control center.

"Ground control, what's wrong?" he asked. "Why has the cave stopped depressurizing?"

"We've lost one of the pumps," came the reply.

"We need to cancel the process and investigate the problem."

Troy slammed his fist onto his armrest. "If it's not going again in ten minutes, somebody's head is going to roll," he fumed. He then thought for a second and added, "When you look for the problem, take some armed men with you. It had to have been sabotaged by Flint and Labeeb."

"Yes, sir," came the acknowledgment. At the same time, the other two pumps began to wind down, and the cave was quickly full of air again.

Troy called Grisha, knowing that he had a grudge against Flint. Grisha responded on his radio, and Troy ordered, "We've got to fix a small problem before takeoff. It would seem that we have a roach. You have ten minutes before we try launching again— would you see if you can do anything about our little pest problem? I don't want any more surprises."

"If you are referring to Flint and Labeeb, I'm on it," he replied.

After a few minutes, the control center radioed back, "We found the problem. Somebody shorted the power by sticking a sharp metal ring through one of the conduits leading to one of the pumps. We should have it fixed soon. So far, though, we haven't seen any sign of the intruders."

"Post guards around the perimeter," Troy called back. "Don't let them slice another conduit."

Then, switching channels, he called, "Grisha, are you on the ground yet?" After listening and getting no reply, he again called, "Grisha, this is Troy. Do you copy?" Again nothing.

Troy was a peeved that Grisha wasn't answering, but he knew his anger was more out of disappointment in not having taken off yet. He suspected that Grisha, whom he placed great trust in, must have turned his radio off in order to sneak up on his un-welcome guests. Troy had no doubt that the Russian would eliminate the two men.

Of course Troy also knew that he would have to find a way of explaining it all to Lydia. But if she persisted in her self-righteous ideology, then maybe it wouldn't matter, anyway. He wanted to share a piece of his work with her. So far his efforts were proving fruitless. Persephone had really messed things up when she revealed herself to Lydia back in Egypt. But even if Lydia was going to be difficult, he couldn't give up on her yet. It seemed to be a waste of his effort if he had succeeded in bringing her this far only to give up on her at the very end, when everything was finally coming together.

After ten minutes had passed, he called the control center again for an update. They informed him that they were splicing the power cables together as quickly as possible, but would need another ten minutes. He then tried calling Grisha again, but still couldn't get ahold of him.

To pass the time, he pulled up security video feeds all around the cave. He saw no sign of Grisha, Flint, or Labeeb. He knew the entrance to the ship was being guarded, but decided to review a few of the cameras from inside the ship. At first he saw nothing that seemed out of place until one of the video feeds pulled up a picture of a man lying face down in the hallway.

Troy sent two other men down there as he re-played the video from the last several minutes. Unfortunately the video angle only caught the man as he was falling to the floor. There wasn't enough coverage to see what had caused the fall. Once Troy's security men were there, they reported that the fallen man was none other than Grisha. Upon hearing this, Troy jogged down to talk to his head of security. The men Troy sent had helped Grisha up by this time.

"What happened to you?" Troy asked.

A dazed and disoriented Grisha replied while rubbing his forehead, "I don't know. Maybe I trip." Then as he remembered where he was going, he exclaimed as he started toward the door again. "I go find Flint!"

"Hold it there." Troy stopped him. "You've been out cold for a few minutes, we're about ready to get going. Just help secure the entrance to the ship so they don't fight their way aboard."

Grisha was clearly disappointed by his failure, but acknowledged his orders. Troy then returned to the helm. As he was going, he got to pondering on Grisha's misstep. The Russian wasn't known for being clumsy. Troy wondered if he really did trip, or if perhaps Flint's stooge, Monk, was somewhere on the ship.

The thought of that emotionless killer brought a chill to his spine. He decided that once they launched, he would conduct a thorough sweep of the ship, making sure that every room and closet got checked. This was no time for a stowaway, especially one as dangerous as Monk.

Chapter 23

Closing his eyes for a moment, Flint inhaled a deep relieving breath of air. The pumps had just turned off and Flint savored the atmosphere that was returning to the underground chamber. As he waited under the ship, his eyes began to focus again and he regained his strength. He didn't have to sit long before Labeeb made it back to their rendezvous point.

"I'm guessing you found a way to postpone their launch?" Flint asked.

"I didn't buy us much time," Labeeb panted. "But we have a few minutes at least to come up with a new plan to stop them. I noticed that you weren't able to keep the ceiling vent from closing."

Flint affirmed, "It's too strong. I think what we need to do is to either get on that ship or into the control room."

"They're both going to be guarded pretty heavily,"

Labeeb said reluctantly. "Any good idea on how to do it?"

Flint thought for a moment then asked, "How well do you think everybody knows each other here?"

"I'm guessing they are at least familiar with each other. Why, what are you thinking?"

Flint expounded on his plan, though he knew it was risky. "The guys in the control center are just dressed in casual clothing, or at least the ones who are dressed. But the ones going to and from the ship seem to be in uniform. If we can get our hands on some of those uniforms, then do you think we could slip onboard unnoticed?"

Labeeb looked bewildered. "I think I liked my earlier plan better, the one where we storm the control center in a final blaze of glory."

"That way we don't stand a chance," Flint reminded. "At least this way, we might get close enough to the ship to touch it before we are gunned down. Who knows, we might just even get lucky."

Labeeb shrugged his shoulders as if to say, *You win.* "How do you think we should get some uniforms?"

"I don't think we should kill anybody for them," Flint replied. "My gun would give us away, and your throwing rings would get the outfits all bloodied up. But I bet you they have extra uniforms in their dorms."

"We better get going, then," Labeeb suggested. "We don't have much time."

"At least that is likely to be the last place that they'll look for us," Flint offered.

They proceeded to crawl in the narrow space between the ship and the floor. When they reached the dorms, they waited for a patrol to pass before they dashed from under the ship. The dorms were arranged in a line about one hundred feet long. Flint started at one end, while Labeeb began searching from on the other end.

Having found nothing in the first two dorms, Flint entered the third toward the middle. Here he did find a uniform, only it was for a female officer; too tight and irregular for his build. He didn't even bother searching further in this particular room. The next rooms were where he had found Lydia and Labeeb, so he passed them by. He was just about to go into the next room when Labeeb opened a door and stepped out in uniform.

He motioned for Flint to come over. When Flint came near, Labeeb told him, "There's one more uniform in here, see if you can fit into it. I'll head back toward the ship and wait for you there."

Flint agreed, but stopped Labeeb before he had gone far. "In case I don't make it on the ship, Monk should be hiding onboard already. Find him, because you will need him."

"We'll both make it on," Labeeb assured. Then he turned back around and was gone.

Flint, upon stepping into the room, found that Labeeb had left the other uniform on one of the beds. Holding it up, Flint immediately knew that it wouldn't fit. It was the major flaw in his plan, which he should have foreseen. Troy had brought men into this group who were clearly descendants of the Martians, and it seemed that the taller the person was, the truer their bloodline.

Labeeb was tall enough to fit into the uniforms, but Flint knew that for himself, he would be a dead giveaway. He was about to try it on anyway when he heard a rush of feet outside the door. He ran over to the door and prepared himself in case anybody came in, but nobody did. A chill ran up and down his spine as he considered that he might already be too late.

He cracked the door open a hair and looked outside. Everybody was racing back to the ship and the control center. Flint decided to abandon the uniform, and he made a mad dash for the only thing close enough that might save him.

Chapter 24

Flint recalled the memory of the last time the launch process had started. He knew that he didn't have enough time to get out the main entrance, especially if anybody was waiting there to take a pot-shot at him. This left only one option that made any sense to him, and he raced toward it.

Along the way he passed a lab. A sudden recollection of what he had seen there earlier struck him, and he had an idea. Without even pausing to consider the consequence of the delay it would cause him, he turned around and ran into the room.

He immediately found what he was looking for. Carefully he wrapped it up in a white lab apron that was lying on a chair. On his way out, he tied the apron in a loop, and put it around his neck and shoulders.

Only one minute ago, escaping with his life was his only concern. Now, if he could just stay alive, he had a plan that could put him back in the game.

As soon he reached the propane man-lift, he knew that lowering the bucket would be impossible. Equally impossible would be to try and climb the greasy boom. His only way to reach the basket at the top was the rope he had used to slide down less than half an hour ago.

The rope started at about nine feet above the ground, and the first time he jumped up, it slid through his fingers. He had never played basketball for any school or community teams when he was younger, but he had played it enough in the past to know that he could at least touch the rim of the ten-foot-high basket. Thus reaching the nine-foot rope didn't seem to be an impractical use of his energy.

With a little more resolve, he stood in place and jumped as high as he could. This time one of his hands gripped tightly around the bottom of the rope. He nearly slid off it, but, grabbing his wrist with the other hand, he did a single-handed pull-up. Just before his grip gave way, he managed to get his other hand on the rope, as well.

The adrenaline of the moment helped him forget about the strain that his first handgrip had caused, and he was able to pull himself up. As he made his way up the rope, he was reminded of gym class in high school. The ropes there were much shorter, and he hadn't had to climb them more than once or twice. But he egged himself on as he ascended, reminding himself that he had easily been able to climb a rope back then.

When he was about five feet away from the bucket, his first doubt began to enter his mind. His hands were sweating, and his arms were starting to struggle with each new inch that he gained. Finally his hands touched the metal railing on the basket, but a mechanical hissing reminded him that he wasn't there yet.

He instinctively knew that the noise was coming from the vent's hydraulic plug as it was being slid back into motion. He only had a few seconds before the plug would completely seal the opening again.

Ignoring the sharp cramping pains in his muscles, he swung his legs over the rim of the mangled bucket and scrambled into it. Without wasting a moment, he then climbed up the bent and broken railing and reached for the thick steel plate that was now a quarter of the way over the vent.

Flint kicked off the basket with his legs, and pulled himself to a sitting position on the sliding plug. His body was now inside the vent, with his legs dangling over the edge. He then saw the flaw in his position. In the narrow vent, he couldn't maneuver his body to pull his legs in also. The steel plate was now halfway shut, and about to pinch his legs right off, just as it had done earlier to the metal railing of the bucket on the man-lift.

His arms were already feeling like spaghetti, but the urgency of survival egged him on. He extended his arms and pushed against each side of the vent, lifting his body up. He just barely managed to get one heel into the vent when he felt the steel door pressing his other leg into the bottom edge of the vent shaft.

Having no desire to abandon his leg, he pushed with his free leg as hard and fast as he could. His other leg shot pulses of pain the whole way up, and he was certain for a moment that he would lose it. His last toe made it out just as the steel trap caught and cut the edge of his shoe off.

Flint stood up in the dark shaft. He could feel a little blood trickling down his leg, but he was positive that he had only scraped some skin off, and that he would be just fine. Below him, he could hear the reverberations of the pumps as they began to pull the air out of the cave.

He wasn't sure how long it would take before the air was sufficiently gone so as to permit the launch. But he knew that once the ship had been launched, the ground crews would open the vent where he stood. His only option now was to continue up. At the same time, he also knew that he needed to rest his muscles.

For five minutes he waited in the narrow vent. During this time he wondered if Labeeb had made it somewhere safe. He had his doubts, but sincerely hoped for the best. In any case he chose not to dwell on the likelihood of Labeeb being dead. His own priority now was to make it out of the shaft.

Visions of the Egyptian well flashed again through his mind as he began to shimmy up the narrow vent. *Why do I always get the shaft?* He joked to himself in an attempt to keep a positive outlook. He was trying hard to remain upbeat about his escape plan. He had already survived the vacuum chamber, but if he couldn't get out of this vent, he was sure that he would die.

Even if he did fall out of the vent into the bucket of the man-lift, he would stand little chance against the armed ground crew that was sure to be looking for him. After what seemed to be fifteen minutes of climbing and resting, he finally made it to the top.

A large metal grate, covered in bushes, barred his exit. Feeling a little despair, he wedged himself in the vent by bringing his knees up and pressing his back tight against the vent wall. Then, preparing himself mentally for the possibility of disappointment, he pushed against the grate. To his surprise, it actually moved.

With a little more effort, he managed to push the grate completely off, and pulled himself through the sharp twigs of a fake bush that had been used to conceal it from the outside world. As his legs were about to clear the vent shaft, he became aware of a large sucking sensation around his ankles. He knew that the plug at the bottom was being removed and that the cave was repressurizing.

His first thought was that if he had still been in the vent, he might have been sucked back down like a moth in a vacuum cleaner hose. Then the realization hit him that Lydia and Troy might now be outside the Earth's atmosphere. Rolling over, he gazed into the dark morning sky, wondering where they might be. He was also glad that he had thought to stop in the lab before making his way to the vent, though it had nearly cost him his life. Because of this, he knew that he still had a chance of seeing Lydia again.

As he stood up, he examined the hole in the ground. There was a small, rarely used road that came almost up to this point. With as easily as the metal grate came off, he suspected that the vent served multiple purposes. One was clearly to give the cave fresh air, but it might also have been used as a means to quickly lower supplies and parts down.

Reaching into his pocket, he decided it was time to let his Chinese friend into the loop. But then he thought better of this, and waited until he had gotten around the guards by the van before calling Lum Fu-han.

Chapter 25

The deafening roars of the great pumps had echoed throughout the whole ship. Lydia felt as helpless as an infant, worried about Flint and Labeeb. After five minutes, the sound of the pumps began to change. She guessed it was due to either the lack of air, which was making it difficult for the sound to reach them, or just the strain of the pumps trying to pump little or no air out. In either case, she knew that they were about to test Troy's ship.

Stepping toward her window, which was located on the lower floor near the starboard bow, she imagined the cruel possibility that the ship might destroy Earth in the same way its predecessor had destroyed Mars. *No*, she told herself. *That won't happen.* But the irony still hit her as strange. A ship like this had destroyed the only other known planet that had been able to support life. Now this one was about to destroy everything that Earth had become.

Even if it didn't harm Earth by fire, it would still be harmed because of Troy's plans. At least it wouldn't be a total obliteration; but destruction of the known civil structure that had developed over the millennia would nonetheless be devastating.

As she pondered this, her legs began to feel weird, and a queasy storm of butterflies filled her stomach. She correctly suspected that the support pillars that held the ship in place were being retracted. Powerful magnets would suspend the ship above the cave floor. Troy had explained it all earlier, and she knew that at any moment the ship would slide out of normal space.

Lydia was looking out the window when the break between normal space was created around the ship. From what Troy had told her on their tour, she knew that nobody could see them anymore. She did, however, find it interesting that she could see out through it. But the cave that once had been dark rock supported by gray steel was now a fuzzy lighted color. It was as if she was looking at the world through a broken television screen. The shapes remained the same, but the clarity and color seemed to be off.

Probably the most disturbing sensation before even leaving the cave was the nausea caused by absence of gravity. Though she should have expected it, Lydia's equilibrium was unprepared for the foreign environment. As they were no longer inside normal space, they weren't bound by Earth's gravitational pull. To keep from drifting about, and with bound wrists, Lydia grabbed a bar that was built into the wall next to her window. As she strained to keep her dinner from the night before from erupting back up, she witnessed the magic of the historic moment as the ship began to move.

Instead of racing into the sky, it seemed that Troy was taking the ship very slowly, and she was able to watch as they approached the ceiling and wall on an upward angle. As they began to touch the cave walls, the rocks, without crumbling, started to part and bend around the ship. Her window didn't allow her to see the back end of the ship, but she knew that the rocks were sealing back together behind them. The ship wasn't really passing through rock; it was passing through space that the rock happened to occupy.

The creepiest part was not the cave but after that, when she saw the ship heading straight for the van outside the cave, the one that had brought her here from the airport. One of the guards standing next to it was drinking a beverage as the ship passed right through him. It seemed to Lydia that his whole body was stretched and parted around the ship. She knew that he probably didn't realize that a ship two stories tall and five hundred feet long had just passed through him.

After this spectacle, no doubt slowed to satisfy Troy's curiosity, the ship began to increase in speed. Her brother must have decided to test the ship by taking it for a joyride before bringing it into orbit around Earth. This she guessed because within one minute they had passed right through the Moon, then one minute later, they were passing through the center of the Sun. Even the intensity of the Sun's heat and radiation couldn't penetrate the pocket of space that the ship was hiding inside of.

Troy had apparently slowed the ship down to more fully appreciate the thrill of passing through the hottest thing in this planetary system. If it hadn't been for the distortion of being just outside normal space, Lydia was sure that the Sun would have been too blinding to look at. However, as it was, she found a dazzling array of colors and movements, far surpassing anything she had ever imagined. It was as if the aurora borealis of Earth had taken steroids and joined with the most amazing trapeze artists.

For a moment she forgot all about her upset stomach, Troy, GRIP, and even Flint. She found herself hypnotized by the majestic display that nobody had seen before now. Then in a moment it was gone, and the ship sped out until it went weaving in and out of the asteroid belt. Troy was racing about the theme park of our solar system. He was a child at Disneyland, and there were no lines to slow him down.

Lydia found herself glued to the window as he danced around and pierced through planets, comets, and asteroids. Finally she recognized that they were sailing slowly above Earth's next-door neighbor, Mars. She watched as Troy wrapped several times around the planet, sometimes flying mere feet above the surface, while the only signs that they found of the ancient civilization were the almost indistinguishable ruins known on Earth as Cydonia.

After satisfying his curiosity, Troy surprised Lydia by disengaging the ship's primary propulsion system, and then maneuvering the ship into an orbit around Mars instead of Earth. Whatever his plans were, he apparently wanted to stay out of reach of anyone back home.

Lydia began to wonder how she could stop Troy when she didn't know for certain what he planned to do. Her only sure bet would be to destroy the ship with her inside. But even that seemed impossible to her. All that she could do was to wait and see what Troy had in store. Actually that wasn't true. There was one other thing that she could do, or rather had to do. Happy to find a plastic bag dispenser mounted on the wall, Lydia hurled the contents of her stomach, managing to trap most of the partially digested food inside the puke bag.

After two more gut-wrenching convulsions, the only thing more bitter than the bile in her throat was the appearance of Kore, who chose that time to come floating in.

Chapter 26

Lydia was having a hard time understanding Kore. The woman seemed to hold her in contempt, yet at the same time tried hard to maintain a degree of professionalism. Lydia already knew that Kore believed Lydia would never come around to see Troy's vision the same way that everyone else at GRIP seemed to. Even the earlier hostile sentiment Kore had displayed was now replaced by a warmer, more patient woman.

Lydia's hands were still tied in front of her as Kore led the way into the hall. With the slightest of effort, Kore drifted perfectly down the center of the corridor. Lydia, on the other hand, found that zero gravity was more difficult to maneuver in than she would have expected. Not being able to separate her hands also came as bit of a disadvantage, and she found herself bumping into walls all the way down.

After she had gone about twenty feet, Kore directed Lydia to the side of the hallway, where there was a ladder going up to the second floor. Lydia went first, only using the ladder to keep herself from drifting out of control. Kore just drifted up behind as if she had been doing this her whole life.

Once on the second floor, Lydia found herself surrounded by a handsomely decorated room. Perhaps it wasn't the most luxurious, but it was still impressive. Beautiful woodwork adorned a few workstations where mostly men were belted down to comfortable chairs. Around the front half of the room and the sides were small windows. Even the ceiling had several small windows from which they could see out. These were much smaller than what she anticipated, but as she thought about it, they made sense. Larger windows would have a much harder time withstanding the pressures placed on them from being in space. After all, this craft was in essence a submarine in reverse. Instead of trying to keep enormous pressure out, it was trying to keep the imposing atmospheric pressure in.

"I hope that you took advantage of the view that your room afforded you," Troy's voice called out. Lydia looked around and saw him almost swimming across the ceiling, passing right over her. "I don't know about you, but the asteroid belt was my favorite part of the trip. Maybe in a few weeks or months we will take a trip even farther into space."

He pulled himself down to his command chair, where magnetic inserts in his uniform sucked him down to corresponding magnets in his chair. He didn't bother strapping himself in, but he still pulled over a small console attached to a swivel arm. It was a simple touch-screen tablet, and he worked quickly on it. He only paused for a moment and looked at Lydia as he mentioned, "By the way, I don't know how you're doing in this environment, but if the zero gravity doesn't agree with you, please let one of us know. I'd hate to see your vomit floating aimlessly through the room."

Lydia had almost forgotten her nausea, and wondered if Troy was saying this out of precaution, or did he have a camera on her earlier and witnessed her upheaval? In either case the return of the memory brought back the somersaults in her gut. She wasn't sure if it was the lack of gravity extending her sick feelings, or just the thought of floating chunks of vomit. But having piloted planes her whole life, and several times putting them into a stall, she was not completely unaware of the sensation that accompanies a lack of gravity. Because of this, her first real experience with zero gravity came as a surprise, but now she managed to suppress the nausea, and within seconds she had nearly forgotten about it again.

"I'm guessing that you sent for me for a reason, and not simply to gloat about your achievement," Lydia said in a hostile tone.

"My dear sister," Troy begged. "This flight is not my greatest achievement. I've tried explaining this to you already. My great achievement is only about to happen. This is a machine using technology borrowed from our ancestors. This is their achievement. Mine will be the unification of all men on Earth. I want you to be here with me while I do this. I want you to see how chaotic Earth is now."

He pressed one more button on his tablet and a projector placed a light on a blank wall. It took a moment for the projector to warm up, taking some of the edge off the suspense that Troy was trying to create. But once the image had come in, it became clear to Lydia that Troy had planned on holding a position around Mars for some time. As the sounds of various reports started to fill the room, the clarity of the broadcasts was so clear that she knew it could only be the result of having a satellite or array of dishes on Earth pointed directly at the red planet. Troy started cycling through several news headlines and broadcasts, most of which focused on the political stability or instability of the world powers.

After about half an hour, Troy turned on another projector. This screen showed a crude diagram of where the international tensions were focused. In the United States, the Republicans and Democrats were pointing fingers at each other for failing to protect the country. The Middle East was ramping up their defenses, fearful that the larger countries would go to war for their oil. Russia was on full military alert, and Europe was falling apart with riots. News coming out of China was being censored by the government, and was deemed unreliable. Speculation suggested that they had their hands full dealing with their own people. Many talking heads were guessing that they were also preparing for possible hostile encounters. It seemed that Africa was the place that showed the least signs of international hostilities. Inner conflict was sure to be taking place there, but much of that would have been happening anyway.

"First thing's first," Troy announced. "We need to send a clear message that oil will not be returning anytime soon."

He pressed a button on his chair, and a voice answered, "Weapons Room."

"Prepare one of the smaller bombs for launch. We're about to begin the next phase of the plan."

The man on the other end confirmed, and Troy pushed his button again to end the call. One of the men sitting at a station in front then called out, "Sir, the broadcast is ready. Do you care to preview it?"

A look of excitement crossed Troy's face. "Lydia, let me introduce you to Bernard Jublein. He is the best computer geek you'll ever meet. He's been working on several special messages for our friends back home. I think you'll enjoy this." He played with his tablet for a second and the newscasts changed to a single announcement. The announcement came from the President of the United States as he began a public address. Currently it was paused, and before Troy played it, he informed Lydia that Bernard had a whole collection of speeches by various political leaders.

He had a unique talent for reading lips, and superimposing different words that could fit into the rhythm of their speeches. In this case it was a former State of the Union address. He had modified the pictures enough to make them look current, and used different camera cuts and movements to splice different parts of the speech together. The finished product was a customized, current announcement meant to look as though the president had just released it. In the address, it appeared as though the president had said the following:

Ladies and gentlemen. A few days ago, I addressed the men and women of our nation. I made a plea with the citizens of our great Union to act responsibly, and with dignity. I also extended this plea to our neighbors abroad. It is, however, with great displeasure, that I have noticed many countries suiting up for war.

We are working with our partners in the Middle East and around the globe to return oil production to our citizens. But in this time of extreme scarcity, many nations have let fear dominate their actions. We in turn have heightened our security, and are committed to protecting our citizens at all costs. To our friends in the Middle East, we ask you to stand down, as we mean you no harm. We will be sending troops to you, but only to protect our citizens and yours as we work together to help you restore your pipelines and oil infrastructures. We strongly urge you to welcome us as friends and partners.

I also wish to address the other rumors that have implied we are responsible for the oil shock, and that we are using it as a means to subdue political structures that don't fit into our ideal democratic model. I want to reassure you that these rumors are unfounded, and completely false.

In the last week, many people of all nations have been hurt, both economically and physically. I do not intend for this message to sound like a warning, but I wish to reiterate my desire to find peaceable solutions to the crisis that faces us all. And I wish to remind our citizens that we are doing all that we can to return our country to the prosperous land that we have all grown to love. Thank you.

Troy was clearly pleased with the video, and Lydia had to admit that it looked authentic. But she was slightly confused, and asked, "I don't get it. You're using false videos to encourage peace, and at the same time you're preparing bombs?"

Troy shook his head and explained. "I think you fail to see the importance behind this video. While it talks of peace, what it is really saying is that the United States is going to occupy the Middle East. It also starts a rumor that the U.S. is the one responsible for the oil shock. Last of all, it makes an egotistical point that everybody loves the U.S. Do you really think that part of the world is going to react well to a message like this?"

"As soon as you release it, the U.S. will denounce it as a fake. Nobody will believe it," Lydia argued.

"I don't intend for everyone to believe it," Troy said. "This is all just one tiny piece of the puzzle. You see, the video will be released in Syria first, and it will mostly serve to disrupt U.S. and Middle Eastern relations. Then as soon as the U.S. investigates, they'll notice that the video has distinctively Russian origins."

Lydia's eyes went wide with understanding. "You're going to pin this on the Russians and try to start a war."

"Now you're getting the idea," Troy said. "Our weapons here are only to add a little powder to the keg." Troy then spoke to Bernard. "Send the video now, and start working on a press release. I want to make sure that the news of Russia's involvement gets released to the public within twenty-four hours of the video."

Bernard swiveled back around, his fingers typing furiously at his computer.

Lydia didn't want to believe what she was witnessing. Troy's plan was now clear. He was going to start a world war. Then, after the nations ripped one another to shreds, he would come in and pick up the pieces. While she hoped it wouldn't work, she could see how it most likely would. Even if she were to destroy his ship now, he had already begun a process that might be irreversible.

Chapter 27

Once Flint had found his way back to the main road, he pulled out his phone and called Fu-han. One hour later, several Chinese military trucks came driving up the lonely road. The first truck stopped right in the middle of the road next to Flint, not that it mattered; in the last hour he hadn't seen another car driving anywhere. Without any traffic coming in or out of the airport, this road served little purpose.

The passenger door of the first vehicle opened and Fu-han stepped out. "Flint, I twuly had not expected to heaw back fwom you so soon." He then did a quick glance about and asked, "Whewe is your othew fwiend, Monk?"

Flint replied to the man who believed him to be a spy, "Monk is busy. As for my calling you, when I came here, I had my suspicions about a group that calls themselves GRIP. They were a little easier to find than I originally suspected."

"And this GWIP is wesponsible fow the wubber oil?" Fu-han asked.

"It's worse than that, but yes. They have a secret underground base about one mi—two kilometers from here—maybe a little more," Flint said, remembering that most of the world used kilometers instead of miles. "They have dozens of armed men, and have just launched a spaceship."

"Spaceship?" Fu-han asked. "Impossibo. We would have noticed a wocket launch. Awe you twying to waste my time?"

Flint had forgotten how impossible that sounded, and he took several minutes to explain the technology, as he understood it. Fu-han listened carefully and asked several questions. Flint answered the best he could. Then Fu-han asked, "Why would they make the oil wubber, then launch such a ship?"

"I don't know yet," Flint replied honestly. "But my guess is that we won't have too long to wait before we find out."

Fu-han thought a moment before he asked, "What do you suggest we do?"

"I'm glad you asked." Flint smiled. "I have a plan, but I'll need to ask a favor from you first."

Fu-han listened intently to what Flint detailed, and Flint hoped that he wasn't requesting too much from his new Chinese friend. Fu-han then asked, "So you think they will weturn in theiw ship soon?"

"I don't know," Flint replied. "My guess is that they can stay in space for a long time, but if they do come back, and they have any intentions of leaving again, they'll have to come to this base. It's the only chamber on Earth that can fit a ship that size and vacuum the air out again for another launch. If this happens, it would be much better for your men to be running that base than theirs."

"We should have little pwoblem taking the base," Fu-han stated. But then he added with hesitation, "As fow getting you down to the Philippines, I feaw that will be mowe difficult. The Filipino govewnment might not appwove."

Flint looked deep into the man's eyes and accused, "So you're telling me that China is afraid of a few Filipinos who, if they actually have triggers on their guns, won't have any bullets for them?"

"We awe not afwaid," Fu-han insisted. "We simply want to keep up good welations with our neighbows."

"That's a bunch of bull, and you know it," Flint rebutted. "You guys have been after Taiwan for a long time now, and you took Tibet. If the Philippines had anything that you actually wanted, you'd have taken them a long time ago as well. But I'm not asking for you to go to war with them, I just need you to spare a plane that can drop me off on the island of Bohol. I'll even parachute in if you're afraid to land."

"That would still be a violation of theiw aiwspace," he argued. "Besides, doesn't the U.S. have any wesources neawby to help you?"

Flint honestly had no idea if the U.S. had anybody near who could help him out. While he had been waiting for Fu-han to arrive, he had also called and updated Fran. But even Fran offered no clue as to how he could get down to the Philippines. Unless he wanted to spend a month rowing down there by canoe, Fu-han was his best bet. He could also see that Fu-han was seriously debating the matter in his head, but he still seemed hesitant. Flint wondered if the man was worried about losing his position due to what might appear to his superiors as a bad decision.

Thus he tried a different approach. "You know,

Fu-han, down in that base of theirs, they have some pretty crazy technology that your government would love to have. It's decades ahead of anything that the rest of the world has yet. Sure, I could have had a U.S. SEAL team come in and take this base without ever telling you guys, and I'm sure that I could pull a few strings and get somebody else to give me a flight to Bohol, but that would take a couple of days, and I'm not sure we have that long. I'm doing you guys a big favor by giving this to you. The least your government can do is loan me a plane. Besides, who's to say that GRIP isn't planning to do something terrible on Chinese soil? You've already seen that they have no loyalties to any nation."

Fu-han mulled this over then told Flint to wait a moment. He pulled out a cell phone and called a number. Flint couldn't understand what he was saying; it was all in either Cantonese or Mandarin. After a couple of minutes, Fu-han ended the call and turned to Flint. "You go back to the aiwpowt and find the jet fwom yestewday. We will take you to Philippines, but you are on youw own after that. We will not bwing you back, and we will not give you any suppowt."

"Just get me there, and I'll make do," Flint replied.

Flint explained for a few minutes how to find the entrance to the base. Satisfied, Fu-han said, "You go now." Then he turned away from Flint and focused on giving orders to his men.

Flint was about to leave, but paused. "One more thing, Fu-han."

The Chinese man turned back around inquisitively. Flint added, "If you find a French-Indian named Labeeb, he's a good guy. If he's there, I doubt that he'll be alive, but just in case, I thought you ought to know."

Fu-han gave a slight look of understanding, then went back to briefing his soldiers. Flint stretched his legs for a few seconds, procrastinating the jog back to the airport. By the time he made it back to the jet, his stomach was grumbling with hunger. Even though he didn't doubt Fu-han's word, he was still relieved to find somebody already waiting for him. "Please tell me that this flight includes a meal," he said to the pilot.

The pilot joked in excellent English, "I suppose you want an in-flight movie, as well?"

"Only if I don't have to pay for the headphones," Flint replied and stepped onboard.

The pilot followed him in and told him that it would be several minutes before some fuel could arrive. He also commented on the pull that Flint had apparently exerted to actually get the fuel and trip from the government. "You're lucky I was still here," the pilot mentioned. "I was told that nobody would be coming or going for several weeks at least." But Flint was more interested in the scarce but adequate snacks he managed to scavenge. Once Flint had a few packages of crackers in his hands, the pilot asked, "So we are going to Manila, yes?"

"How about Bohol?" Flint countered. "There is a town there called Tagbilaran. Last time I was there, it sounded like they might have a small airport."

"I was told Manila," the pilot replied more seriously. "Even if they have a runway long enough, I don't know if I can go that far down."

"If you can't get me there, then at least get me to Lapu-Lapu," Flint told him.

The man looked grave as he repeated, "They told me to go to Manila, and return immediately. I'm sorry, but that is the best I can do."

Flint was disappointed, but he knew that it would do little good to argue with the pilot—for the time being.

Chapter 28

After Troy had sent his phony video message, Kore escorted Lydia back to her room. Neither woman had said a thing to each other. Kore had a self-righteous look of superiority painted all over her face. Lydia, being tied up and confined, had little prospect of a future. She knew that she would never approve of Troy's actions. In her current predicament, she felt more like a cow being led to slaughter. The way she saw things, it was only a matter of time until either they killed her or she found a way to stop them by killing them all. In any case, she had abandoned any possibility of returning to any real life after this.

Before leaving Lydia in her room, Kore gave a small lecture, something to do with the nobility of the whole thing, plus some other details that Lydia tuned out. Her inattention only added to Kore's annoyance. Lydia couldn't bring herself to focus on the woman's ranting; she was still trying to digest everything she'd witnessed in the last few hours.

While only a few days ago, Lydia had still felt some discord with her life, everything at least made some sense. In just the last twenty-four hours, nothing seemed to fit anymore. A small spark of hope had flickered for a couple days during the reunion with the man who had once been hers, but now he was probably dead. Her brother was insane, and all the good she had thought she'd been doing had been preparatory to setting up that maniacal sibling to be ruler over the whole world.

At the same time she was mentally scolding herself and her brother, she remembered witnessing the awe-inspiring journey through Earth's solar system. She almost hated herself for the profound amazement and admiration she had felt as they had passed in and around everything, since it had been Troy who made it all possible.

After thinking things over, she found herself gazing onto the red planet below. It was almost impossible to believe that this world had once been similar to Earth. Mars still appeared to be more of a red-rock planet than the scorched wasteland it really was. She wondered if any structure, library, or any remains at all could have survived underground. She doubted that any life form could have survived. Even if it had, there would be no way to sustain it for the many years since the atmosphere had ignited.

Lydia allowed herself to float away from the window. She finally began to feel relaxed enough to clear her head. As she analyzed everything, she could see how Troy might feel. The simple view of looking down on a planet, which now seemed so small, could be intoxicating. The feeling would be the same on Earth as here. Troy undoubtedly must consider himself conqueror already. All that was left to finish the job were minor housekeeping issues. She turned this in her head, and wondered if his sense of accomplishment, or his overconfidence, might provide an opportunity to not only stop him, but also undo some of the damage.

The more she thought about it, the more confident she became. No longer was she a victim, or a pawn, but rather a joker in his deck of cards. She wished that she had started off the journey with the wisdom that Labeeb had demonstrated. He had nearly won Troy's confidence. If he could do it, then maybe she could. After all, Troy wanted so badly to bring her in that his ambition in this matter might help her more easily win his confidence.

Having learned to control her emotions as a result of her military and personal training, she began to meditate in the middle of the room. She committed herself to being agreeable to not only Troy but Kore and Grisha, also. The latter two would be harder to convince, but since Troy was the head of the whole organization, she hoped to gain just enough trust so as to sabotage their efforts. She knew that Troy would tax her resolve, but she didn't realize how much until he let himself into her room.

He asked, "Didn't Persephone tell you about the uniform?"

"I'm sorry," Lydia responded sincerely. "I didn't think that I would be privy to wearing your uniforms."

"She was supposed to explain how it's not just a uniform, but that it actually has some practicality built in." Troy explained that the uniforms were designed with built-in magnets, which served to keep everyone from floating aimlessly around the ship. The chairs had corresponding magnets, and it would be difficult to work without them.

Lydia went to a cubby and opened the door. Inside she found a couple of the full-body suits. "They look like my size," she observed.

"I had this room in mind for you from the beginning," he replied. "The uniforms are your size, and the view is one of the best on the whole ship."

"I'm flattered," Lydia admitted, and she was. But then again, it made sense. Had Troy's plan worked out perfectly, she would have been a willing member of this crew, even if she didn't condone his methods. He may even have had plans to keep her useful without letting her see some of the tricks he was pulling to start the war.

Troy drifted over to her and pulled out a small sheath knife. "Nothing funny now," he warned as he cut her zip ties off. "To be completely honest, I thought you would have found a way to break those off already."

"Let's just say that I've had a lot on my mind for the last couple of hours," she replied. "And since I'm not going anywhere, there wasn't much use in trying to escape."

"Well, I hope that this time to think has helped you consider things in a new light," Troy said.

"It may take a little time, bro," Lydia replied, calling him *bro* in hopes of bringing a friendlier tone back to their relationship. "I know I've been ignorant of this all, but I can see that you've put things in motion that can't be stopped. I'll try to consider everything as best I can, but like I said, you might need to give me some time."

"An open mind is all I ask." Troy smiled.

Lydia added, "If that's all you ask, then all I ask is that you be honest with me in everything. I don't like being deceived, and that has been the hardest part of this whole thing."

"I'll do my best to include you in the loop from now on," Troy promised. "And as long as we're talking honesty, I have to admit the real reason why I came here to your room."

Lydia felt a little nervous. With hesitation creeping into her voice, she said, "Go on."

Troy gave her a very grave face and confessed, "You see, I'm very truly and honestly starving." Then, with a smile working its way onto his face for having made Lydia a little nervous, he added, "I was hoping that you would want to join me in the cafeteria for lunch."

Lydia sighed. "I was hoping you didn't leave in such a hurry that you'd forget the food."

"Yeah, we kind of missed breakfast this morning. But get dressed—food will only be served for another forty-five minutes."

Troy didn't leave the room; he simply turned a trusting back on Lydia while she changed. He must have known, as did she, that it would have been foolish to attack him at this moment, even if she really wanted to.

The cafeteria wasn't like anything Lydia had expected. When Troy had given them a tour, he'd failed to do more than show them where the room was. Inside, the ceiling and floor were covered with wire mesh. A large, albeit slow, fan kept the air circulating from the ceiling down through the floor. When she asked about it, Troy took great pride as he boasted about the design of the room.

Since he planned to spend a lot of time on the ship, he didn't want to be stuck eating food that came in a squeeze-paste form. "That stuff might be okay for NASA," he said, but if he was going to go cruising around the galaxy in the most advanced ship ever, he needed to make sure that the dining arrangements were more becoming to one who possessed the best technology around.

But eating in zero gravity presented a few problems. The large fan in the ceiling kept any stray food particles from floating randomly throughout the ship. It blew the crumbs down through the wire mesh in the floor. There they were collected and combined with the sewage, and composted. The nutrient-rich soil was then used in the hydroponics room, where many of the ship's vegetables and fruits were grown.

The tables and chairs of the cafeteria were also made of mesh material. Lydia found it interesting how well the magnetic uniform secured her to her seat. Troy let her sit for a moment before returning with two trays of food. Each tray was partitioned with a few different metal covers. She learned that these, too, were held on by magnetism.

When she lifted one of the covers, a corn dog started to float up from the tray. "It may not be fine dining, but I suppose it's better than hotdog-flavored toothpaste," She said.

Troy raised a sippy cup and clinked it to hers. "To a child or an astronaut, this is as good as it can get."

The rest of her meal consisted of a hard roll with butter, a sticky fruit salad, and two carrot sticks. The soft drink that Troy had given her was in a sippy cup not too different from an infant's. To get any fluid out, she had to suck on it like a bottle. But considering the circumstances, this dining experience wasn't bad, just unique.

When she had finished eating, she found Troy in a playful mood. He kicked himself up against the flow of the fan. As he gently reached to the ceiling, he unscrewed the lid to his cup. He then allowed the last bit of his drink to float out. Following it toward the floor, he sipped the fizzy bubble of liquid all the way down. The last droplet of the sparkling drink fell through the mesh, and disappeared.

As they left the mess hall, or *mesh hall* as Lydia started calling it, she commented on how it was nice that Troy didn't have to worry about a weight limit for his ship. He admitted that it did allow a little more flexibility on the comforts he could enjoy while in space. But he was starting to lose that fun brotherly attitude that she had just started to glimpse. She suspected that he was about to go back to work, and though she hoped he would bring her with him, the fear of what she might witness next gnawed at her like a swarm of mosquitoes.

Troy led the way out of the cafeteria and down into the weapons room. "You want me to be honest and keep you in the loop, so forgive me if I comply. Just understand that the harder we hit now, the higher the chances of this impending war ending soon."

In the weapons room, she found Grisha, Kore, and one other man she hadn't met yet. Lydia locked eyes with Grisha, his betrayal finding condemning accusation under her scrutiny. Pained feelings of misplaced loyalties drove her scornful attention to Kore. Hate simmered under her brow when Troy said, "I think we're ready." He then turned to Lydia. "What you see here are all of our weapons, but I want to assure you that we have no intention of hurting anybody right now."

Lydia remained silent as her attention drifted back to her former partner. She watched as Grisha and the other man loaded one of the smaller bombs into a chamber and sealed it. She then ventured a question. "If you're not killing anyone, what are you going to bomb?"

Troy answered that it would be a communications satellite, and that they would launch one more after that to take down a strategic communications cable. They were trying to cut Russia off from the United States. "You see," Troy explained, "the U.S. has already started denouncing the video from earlier. Riots at U.S. embassies are starting, and there is a lot of political unrest forming in the Middle East already over it. In a matter of hours, the United States will discover that the video originated in Russia. When this happens, the President will likely try to get in touch with the Russians. Tensions will be hot, but the most likely outcome will be another Cold War or stalemate. This will go on until one of them cracks. We're just going to speed things up a bit."

Troy pulled a radio from his pocket and called Bernard Jublein. "Bernard, are you ready for that call to Russia?"

The radio squawked back affirmatively. A television was on the wall, but as he turned it on, Troy said that this time the message would be audio only. Lydia waited as she heard a phone ringing. As soon as the phone was picked up and the transfer was made to Russia's President, Bernard's fake U.S. President began to accuse them of stirring unrest.

He suggested that in such unstable times, the Russians were irresponsible and bullheaded, and that this type of behavior would not be tolerated. He also mentioned that though the U.S. didn't want war, they would ensure that Russia couldn't continue to send out anti-U.S. propaganda, and that they would do all in their power to prevent Russia from attempting to disrupt world peace any further.

Because Bernard's fake president was simply a recording, and the delay in reception, which came from being as far away as Mars, he'd made it so that the President sounded too irritable for conversation. Thus each time Russia's President tried to inject a comment or defense, Bernard's President cut him off with more accusations and hotheaded remarks.

Once the recording was finished, it automatically hung up. Lydia knew that what she had just heard would be taken as a precursor to war. Then, with Troy giving the signal, one of the chambers that the bomb had been placed in began to hum. When a red light turned to green, there was a popping sound, and then the chamber opened up again, revealing empty space. Troy might be crazy, she thought, but his plan seemed like it should work.

Grisha brought another bomb over, and they loaded it into the chamber. The loading process was repeated, and Russia would now suspect the U.S. of trying to create hostilities. To them, the U.S. would appear to be the aggressor, and they would make preparations for war. The U.S. would see these preparations and, unable to contact the Russians, would assume that the video had indeed come from them.

"Very good," Troy said approvingly. "The U.S. and Russia will start getting ready for a showdown. The Middle East is already starting to tear itself apart. Now it's time to invite China and Europe to the party."

Chapter 29

Since Monk had found his way onto GRIP's spaceship, he had been forced to hide. There had been people going back and forth all over the ship. He knew that if he was discovered, they would assume his best friend Flint was also either on the ship or in the base. For this reason, he crept about, keeping as low a profile as possible, while still trying to memorize the ship's layout.

Only once before launch had he dared exposure, when he had overheard Grisha talking about finding Flint and killing him somewhere in the base. Monk had allowed Grisha to pass him in one of the corridors, and then stealthily approached from behind. With a carefully executed maneuver, Monk was able to both trip Grisha and then force the much larger man down hard, slamming the Russian's forehead into the floor.

The hit had been enough to knock the man unconscious, buying Flint a little more time outside the ship to find Lydia and Labeeb. Continuing his search of the ship, Monk had started at the front and worked his way back. He didn't find Lydia, but he did find several things that interested him. The bottom floor was mostly filled with smaller rooms. Some were clearly meant to be sleeping quarters, and a few were meant as labs for some purpose or another.

A couple of rooms were reserved for the functioning purposes of the ship. One room appeared to be a dining room, though he wondered why they would have chairs and tables in space. One room appeared to be fully mechanical in nature. There were tanks and machines that were in the process of circulating sewage, water, and other things. One room he guessed was meant for weapons. It was filled with several six-foot-tall objects, and even more of some smaller three-foot-tall objects. His hypothesis that this was a weapons room was further supported by the presence of two chambers in the room. Each chamber matched the size of the stockpiled objects, and they seemed to be vacuums. The only reason they would have vacuum chambers, in his mind, was if each of the objects was capable of flight in the same manner that the ship was. Thus he determined that the small objects were bombs, and the larger ones were bigger bombs.

Most of the living and working spaces were along the outer edges of the ship with windows. The inner rooms were more for storage, and Monk took advantage of them several times to hide from the crew when he suspected them to be near. One time he even found himself hiding behind a box as somebody came in to stock the storage closet he was in. He wasn't concealed very well, but luckily they weren't looking for him, and he avoided detection.

When he made his way to the upper floor, he found the ship's control center at the very front. There were many people walking in and out of this room, and the congestion made it impossible to get a good look inside. Behind the control room was his favorite part of the ship.

The control room only took up about fifty feet of the ship's upper deck; the rest of it was a large room filled with vegetation. Clearly it was meant to be a greenhouse of sorts. Bright lights, some of which were ultraviolet, filled this man-made Eden. Undoubtedly the power required to maintain the lighting was derived from all the moss that covered the interior of the ship. The moss looked slightly different than that of the cave he had been in only one and a half days ago. He knew, though, that it must serve the same purpose, mostly because when he had first entered the ship, he'd felt the shock associated with stepping into the electrical field. It was like taking a step back into the Egyptian cave.

Though trees of all sorts filled the interior of the green room, most of the plant life was in the form of vegetables and fruits. One of the crew seemed to be a full-time gardener, but with the room being so large, it wasn't hard to avoid him. The air smelled fresh throughout the whole ship, but in this room, it was intoxicatingly delicious. Monk suspected that he wasn't the only one who found the room suitable for rest and relaxation. Scattered throughout the room were various chairs, some anchored to the floor, others to the ceiling.

The soils for the plants were contained in bags, and several vents with filters kept the air circulation going strong. This was where Monk had stayed when the ship launched, and as gravity disappeared, he saw how the filters collected any floating debris from the massive garden.

The feeling of weightlessness intrigued him. When the gardener had left briefly, Monk used the opportunity to adjust to his surroundings. Had anyone walked in on him, they would have thought he was a child at play. But as he bounced from floor to ceiling to wall, he was just making sure that he was comfortable moving in the new environment. After all, he knew that sooner or later he would have to confront the crew. Just as usual, he learned very quickly. During the couple of minutes that the gardener was out, he gained a complete confidence in his ability to move and react.

However, now that the ship was in space, he decided that he should make another sweep of the rooms. If Flint had gotten onboard, he needed to find him. Regardless of what had happened to Lydia earlier, she would surely be here now. It was only a matter of time before he found her.

Before leaving the upper deck, he took advantage of some of the fruits and vegetables. Monk had always preferred fruit in the mornings, and a blackberry bush conveniently satiated his hunger. But he wasn't sure when he might get back up to this deck for lunch, so he stuffed two carrots and a zucchini in his pocket for later.

Moving from room to room with all the activity on the ship was tedious, and slow. Monk knew that most people would find the pace difficult, but he didn't mind at all; patience was one of his stronger attributes. On the way, one opportunity presented itself that Monk simply could not ignore.

While waiting in one of the multiple closets he'd used for the slow trek, two of GRIP's crew came down the hallway and stopped in front of his closet. Not a problem except they would not move on. Troy may have ambitions to run the world with an iron fist, but these two people were just wasting time with gossip. With a little light filtering in from beneath the door, Monk was able to survey his tight surroundings. This was a supply closet with everything being clamped or tied down to metal shelving. The shelving itself was held onto the wall by some large bolts. The large bolts may be useful where gravity applied stronger pressure on the shelving, but here the size was overkill. Also since there was no downward pressure on the bolts, Monk was able to spin them quite easily. As long as the two people in the hall chose to linger, Monk was content on removing the bolts.

This contentment only lasted until he had three bolts removed. With each bolt being about the size of his pinky finger, Monk imagined that a bolt similar to these could reasonably be used for something more structural than shelves. Granted, the bolts didn't provide any real structure to the ship, but the back of the closet was really close to the exterior hull. As long as the two people didn't look into the closet, Monk wouldn't have to hurt them. But even if he did have to hurt them, the trick was worth it. Maneuvering with as much silence as possible, he placed his body just above the bottom of the door. The lightened gap was just wide enough to throw one of the bolts through. With a reverberating ping, the first bolt found its way into the hallway. As it bounced from wall to wall, the two people went silent.

"Grab that," one of them ordered. After a minute of fumbling, that same voice asked, "What is it?"

"It's a bolt," her voice trembled slightly.

"It's nothing. Maybe it just never got cleaned up

before launch. It's probably been floating around here since we launched."

"Are you sure about that?"

"Of course, I'm pretty sure we'd hear something if the ship was starting to fall apart."

A low metallic groan silenced their voices again. Monk let go of the shelving. It made the perfect noise. Curling over, he skipped the second bolt under the door and into the hallway.

"Another one, the ship's falling apart! We're going to die!"

"Calm down, it's okay. I'm sure it's nothing. We'll just take a peak and see what's happening."

Monk couldn't allow them to open the door. With the last bolt between his fingers, he started clanking it on the closet wall while bending another shelf to add the metallic groaning noise again. His rattling of the bolt started out slow, and picked up speed.

"Uh, I think you're right. We need to get someone down here quick," panic was now in the man's voice.

Monk could hear the woman panting hard, but she only seemed to whimper a reply. When Monk sent the last bolt pinking out from under the door, she screamed and gasped at the same time. This kept her response much more quiet than Monk could have guessed possible.

"Come on, we got to hurry," the man urged as they scrambled away.

Monk opened the door. The coast was clear. Two of the three bolts were still bouncing down the hall. Very soon, somebody who knew more about the ship's construction would be back here to examine its integrity. As Monk made his way farther down the hall, he reached out and grabbed one of the bolts. Maybe it would come in handy later.

While moving, Monk checked each room in sequence, until he heard a familiar voice coming from the room that he had earlier suspected of being a weapons room. It sounded very much like the President of the United States, and from what Monk could tell, he wasn't very happy. The President appeared to be communicating via a telephone call, but Monk didn't recognize the voice on the other end. It also appeared that both of them were somewhere else, and that somebody here was just eavesdropping on their conversation.

He tried to get a little closer, but the going was slow. When he finally did get close enough to peek inside the room, the call had ended, and there was some other mechanical noise coming from inside. Monk had no fear of looking inside the room. When people were focused on an important task, they often became oblivious to everything else around them. If this was a weapons room, and that was the President, then whoever was in there would clearly be focused on something of importance related to them. So he poked his head in.

As he suspected, Grisha was helping another man load one of the smaller ordinances into the small vacuum chamber. Troy and Lydia were there watching as the second object was sent out of the ship. Monk wondered if they were trying to target the President by tracing a phone call, or if the call served some other purpose.

Monk had seen enough and was about to move back out of sight when Lydia, being the first to turn around, caught a glimpse of him. Her eyes went bright with recognition, and Monk put a finger to his lips, signifying that he wanted her to be quiet, and then he signaled her to turn around so as not to draw attention to himself. She understood and complied. Monk then crept back into the hall, and found a closet to conceal himself in.

Not long after that, a few members of the crew came into the hall and were examining where they thought a bolt had sheared off the ship. Monk was content to see that his little joke was still causing some of the crew to be nervous. However, this prevented him from being able to follow Troy and Lydia as they exited the weapons room. Monk knew that he would have to start slowly making his way back to the front of the ship again to find her. But at least he knew that she was here, and he had a fairly good idea of which rooms she would not likely be occupying.

Even still, as soon as the crewmen in the hall had nervously given up interest in the bolts, claiming that it wasn't anything to worry about, Monk left his closet and ducked down a side hall, but not before hurling the bolt that he'd retrieved only minutes ago. He couldn't see the crew anymore, but he heard one of them yell out as the bolt struck home. In the head if Monk's aim had been accurate, which it usually was. As expected, this sent off a whole new fervor of space ship paranoia among the crew members. Content with his practical joke, Monk continued toward the back of the ship. He knew Lydia was here now. He'd catch up to her later. Maybe with any luck, Flint had found a way onboard before launching also.

Chapter 30

The entire morning after Flint had left Dusty alone on the yacht with Fran, she had been in a high state of agitation. She'd woken up early, and explored the boat. It soon dawned on her that she was alone with Fran. Flint and Monk had ditched her sometime that night after she'd fallen asleep. Monk, she didn't care much about. But Flint, she felt like they were reaching a new degree of comfort in their relationship. He might even stop thinking about Lydia and choose the more steady option. For the last several years she had spent her time laboring with Marshal Steel. The selfish grave robber. Doing Shen Mao's dirty work, he was an ugly scab on anthropologists everywhere. Ever since that chapter of her existence had appeared to be ending, she'd been looking for the next place to move on to with her life. She only hoped that Flint was just off the boat, running a quick errand. But if that was the case, *No, it can't be,* she realized. They were too far away from shore. Not only that, but they weren't even anchored near any harbor. Where was Fran taking her?

Flint seemed to be an exciting man, and she had hoped that something might work out with him. At the same time, she wasn't sure if she wanted him just for the sake of being with him, or if it was to give her life some direction. Now that he had ditched her, she began to seriously contemplate her future. Her family had grown up in the United States, and she used to call the South home. Finding her way back there now seemed to be next to impossible.

Even if I do go back, what's even there for me? She had wondered. Her family hadn't been very close, and she feared that she wouldn't have a livelihood. Her life was more in tune with the Middle East now. Even here, where she had made a few connections, she felt all alone.

As the sun brightened the horizon, Fran woke up and joined her. Throughout the rest of the morning, he had been more than accommodating to her, even sympathetic at times. He must have noticed her conflict, but he still seemed distant to her. She didn't feel that she could open up to him. His style was too like a politician. Everything he said was meant to sound inoffensive. He always had a motive for everything he did, and one could easily see that there was much more going on inside his head than he would ever divulge.

Fran didn't waste much time. A few welcoming words to Dusty, a splash of water on his face, then Fran put on an apron and got busy with breakfast. He served her a much nicer breakfast than she would normally have expected to find on a boat during these times of turmoil. Frankly the food was better than most breakfasts Dusty was accustomed to, period. Fran was obviously a man of appetite, having prepared the morning routine out of smoked fish, poached quail eggs on English muffins, sided by a generous portion of kiwi, melons, and raspberries covered in a semisweet cream sauce. While her belly relished in the treat, Fran explained the disappearance of Flint and Monk. In a futile attempt to spare her any grief, he told her what she had already guessed, that she'd been ditched while she was sleeping. To keep her from falling into a deep melancholy, he elaborated on how she could make herself useful. Since they needed to get samples of their precious moss distributed to those who could make the best use of it, there would be plenty to do.

He laid out a plan for delivering it to the various continents. If she was to come with him, she could work on propagating the sample into larger quantities so they could distribute it to more places along the way. Since she had nothing else to do, and no place else to go, she agreed to it. But this didn't fill her with the sense of purpose that she knew was needed.

She was lonely. Fran would never be the one to fix that; he was too old and reclusive. Flint could have been the one, but after dragging her over and under countries, he'd abandoned her without even saying a word. Then the memories of Marshal came back to her, and she remembered how he had treated her. *Am I one of those girls?* She thought. *The type that men can use for a short time, then drop without even thinking twice?*

The more the morning progressed, the more she dwelled on these types of thoughts. She felt depressed, and even welcomed it. Right before noon, in the confines of her little room, she let her emotions erupt and sobbed for over an hour. When the tears stopped coming, the rocking of the boat gently lulled her to sleep.

She woke up a couple hours later and stepped out onto the deck. The sun was high, and on land she would have been hot. Surrounded by water, the smallest of breezes prickled the skin on her arms and legs. The water took on a magical glitter. She stretched her whole body, and soaked in the afternoon rays. The thoughts from this morning were still fresh in her mind; however, the cool ocean breeze rejuvenated her. Each deep breath brought on a new determination to live and have joy in doing so.

She wrapped her arms tightly around her chest, partly due to the chill, but also because it felt comforting, as if she didn't need a man to add meaning to her life. She could give herself that reassuring hug and tell herself that she would be alright. The thing is, she was starting to believe it too. Fran stepped out to greet her. "Good afternoon, you're looking much better already," he observed.

"I feel better, also," Dusty replied with a gentle smile.

Fran put a hand on her back, and though she didn't care for it to be there, she didn't pull away. He seemed to have an almost fatherly attitude toward her, and she wanted to break the barrier that she knew must come down. If she was to spend the next couple of months with the man, she might as well be his friend.

"Do you really think that this little plant will keep the world from tearing itself apart?" she asked.

"To some degree, yes," Fran said. "I think that the next several years will be very difficult. The proverbial rug has been ripped out from under the whole world's economy. A global depression has started, and we will see the best and the worst coming from many individuals and nations. Oil production, or should I say oil distribution, will eventually come back, but there will be several hard years ahead first. This plant that you succeeded in bringing back, it will serve more as a beacon of hope. In time it may eventually decrease our dependence on oil, but even that may take years. I don't doubt that botanists will eventually find ways to modify it for more widespread uses."

"What about GRIP?" Dusty asked. "What do you think their plan is?"

Fran stepped away from her and leaned over the railing and looked at the water. He then ventured a hypothesis. "My guess is that they used the oil plot as a catalyst for even bigger plans. Most of the men who serve that organization were related to people who had belonged to a secret fraternity of Martian descendants, as you are well aware. For one reason or another, none of them were brought into that fraternity. Like Troy, some of them had extremely radical ideas and power-hungry motives.

"With the help of Labeeb, and a few other observers, I've been trying to piece together their activities. All that I've been able to understand so far is that they have been trying to gather an assortment of ancient technologies. I tried a few ways to stop them from getting too much, but I fear that not enough was accomplished to that end.

"The oil scheme was one of the more obvious, because that was where Labeeb was focused. Unfortunately we had only begun to figure it out just as they were enacting that paralyzing blow. It was too late to stop them. So if you ask me what they are trying to do, I would say that they are probably trying to find a way to exert some degree of power over the world. For them, bringing about a global change in environmental awareness wouldn't be enough or anything at all really. They don't really care about that sort of thing. Since they already have amassed a great deal of wealth, it seems inconceivable that money is the higher motivation. The only thing left is power."

Dusty laughed, but with a serious note. "You know, that sounds so cliché. They want to take over the world. I kind of doubt that the world will just bow down to them."

"One thing I've come to believe," Fran noted, "is that you can never underestimate the power of determination."

"I mean, people are suffering, maybe even dying. Even more might if they keep pushing. What kind of power-hungry determination can cause that?" she wondered.

Fran thought for a minute then argued the point. "Though the world is filled mostly with good people, it is also home to some really bad people, but most of them don't consider themselves bad. Most of them feel that what they are doing is right. Maybe they think that they are doing the public a service. Even some of the most hardened killers are able to justify their motives."

"It still makes no sense to me," Dusty answered as she joined Fran by the railing.

Looking into the water, she noticed a large jelly-fish drifting by. The calm movement of the creature had a soothing effect on her. She wondered if this gentle-looking life form could also be one of the more dangerous varieties. Without taking her eyes off it, she asked, "Do you think that Flint stands a chance of stopping them?"

Fran looked at her and said, "The only way to halt anyone as determined as GRIP is to send somebody who is equally determined to stop them. With the very little that I've learned about Flint, I know that he is the sort of man who will stop at nothing to accomplish what needs to be done. He is intelligent and willing to take the risks that most people would shy away from. Most of all, he can and likely will adapt to the needs of the moment.

"He may have left to save Lydia and Labeeb, but as he learns what GRIP is doing, I don't doubt that his priorities will include stopping them. If I knew of any black-ops teams in the area, I would have still sent Flint. I might have requested to send them as a backup, but I would put my cards on Flint. There aren't many men who give me the sort of impression that he does. If anyone stands a chance of stopping them, it will be him."

Dusty fought back her feelings, both for loving and for hating Flint, as she added, "I really hope you're right about him."

"Well," Fran said, straightening up. "We have a lot to do. We'll just have to trust him to do his part while we do ours."

Chapter 31

Flint and his pilot had taken off in their jet and left Chinese airspace. After forty-five minutes, the pilot prepared for the descent into Manila. Flint chose this time to remind the pilot that he needed to be farther down south.

As before, the pilot refused to acknowledge Flint's request. Since the pilot was reluctant to comply, Flint took the only measure that seemed available to him. He stepped away from the pilot long enough to reload the pistol that he'd taken from one of Troy's men. Then, careful to leave a bullet out of the chamber, since he didn't actually intend on using it, he returned to the pilot. Though reloading the gun seemed unnecessary to prod the pilot along, he felt it would nonetheless be smart so he didn't forget to reload it for when he might actually need it.

With the short barrel pressed firmly into the pilot's neck, Flint interrogated, "What did they tell you about me?"

The pilot was obviously scared, as his English became more broken, "They say you spy, American spy. Please, I have family." He then mentioned, hoping that it would elicit some mercy, "Besides, you need pilot."

Flint pressed the gun harder against the man's neck and replied, "I can fly one of these jets just as good as you can, and since you know that I'm a spy, you should also know that I value my mission more than I value your life. You will take me to Lapu-Lapu, or your family will lose a father and a husband."

Flint had no real intention of hurting the man, but his bluff was convincing enough, and the pilot held off his descent.

The pilot made as if to adjust his instruments, and Flint had to grab the man's hand before it snuck over to the transponder. "I know what that piece of equipment does, and you don't need to change it," If Flint allowed the pilot to change the code on the transponder, then any air traffic controller would know that the jet was hijacked. The last thing he needed was a military presence at the airport when he landed.

After another forty-five minutes, they finally began to give up their altitude. The air-traffic controller wouldn't respond, and Flint guessed that the airport, like so many others, was completely shut down. This pleased him; it would give him the chance to land and find his way out while avoiding any type of customs. He knew that it would also please his new pilot friend, because he didn't want to hang around an airport without the proper clearance, either.

Once they had touched down, Flint thanked the pilot, who stayed glued to his seat. Flint didn't expect a response, since the man was obviously infuriated at having been hijacked. But no real harm was done, and Flint was that much closer to his goal now. As soon as he was off the jet, it turned around and was back in the air, heading home to Hong Kong, with the pilot undoubtedly informing his superior about his forced detour.

Flint knew that finding a powered ride to Bohol would be next to impossible. As an oil importer, the already struggling Philippines economy had been crippled even further. Still, he checked a couple of the smaller planes at the airport, but found that any fuel that may have been in them had been siphoned out.

Pulling out his phone, he placed another call to Fran. It seemed like a long shot, but he hoped Fran might still have enough connections to get him some transportation to the neighboring island. At first he got no response, so he left a message. A few minutes later, Fran called him back. "I was just talking to Dusty about you. I assume you made it to Hong Kong all right?"

"Yes, thank you very much for that," Flint responded. "How have things been with you and Dusty?"

"Oh, fine," he said. "She needed a couple hours to get over you, but she's fine now."

"Only a matter of hours?" Flint joked.

"Well, I'm sure she still thinks about you. Right now we're just about to head up the Suez Canal and start dropping samples of the moss along the way. We'll hit Africa and Europe, and then head over to America. We'll probably hit China last, since we don't want to end up around Somalia. I hear the pirates there are becoming increasingly desperate and dangerous."

"If I were you," Flint said, "I wouldn't worry too

much about China. I sent their military into Troy's compound, and I have a funny feeling they'll find a similar moss that Troy genetically engineered. I also wouldn't be surprised if they find a few other surprises, but that's not why I called you. I need to know if you by any chance have a little extra pull to get me a boat in the Philippines?"

"Why do you want to go to the Philippines?" Fran asked.

Flint was wondering why Fran was asking, but he guessed that Fran just wanted to know the details. "I thought you could track my phone."

"I haven't had a free minute to look you up," Fran replied.

Flint went ahead to explain, "Well, it didn't take long to find GRIP, but they launched their ship before I could stop them. I'm in the Philippines now, trying to get to the island of Bohol."

"Ah," Fran expressed with an air of understanding. "You're going to Shen Mao's compound, aren't you? I thought that ship was damaged. Why would you go back there?"

Flint wondered why he felt surprised that Fran would know about that experience. But he assumed that Dusty had simply told him about it. "Other than his own version of the moss, Troy had also used the broken pieces of the device that Mao used to develop his own propulsion device. I found that broken unit in his base. It seems that Troy did a crude repair job when they were reverse engineering it. I don't know if it'll work, but I have to give it a shot. Something really big is about to happen, and I need to stop him if I can."

"I hope you are very careful. That technology is dangerous," Fran warned.

"I know all about it," Flint said, then described

how he had been eavesdropping on Mao when it was all explained. "But what about that ride? Do you know anybody around here who could help me?"

"I'm afraid you're on your own this time," Fran informed. He then asked, "Where do you think Troy's ship is right now?"

Flint had wondered the same, but hadn't figured out how he would find them. "I'm not sure yet."

"Space is a large place," Fran reminded.

"I'm working on getting up there," Flint stated. "But I'm not beyond listening to any suggestions on how to find them."

"I'll do what I can," Fran said, which Flint took as meaning, *I know people, who know people, who should be able to find them.*

"Good enough. Call me if you find out anything," Flint said before each gave their ending remarks.

Upon hanging up the phone, Flint headed for the shoreline. It took a good hour and a half to walk into the more populated portion of the island. Little had changed since his last visit. The only difference was that there weren't any automobiles on the road. Rickety old bicycles with sidecars had replaced them. The first one to pass him slowed down and hollered out in English, "Hey, Joe, you ride?"

The man's English was limited, but it was a start. "I need to get to Bohol," Flint said. "Do you know of any boats going there?"

"Bohol?" The driver gawked with a look of insult. He then waved a hand of dismissal and pedaled away.

The next trikse-cab coming down the road saw the other ride off, and decided to capitalize on the situation. "Hey, Joe," he too called out. "Where you going to, man?"

Flint liked this driver more. He was younger and

more energetic. "I need to find a way to Bohol, any idea how I can get there?"

"Sure, Joe, my uncle, he has boat. You have money?"

"I've got a little," Flint told him. The teenager motioned for Flint to get in, and he started pedaling the heavy bike down the road. The first ten minutes went well. The boy was putting his whole heart into the job that would likely be his best client for days. However, after he had gone for fifteen minutes, Flint could see that he was starting to fatigue. The life of a trikse-cab driver was a poor one, and he suspected that his skinny driver rarely ate well. *Why not*, Flint thought, and ordered the young man to stop.

His driver was slightly confused at first, but then took great pleasure in letting Flint pedal the trike for the next fifteen minutes. The teen occasionally gave directions as he joked with his American chauffer, and by the time they reached their destination, Flint had gained a new appreciation for the young man's line of work. With sweat drenching his whole body, partly from the heat but even more from the exertion, he dismounted the coconut shell that served as a seat on the old bike. He then surveyed the hut where the boy had led him.

It was a simple little house, no larger than a backyard shed in America. The wall was constructed from a single layer of woven palm fronds with larger poles made from bamboo acting as corner posts and supporting beams. The house stood on four short pillars of the spongier coconut wood, with the roof being overlaid with several layers of thatched palm fronds. A single wire ran into the house, and directly powered a small black-and-white television. The only toilet was detached, and appeared to be a community outhouse. The stove was just a stack of cinder blocks with a small pile of twigs for burning. Running water was a luxury that still hadn't made its way to this small neighborhood. Every home here was built around a community well, where there was a woman doing laundry and another girl, dressed in garments sufficient to give herself privacy, taking a shower by dumping buckets of water over her head.

In one respect, Flint pitied the living conditions that his new friend endured, but on the other hand, he almost envied the simplicity. The young man didn't waste any time and led Flint along a dirt path to another little shanty closer to the water. *"Ayo!"* he called out, which seemed to Flint to be the way they knocked on doors, since many of their doors wouldn't stand up to a fist pounding.

A poverty-hardened woman came out. She had a stern but pleasant appearance. Her palms were callused from decades of washing laundry by hand, and her clothing looked like old secondhand rags, which they likely were. The young man, whom she called Dodong, asked her something that Flint couldn't understand. Dodong in turn walked up and gave her a proper Filipino greeting, which Flint later learned was done out of respect for their seniors. Dodong did this by taking her hand, palm down, and bowed as he pulled her knuckles to his forehead. He then spoke to her for a minute before turning to Flint. "You are in luck—my *tio* is still here. Come, I take you to him."

Flint followed the excited youth until they were on the beach. It wasn't nearly as pretty a beach as some that Flint had seen during his last visit to this country; in fact, he found this beach to be so polluted, he wondered how anyone could live a healthy life with all the garbage that collected here.

A little way down, they found a few people sitting

near what they called a pawn boat. It was an ocean-going vessel that seemed like a large canoe with a hint of Asian influence. It couldn't have measured more than thirty feet long, and had outriggers on both sides for stability. Flint had seen and ridden in many boats before and had never been nervous, but he remembered how long the trip was in a ferry from Cebu to Bohol and back. The thought made him a little leery of sailing that far in a rickety canoe, especially one held together by little more than pieces of twine or rope.

Looking into the boat was even less reassuring. The bottom of it had small pools of water already sitting. Dodong explained to his uncle what Flint wanted, and then the man stood and loosely started shaking Flint's hand with both of his. Flint could smell the nauseatingly sweet odor of *tuba*, a home-made palm wine, on his breath. It was evident that the man was drunk, and the way he persisted in shaking Flint's hand much longer than was neces-sary confirmed that he was less than a drink away from passing out.

He went on saying things like, "You are a hans-ssome Merican. I have a daughter, sheez very prity, eh?" Flint tried to reassure the man that he was only looking for a ride to Bohol. All the while he seemed to agree, stating that it was no problem. Finally, how-ever, Dodong stepped in and suggested they wait a few hours. He would try to sober his uncle up, but in the meantime, Flint should relax. Dodong even went as far as buying him a bottle of Coke, which Flint knew must be a sacrifice for the poverty-stricken family. But in an effort to not offend, he graciously accepted.

While Flint waited, he tried to appreciate his humble surroundings. If there was any place like this back home, he knew that seagulls would be scrounging the whole area. This train of thought led him to notice that there wasn't a single bird in sight. In fact, he couldn't recall having ever seen a bird of any type during his time in this country. Wanting to ask Dodong about it, Flint started opening his mouth, but then he noticed the waves of the sea behind the little pawn boat. This contraption that was meant to carry him to Bohol looked like the most risky adventure he'd committed to so far. He tried to imagine another scenario that would afford him a trip to the island with less chance of drowning. Flint had to get to the late Shen Mao's mansion. Aside from the pawn boat, he found no options, and therefore no solace.

Chapter 32

Heading north up the Suez Canal was less difficult than Fran expected. The anticipated obstacles were few along the way, and soon he and Dusty were breaking water on their way to Italy. The moss was growing surprisingly fast, well enough in fact that a sample might be spared as soon as they reached the boot of Europe.

En route he placed several calls to various contacts, some in NASA, others in different governments. He explained who GRIP was, and that it was urgent to locate them. Within the next five hours, he hoped to have as many telescopes searching the sky as he could get. Troy was up there, and he was planning something big.

In the meantime international relationships were starting to degrade. That morning, right after having talked with Dusty, he checked on the world news. The U.S. President had given a surprise address, wherein he had all but said that the U.S. would start an occupation of the Middle East. This started more riots and anti-U.S. protests that were turning increasingly violent. Even with all of Fran's contacts, he hadn't been able to get any answers from the U.S. side on the provocation for such an announcement. Fran knew as well as anyone that the Middle East wasn't even that critical anymore. If the U.S. needed oil, it had plenty of resources. The announcement just didn't make sense to him.

By noon Fran began to notice that tensions were escalating all over the world. Rumors were floating about that Russia had faked the presidential announcement, and the U.S. had retaliated by bringing down one of their key communication satellites and destroyed a major communication cable running into the capital city of Moscow.

Everything was speculation at this point, but it seemed as if everyone was getting jumpy. If it was true that Russia had been the early aggressor, then it might use the attack on its communications as a reason for going to war. It wouldn't take long before all of Europe was involved, and he wondered how things would shape up if China also found its way into the picture. The large country had taken a backseat during the last few major wars, but he found it unlikely that they would be unaffected by another major world conflict, the likes of which was beginning to brew.

Fran used his satellite uplink to send off thousands of e-mails to everyone from among his political contacts to news reporters. He had a war to stop, and he was sure that the energy crisis was catalyzing the hostilities. However, despite his best efforts, it seemed that Russia, the Middle East, and the U.S. conflicts continued to dominate the news, with his announcement only taking a five-second slot in be-tween news updates.

While all of this was going on, he wondered if Troy had anticipated the global tensions in his plans. Without knowing what GRIP planned to do, Fran couldn't quite picture their role in the world economy yet. But he was certain that he wouldn't have long to wait. Troy was already up in the sky somewhere, and he wouldn't be there if he wasn't ready to make another move.

The moss Flint had brought him was growing well. Already it had increased about ten percent in size, and Fran was certain that in a day or two, he would have sufficiently large samples to share with not only the Italians, but every country he came to port in. The afternoon was still young enough, and with the winds favorable, he believed that he might make Italy sometime during the night or early the next morning. He didn't much like the idea of sail-ing all through the night, especially when his focus was needed so badly on the political issues. He was in a race and time was his enemy. The thought oc-curred to him that Dusty might be able to lighten the burden a little, and he wondered if he should teach her how to sail and navigate so that they could take shifts.

At the top of every hour he checked to see if any-body had located Troy's ship. Though most every ob-servatory around the globe was searching the skies, none had found any luck in locating it yet.

About 6:00 in the evening, Dusty brought Fran a light dinner. "I found some food in the galley," she said as she offered him a plate. "I'm not much of a cook, but I thought you might be hungry enough by now that it wouldn't matter."

Fran thanked her and invited her to sit down

with him. As they ate, he asked if she wanted to learn how to sail.

Chapter 33

At around 1:00, Flint had been offered a light lunch consisting of ground corn and a thin leafy soup to put on it. The flavor was good, but he had seen them prepare it and knew that it was flavored with almost a quarter cup of MSG powder. But it tasted good, and he didn't want to offend.

After lunch, not entirely to Flint's surprise, the drunken uncle lay down on the floor and was asleep in less than a minute. The part that did strike him as odd was that everyone else went down for a nap, too. Flint knew that in many Spanish cultures it was customary to take a siesta in the middle of the day. Since the Spanish had owned the Philippines for nearly three and a half centuries, he decided that these people must have more Spanish influence in their culture than Asian.

While he wanted to get on his way as soon as possible, he couldn't complain. The uncle would need some time to get the alcohol out of his system, and Flint enjoyed the rest. There was far too much on his mind to fall asleep, but he did get to relax for a couple of hours and think about what he was going to do. Since his plan still involved so many unknown variables, a concrete idea was hard to put together. Too much of his activities had followed this pattern of acting on too little information. This was fun for an adventure, but not when people's lives were at risk.

First, he didn't know where Troy's ship was. Second, even if he was able to find it and get Shen Mao's little ship to work, he didn't know what he would be able to do once he found his way there.

After two hours everyone except the uncle was awake. Dodong's aunt tried to wake her inebriated husband, but he wouldn't budge. She even began swatting him with a short broom, but all he did was stir a little and turn over. Seeing that it was useless, she gave Dodong a few instructions, and he started to run around the neighborhood, for what reason Flint could only guess.

Fifteen minutes later he was back, carrying two large bamboo poles. Each pole must have been a good twenty or thirty feet long. The aunt in the meantime had continued working at a foot-driven sewing machine. When the uncle finally did wake up, he was still drunk, but had a little better presence of mind. Flint could hardly stand being around him because he stank so badly, but at last the uncle began to work on his boat.

Flint lent a hand as they prepared for the trip, careful to avoid the man's flammable breath. The aunt finished making what was apparently a sail, sewn together from several bed sheets. Flint wondered where she had found them, since he had yet to see a single bed. They then attached the sad excuse for a sail on two thin bamboo poles before tying them off to a larger bamboo mast about the thickness of his wrist. The scale of the sail on the pathetic excuse of a fishing vessel made Flint wonder if he would be swimming half the way.

The uncle had clearly thought the whole thing through before Flint had entered the picture, but it still seemed evident that he didn't know what he was doing. The pawn boat had a small gas engine that he no longer could get fuel for, and he doubted that the man had ever gone on the ocean by wind power. Flint looked up and down the beach, but couldn't see anybody else who might be better equipped to handle the voyage.

By the time they were done, the pawn boat looked like a sea canoe with a large pair of open scissors, covered in cloth, pointing on an angle into the sky. They finished loading it with some food and water, being generous enough to include some bottled water for Flint, since the water they were drinking was full of amoebas and could have given him the worst stomach and intestinal problems he'd ever experienced. Then, for the trip back home, the uncle packed a fishing net, as he was determined to make a living on both legs of the journey.

So with Dodong, his uncle, and one other man named Joseph, they cast off and were on their way to Bohol. Their boat was blown back to shore twice before they were able to get the hang of traveling by wind power, further discouraging Flint's confidence in his travel companions. Another fifteen minutes later, Flint was manning the sail, having caught on much quicker than the other men. Instead they resorted to navigating. They had no compass, but they had a lifetime of experience in blind reckoning. Flint reluctantly trusted their judgment on direction as he zigzagged his way to Bohol.

The island, which was only about fifteen miles away from Lapu-Lapu, took twice as long to get to than if the winds had been favorable. But after a couple of hours, they sighted land. The uncle then asked Flint which town he was headed for. When he replied that it was Jagna, the man looked surprised. "Jagna is back of Bohol," he protested. But Flint was insistent.

The men gave in to Flint's wishes, reluctantly accepting their charge to sail around the island. Since Jagna was on the complete opposite end of the island, it added another eighty miles to their voyage. But they only had to go about forty miles around before they found themselves moving along more easily with the winds. Unfortunately, this was about the time the sun was setting. As they made their way to shore for the night, Flint couldn't help but be fascinated by the bioluminescent water. In their wake the oxygen was being mixed, and the bacteria common to these waters were creating a neon-blue light. When Flint got to looking closer, glowing outlines of fish came into focus as they swam beneath the magical ripples.

Flint had heard of this phenomenon, but had never yet experienced it for himself. He dipped his hand over the edge and watched as the water around his fingers glowed with a glittering green. He was suddenly overwhelmed when he realized the boat was already to shore, and the whole shoreline was lit up by the gentle waves. In all his life, the only thing that he could come close to relating the experience to was seeing the aurora borealis in Alaska.

The uncle threw out his net and Flint helped drag it in. They were able to catch a few small fish, nothing that would have passed for food in America, but they weren't in America, and his hosts seemed content with their bounty. The uncle even grabbed a small flat flounder from the net as soon as it came in and began eating it like a potato chip before it even stopped wiggling. Joseph was entertaining everyone by playing with either a sea snake or an eel that came in with the net. He held it by the tail and threw it around, or wrapped it around his arm before swinging it around somewhere else. Flint didn't know, but he guessed by the way the man was showing off that the creature was a poisonous sea snake.

After bringing in the net, Flint entertained himself by trying to guess which fish they were planning on eating for dinner. None of them were over four inches long, and to his surprise, they built a small fire and started cooking them all.

This was the first time Flint had ever eaten such a meal. The Filipinos had packed some rice, wrapped in woven palm fronds, then dropped the fish directly onto the coals. When the fish were sufficiently blackened, the men would start eating them, skin and flesh. They even picked at the tiny flecks of flesh on the top of the heads.

Flint vowed that if he ever got back to America, he wouldn't take for granted the larger fish he'd been privileged to enjoy there. Here the men were content with even the smallest fishes. They just held the things in their hands and picked them clean. With some of the smaller ones, they didn't even bother pulling off the bones; they just ate the whole thing. Admittedly, they were the freshest fish Flint had ever tried and they tasted amazing. He had polished off close to a dozen of them before finally retiring for the night.

His companions all slept soundly on the beach.

The glow of the ocean had turned faint in comparison to the unbelievably clear sky. The stars were brighter than he remembered ever seeing them. He knew that up there someplace, Lydia and Monk were drifting along, looking down on them. As he began to drift off to sleep, he tried to imagine what it would be like to see the Earth from space. If things worked out, he might even get the opportunity. He imagined that it would be mostly blue, with large white patches, similar to what most pictures depicted. The only real difference would be that his vision would be more powerful, because a picture rarely did anything justice.

He then wondered how the other planets would look. Jupiter with all its moons, and that large bright spot in the middle; Saturn with its rings. He then thought of the red planet, Mars, where the seeds of all this had been put into action several millennia ago. If it was true that Mars had in fact looked like Earth at one time, he wondered if that perspective would change how he looked at the scorched planet. As sleep overtook him, he got an important idea. But the day had been a long one, and from being on the ocean with the sun beating down on him, he found it difficult to stay awake. His eyes fluttered once more before dreams replaced reality. All the while, visions of luminescent water swirled through his sleeping world.

Chapter 34

After dinner, Troy led Lydia back to her room, he prided himself on the accomplishments of his day. "Tomorrow," he mentioned, "with or without our help, the Russians will retaliate against the United States. The UN will attempt to mediate, but as they are attempting to do so, China will receive a rather nasty little surprise. When the U.S. starts their war with Russia, the U.S. will find it difficult not to default on their debt obligations to their former trade partner. China will have little recourse but to attempt to foreclose on the U.S. From there it's just a matter of picking sides for the leftover countries."

Lydia could see that Troy had everything planned out perfectly. He was so convinced about his future chain of events that he believed nothing could possibly go wrong. And if it did, she knew he would find a way to justify the rogue variable as being all part of his grand scheme. Such was the type of man her brother had become.

Troy managed a completely sober face while he mentioned, "As soon as nuclear strikes begin, citizens of each country will lose faith in their leaders. It is a sad but necessary evil which will allow people to unite behind one who can put an end to all of it."

"And you will humbly take on the role of savior," Lydia surmised.

"GRIP will herald in a new era of responsible progression for all mankind. Had our ancestors not come to this planet when they did, Earth might still be full of the same primitive men that roamed this world millennia ago. It's only fitting, since we brought higher degrees of thinking to them, that we also show them how to handle those advancements in science that accompany higher learning."

Lydia quietly scoffed at his egotism. She still was trying to keep up appearances to be allowed a little more freedom onboard the ship. But alas, upon returning to her room, Troy locked her in. He told her that he would be back in a few hours, and she should attempt to relax and enjoy the Martian view.

Like I'm going to just sit around like a caged pooch, she thought. As soon as Troy left, she explored every inch of the room for a way out. He had at least refrained from tying her up again, which she was grateful for, but the door to her room allowed no apparent means of egress. She needed to find Monk. How he had gotten onboard without detection, she could only wonder. But if she were to stop Troy from further disrupting the now delicate nature of Earth's governmental powers, she would need Monk's help.

For the first time in several hours, hope was again beginning to surge through her veins as she desperately searched for a way to escape. When the door proved fruitless, she checked the ceiling, floor and each wall, looking for an air duct or anything that might be a weakness to her prison. As if to dampen her optimism, the ducting was a high-pressure air system with holes only large enough to place a couple of fingers in. She then tested the walls. Behind the metallic mesh panels that supported the moss, there appeared to be a separate wall constructed from a sprayed-on fiberglass. By pressing up against it, she was able to determine that it wasn't very thick, and that every two feet or so there was a firm wood, or more likely metal, stud supporting the wall. What she needed was a way to cut through the fiberglass without drawing attention to herself. The metal paneling was too large and heavy, making it impossible to use the corners as a cutting tool.

After floating throughout the room in search of something else hard and sharp enough to do the job, she decided that her most useful tool would be the diamond ring Flint had given her when they got engaged. Lydia had kept it on a necklace, hidden under her shirt, since putting it on her finger made her feel like a hypocrite and a monster. She went up to her closet, with the idea that if anyone came in, she could close it, and they wouldn't be any wiser to her actions. The closet wasn't like anything back where gravity could hold clothing to a hanger. This closet required you to fold all your clothes and place them in magnetic boxes, each just small enough for a single day's outfit. She had to pull most of these boxes out, attaching them to the floor outside the closet before she could start. Then, after taking off a panel, she took out the ring.

Hesitating, she stared at it for a minute. In financial terms, the small piece of jewelry was worth maybe four or five thousand dollars. In sentimental worth, it was priceless. For the last couple of years, the diamond ring was the only physical reminder of a life wherein she had truly been happy. But if she was going to die up here anyway, the sparkling sentimental rock would be of little consequence. Carefully and deliberately she began to dig the diamond surface into the fiberglass wall. Progress was slow and painful as she used the edges to scrape away the epoxy from the wall.

To begin with Lydia scratched the outline of where she wanted her hole. It just needed to be large enough to fit through. Then over the next thirty minutes, she labored away, scratching deeper each time, hoping that the wall wasn't any thicker than her first estimate. Aside from the tedious and slow progress, Lydia had to be careful not to break the ring outright. It held up longer than she might have expected, lasting a good forty-five minutes before the diamond became dislodged. She pocketed the stone and continued the gouging process with the small sharp angle where the mount used to hold the diamond. The softer metal was much less effective, and frustration began to set in. The room was so devoid of anything sharp or hard that she wondered if she would ever put a hole in the wall.

Losing all patience, Lydia flipped around in the air and tried kicking the center of her closet where she had been clawing. Instead of allowing her feet to take the brunt of her aggression, the exertion launched her body into the wall at the other end of the room. Clearly there were still a few hard lessons to learn about maneuvering in zero gravity. When finally her hands were able to grab the bed frame and keep her from bouncing, she took a moment to rest. Bruises covered her body from all the collisions when she'd been slammed from wall to ceiling to floor and back to the wall again. Then, carefully making her way back to the closet, she sighed and tried to prep herself for another attempt at making a hole.

When she stuck her head into the closet, she found that a small crack had finally appeared on a portion of the wall. Hoping that nobody had heard her before, she began to work fervently at enlarging the crack. It took several minutes, but she was finally able to create a hole large enough to stick her finger in. Then, using all her strength, she first pulled then pushed at the area until the crack spread. After another half of an hour doing this, she managed to break off a small portion of the wall. The hole was still not nearly large enough to fit her body through, and inside she found it full of insulation. Parting the irritating fiberglass, which must have been used more for sound than temperature control, she discovered some wiring and plumbing for the humidifiers that misted the outer metal mesh walls.

Again her hopes were dashed when she discovered that behind this mess of insulation and plumbing, there was another wall similar to the one she had just broken through. Her ring no longer had any prongs or sharp points on it, and she knew that even if she did manage a hole large enough on her side to fit in, the next wall would be impossible, given her means. With a grunt of disappointment, she wondered when she'd be let out again, and if she'd be able to kife a sharp enough object from somewhere on the ship to finish the job.

If she could just wait until the next mealtime, she might be able to find and confiscate a fork or other utensil to continue the work. Why hadn't this thought occurred before? It would have prevented her from destroying the engagement ring. A sick feeling crept over her, and even as she reminded herself that both she and the ring would be destroyed if she succeeded, she couldn't stave off the feelings of regret and betrayal that came with breaking the symbol of her husband's love.

Giving in to her reality, she decided to cover up the hole in the closet before anyone discovered her little endeavor. But as she was grabbing the metal panel that went into the closet, the door to her room swung open. From the vantage the door provided, Lydia knew she would be discovered, so instead of allowing herself to be found out and tied up again, she used every effort to throw the metal panel at the person about to enter the room.

The panel left her hand slower than she would have expected, because at the same time it had caused her to fly backward. This, however, gave her another advantage as her legs came up against one of the walls. Since she'd already learned the hard way about bouncing off walls, her legs were now flexed and prepared to spring off into the doorway. Whoever was coming in, whether it was Troy, Kore, Grisha, or someone else, they would be in for a surprise. If she was lucky, she might even be able to lock them in the room, and get herself into the hallway where she wanted to be. Let them try breaking through the wall to get out for a change.

Chapter 35

August 10th

The sky was still dark when Flint awoke to what sounded like a growing white noise. It took him a minute to clear his mind. Then came the realization of what the sound meant. But by the time he figured it out, the storm was already upon him. The unrestrained curtain of rain flooded out their camp, and he scrambled for shelter. Within only a few minutes, the rain was coming down harder than any storm he could remember. Nothing was visible beyond fifteen feet, and even that may have been stretching it.

He approached Dodong and asked how long these types of storms usually lasted. The response he got back was not pleasant. Dodong related that a storm like this would last at least all day, and maybe into the next day, as well. Nobody seemed willing to test the waters with their makeshift sailboat. Good thing, too; already the pawn boat was half full of rain water, and would probably fill up the rest of the way within the next minute or two. Everyone else was reluctant to provide Flint with a straight answer when asked how much farther they had to go before reaching Jagna.

Flint knew that only a fool would be out driving a car, let alone a boat, in such a storm, and that if he wanted to get anywhere, he would have to walk. He didn't like the idea of moving about in such a downpour, but since he was already soaking wet, and there was no chance at falling asleep again, he couldn't see any reason not to. Since waste removal still left something to be desired, and since littering was a common activity, Flint had no hard time in finding a discarded plastic bag. Taking the small plastic bag, he wrapped up the satellite phone and his little bundle for Troy's lab to keep it all as dry as possible. Then, without waiting for morning to break, he paid the men every last dripping dollar he had. Taking leave of his sailing companions, he walked in the direction that he believed Jagna to be in.

The walk was refreshing in an odd sort of way. He was soaked clean through, but because the rain wasn't cold, his body temperature stayed comfortable. The sound of the wall of water as it came down was unlike anything he could describe. Not only was his vision limited, but also the sound blocked out all other noise. The whole experience was as if he were in a small dark shower with fifty nozzles aimed directly on top of him. Add to that a television speaker turned to full volume on a blank channel.

The only reason he managed not to get lost was the simple fact that the road, which ran along the ocean, was the same road that should lead to Jagna. He remembered traveling it, coming from the other direction, only a week earlier. After two hours of walking, he came to a sign that indicated he was in a town called Duero. By this time he could make out a couple of other people as they too braved the elements. Most, however, were sheltered in faintly glowing bakeries or shanty-style homes. No doubt this would be a boring day for most of them.

His feet sloshed in the murky water as he trudged up to the first bakery that had an awning over it.

"*Hoy!*" she said loudly, almost jumping at the sight of him. Her smooth creamy brown face blushed dark red. Then, trying to make up for her bewilderment, she said in broken English, "Is rainy, you very wet, oh."

Flint had startled a young woman. She probably would have been surprised to see anybody, let alone an American braving the storm, and finding his way to her little shop. Flint smiled wide, trying to imagine how silly he must look with water streaming down him. This, however, only served to make the young woman blush even more. Her bread smelled delicious, but he hadn't come looking for a breakfast. Even though he would have loved to sample the morning pastries, he remembered that he had already given his last dollar away. Instead he just asked, "This is Duero?"

She confirmed that it was, and Flint added, "I'm going to Jagna. How far away am I?"

"Jagna?" she said. "Yes, Jagna that way." She pointed down the road.

"Yes, but how far?" Flint repeated.

"Maybe nine oh ten kilometer," she replied.

Flint did a quick calculation and realized that he was only about five or six miles away. He was closer than he would have expected. He raised his hand and said, "Thank you," as he began to walk away.

The girl mustered up a little more courage and called out, "*Hoy*, Joe, you no want bread?"

Flint turned back to her and replied, "I have no money."

"*Hoy*," she said again in disbelief. "Americano is rich, Filipino is poor."

Flint shrugged his shoulders. "This Americano is poor, too."

She didn't let it end at that. Instead she flagged him over and took out a small plastic sack and filled it with three sugar-covered rolls called *ensaymadas*. She then handed him the bag, making sure to rub her hand across his as he took it from her; and smiled, making sure that he understood her flirtation. Flint thanked her for the gift, and she asked, "You come back soon?"

"I don't know," Flint replied honestly. "Anything is possible."

He left the shelter of the bakery and ventured once more into the rain. The pastries were heavenly and Flint's confidence was high as he walked. He even thought, *I could really get used to this place if the women are all like this.*

However, in the next couple hours of walking, reality took hold of him again. The morning had grown considerably lighter, even if the sun couldn't push through the storm. At least he could see more clearly through the rain, but he was getting tired of the sloshing as his water-filled shoes began to wear on his soaking feet. As his attitude muddled with the weather, he caught himself doubting his plan. What if the part that he had stolen from Troy's base didn't work anymore? *Even if it does work, what are my odds of finding their ship?* He had come too far to give up on his plan, but this and other thoughts plagued his enthusiasm.

Eventually he found himself standing on the road outside a large Catholic cathedral. He determined that it must have been built sometime in the 1800s. He continued on his way for another ten minutes before he realized he had gone too far. Turning around he quickly remembered where he was. Everything looked slightly different from the last time he had been here, but he remembered well enough that he was able to find Shen Mao's compound after only a few wrong turns.

The tall steel gates to the compound were locked up. The only people who could possibly be inside were either police guards or squatters. He doubted the first two, in lieu of the weather, but he didn't doubt that some squatters might have found their way in. Wasting no time, he skirted the perimeter, looking for a way inside. The metal gate was too wet to attempt climbing, and the tall concrete wall offered little chance of scaling it. He also remembered that there was broken glass cemented into the top of the wall to keep intruders at bay.

This hadn't stopped him the first time when he'd raided Mao's mansion. He'd had help then. But alone, and with everything being wet, the odds of getting hurt went up dramatically. At length he found a large stack of cinder blocks near a neighbor's yard. They were preparing to construct an addition to their home. Since nobody seemed to be watching, Flint decided to borrow the blocks for a moment. He began to stack them in the same place where he had crawled over when he last assaulted the mansion. Not because the wall was shorter here; on the contrary. But he remembered that he had broken and scraped away several of the razor-like shards of glass that threatened intrusion.

He was careful to stack the blocks quickly but

firmly. On one hand, he didn't want the neighbors to find and call him out; on the other hand, he had to stack them pretty high in order to reach the top of the twelve-foot wall. After making two stacks, one at about three feet high and the other at six feet, he used the smaller stack to climb onto the taller stack, the whole while trying to balance himself from tipping over the several blocks below him. Once he was standing upright on them, he concentrated and jumped. The pile of blocks below him went crashing to the ground, and he nearly did also. Had it not been for one of the pieces of glass on top of the wall, Flint would have lost his grip on the slippery surface. As it was, he now had a large gash in the palm of his left hand, but a secure grip nonetheless.

The adrenaline that suddenly kicked in helped urge himself up and over the wall. Upon falling on the other side, he inspected his hand, allowing the stinging rain to clean the wound. The glass hadn't cut as deep as he suspected it would have, and he considered himself lucky that the shard had actually been there, or he might have tumbled onto his back, severely injuring it on the mess of cinder blocks below.

His first task was to break into the house. This wasn't difficult, and he soon found a clean rag and was able to tear it into a bandage. Then, upon not finding anyone there, he helped himself to some dry clothing. It was of course all too small, but a pair of stretchy basketball shorts and a tight T-shirt seemed better than the wet clothing that Fran had given him the other day.

Once he was dry, he began to look for some food. The police had scavenged the area well, and had apparently helped themselves to much of Mao's house. But a half-eaten box of crackers made for a satisfying snack. He then pulled out his phone and pressed the Call button, directing him to Fran. Fran was quick to pick up the phone this time, and Flint was happy to hear that they had already dropped off one sample of the moss in Italy and were planning on making their way to the U.S.

Flint informed Fran that he was inside Mao's compound and needed to know if they had found Troy's ship yet. "You won't believe this," Fran said, "but a thirteen-year-old girl thinks she might have found them."

"Not much surprises me anymore, but let me guess," Flint ventured. "They're not somewhere around Mars, are they?"

Fran sounded flabbergasted. "How could you have known that? I had every observatory searching the sky. This girl was just a fluke. She wasn't even looking for them, but her parents, some amateur astronomers, had a thirty-inch telescope and were showing her Mars when they saw something that looked like a third moon. They called it in to an observatory, and now we're trying to reposition the Hubble to get a better look at it."

"Well, I'm heading up to Mao's ship now. Let's hope I can get it working. I think he's got some type of computer navigation control on it, but you might have to talk me through it, because I'm not sure how to find Mars yet."

Fran hesitated, then asked, "You don't know where Mars is, but you knew they would be there? How does that work?"

"As I was going to sleep last night, I was appreciating everything around me on this beautiful world," Flint explained, suddenly feeling a little weird at how he described his train of thought. "Then it occurred to me, if I was the proud Martian that Troy considers himself to be, and if I could go anywhere in the galaxy I wanted, I'd probably go visit my home world, Mars."

"I wish I'd have thought to look there first," Fran admitted.

But right as Flint was about to comment back, he heard a small rustling. "Fran," he whispered, "I gotta run—I'll call you back when I get Mao's ship ready." After hanging up, he quietly searched for whoever was inside the mansion with him.

He had no doubt that the other person had heard him talking, but what business could someone else have here besides himself? Pulling out the pistol he'd confiscated from Troy's base, glad to have reloaded it on the airplane, Flint began to ease himself in and out of each room, clearing them in succession. As he slipped out of one room and approached the next, he felt the distinct point of a knife blade as it gently announced the presence of someone behind him.

Chapter 36

The door opened a little wider, and Lydia kicked hard against the wall, putting her body into a controlled spin so as to also hit the person entering her room. She followed the metal mesh panel by only two seconds as it flew toward the man at the door. She realized only too late that her guest wasn't Troy or Grisha, or someone else from the ranks of GRIP. It was Monk.

Lydia seemed more startled than Monk did, though she could never really tell with him. In the fraction of a second that he had to react, he dodged the perforated wall panel, and allowed his body to float up slightly to catch her by the knees. Then, using his own legs, he cushioned their combined momentum against the other side of the moss-covered hallway.

Lydia was surprised that Monk had so effortlessly countered her attack, and wondered if the result would have been the same had the intruder been Troy or Grisha. "Sorry," she apologized. "I thought you were someone else for a minute."

Monk then quoted, "Luke 3:9. 'And now also the axe is laid unto the root of the trees: every tree therefore which bringeth not forth good fruit is hewn down, and cast into the fire.'"

Lydia believed she understood and replied, "If you mean that it's time to put an end to GRIP, I think you're right. But unless you know of a better way, I can only think of one way to stop them, and that means destroying this ship—with us on it."

Monk replied with a familiar quote that referenced the willingness of the biblical Isaac to submit to his father before being offered up as a sacrifice. "'And Abraham took the wood of the burnt offering, and laid it upon Isaac his son; and he took the fire in his hand, and a knife; and they went both of them together.' Genesis 22:6."

"I don't know if I would ever understand you, even if we did get to live out a full life. But even still, I think that I'll be going out in good company,"

Monk put a comforting hand on Lydia's arm, and even though the zero gravity made it somewhat awkward, a gentle but powerful squeeze from his hand accompanied by a penetrating look from his eyes made her feel secure. This man whom she had never known to show any emotion had just proven to her that he understood and was capable of normal emotion. His face may not have reflected it, but she knew that somewhere inside his mind he had similar fears, compassion, and noble desires.

"Well, let's do this," she sighed, almost impatiently. "I don't think we can hijack the ship, but we might be able to make our way to the armory. If we can do that, then we might be able to rig one of their bombs or missiles, or whatever they are."

Monk agreed, and they shoved off, gliding down the corridors to the weapons room. While Lydia had been on the ship just as long as Monk, she noticed that he seemed more at ease with the lack of gravity than she was. Every effort he made was simple and exact, while she found herself still struggling as she bumped around the hallways like a drunken bat. Luckily for her, most of the crew onboard was nearly as clumsy. When they ran into two of them in one of the corridors, she was able to pounce on one, and eventually subdue him. Monk took the man's companion out much more swiftly, though she didn't see how because of her preoccupation with the first man.

Her biggest cause for alarm was that during the small fight, the crewman had called out for help. They seemed alone, but she knew that the ship couldn't be so small that nobody would hear. With increased caution, they made their way down the remainder of the hallway until they got to the weapons room. Nobody seemed to be guarding it, which Lydia thought was strange. Only when she and Monk were both inside did she realize why.

Floating slowly into the room, they had little hope of pushing off any walls or ceilings to escape when Troy, his friend Jublein, and Joseph appeared from behind some ordnance. "Lydia," Troy said sorrowfully, "I was afraid you might try to sneak back here, and I'm surprised to see that you brought Monk with you. I was going to let you share in our victory, even be a queen of sorts. But I doubt my dear Persephone will be heartbroken. What could have been yours will now be hers. I'm very sorry, my dear sister." Lydia was about to protest when Troy and the other man pulled out stun guns. There was no hesitation in her brother. The moment she recognized the stunners for what they were, painful jolts of electricity were shocking both her's and Monk's nervous system.

When she came to again, she found herself bound to a wall, with Monk on the other side. He was still unconscious when Kore entered the room. A wide, condescending smile was framed by the high cheekbones of her face. "Good morning. You really couldn't play the game well, could you?" Kore taunted, as she got right up into Lydia's face. "Well, now you're stuck with me. Troy has given me charge over you again; only now I have no real use for you." She finished by delivering a quick slap across Lydia's face.

Morning? Had she really been out that long? Or had she spent the whole night trying to etch a hole out of her room. Everything seemed a blur. Everything that is except for the hatred she felt towards Kore. Tears of anger stung in Lydia's eyes as she responded. "Troy's probably just using you, the same way you both were using me. When he's done with you, you'll find that you're no better off than me."

"Just a little secret, between you and me," Kore replied. "A king may rise, and a king may fall. If, or should I say when, that happens, the queen will inherit all."

Lydia wanted to struggle free of her bonds; however, she knew it would be pointless. "The only thing worse than having my demented and sociopathic brother rule the world would be to live under you."

Kore did a floating spin, clearly enjoying herself as she replied casually, "I never said you would get to live, either." Then, as if to rub salt in her eyes, Kore added, "By the way, I thought you might like to know before you die, but I'm the one who hit your car when you were going to the hospital to have that baby of yours two years ago."

Lydia's eyes went wide with disbelief. Though she couldn't remember the accident two years ago, she remembered every eye-witness account of the fateful day. How an attractive, but emotionless woman had approached her after ramming into her with a stolen truck. How that woman seemed to offer some sort of aid, then disappeared without a hint as to who she was or where she went.

Kore continued, "Troy and I thought it would be a perfect way to enlist you here. Did you know that your baby might even have lived, had I not intervened while you were unconscious?"

Lydia tore at her restraints, only mildly aware that the screams in the background were coming from her own mouth. Kore had successfully extracted Lydia's broken heart and driven it through a meat grinder all over again. A mix of fury and regret made Lydia vow that Kore would not live past this day.

Chapter 37

"Drop the gun, pardner," the voice demanded with a bad Western accent.

Unsure of who his captor was, Flint decided to play it safe, and he dropped his pistol. He then brought his arms up to a square, not wanting to raise them all the way, but just enough to calm the person behind him. Then with a smooth, unalarming turn, he pivoted to see his attacker. Since he didn't want to give away any advantage that he might have, he decided to act quickly. Without looking directly at the person's face, he focused instead on their build and weapon of choice. It was a man holding a large steel machete, and Flint guessed that he could take him down quickly.

In a lightning-quick move, Flint straightened his fingers out and slapped his hands inward as if to clap as hard as he could. Instead of bringing his two palms together, though, he staggered them, so that when his hands met in the middle where the machete was hovering, his opponent had no time to react and the blade was ripped from his grip and went spinning up in the air. Flint then bulldozed his shoulder into the thin Filipino, and with a stroke of luck more than skill, he caught the machete by the handle as it fell back down, and brought it to level against the young man's throat. For a split second, he even allowed himself the pleasure of pride in his move, which he doubted should have worked as well as it did. Like accidentally spitting a watermelon seed into a thimble at ten feet, this was one of those times where he wished that more people could have seen it. Never again would he likely be so lucky as to have repeated the act, even if he tried.

But now that he had the smaller man's wet shirt within the clutches of his bandaged hand, and the machete ready to pierce his neck, he noticed the expression of horror on the person's face. It wasn't a man at all, but only a teenager. In fact, it was the same boy who had accompanied him from Lapu-Lapu. "Dodong!" Flint reprimanded. "What are you doing here?"

The boy stammered with tears in his eyes, "S-sorry, I follow you, I sorry—"

"Yeah, you followed me, but why?" Flint interrogated.

Dodong was now sobbing like a schoolgirl, and barely able to speak English coherently. "The rain, we no go home, I follow *kay kuan,*" he hesitated as if searching for the right words. "I no have better thing to do today. Please no kill, it was joke-jokes only. Friends you and I still."

Flint realized that he still was holding the boy at knifepoint, and began to relax his grip. "It's a dangerous game you just played," Flint reprimanded.

"How did you get in?"

Dodong wiped his face and replied, "I fit through front gate."

Flint shook his head. "Yeah, I guess you're thin enough. Listen, I've got important work to do, you should head back to your uncle."

"Are you spy?" Dodong asked. His red eyes became all wide, the way a young child's would at the peak of their curiosity and interest. "I want to stay, I help you." He then bent down to help pick up Flint's gun, but a quick flick of the machete reminded him that he was not to touch the firearm.

Flint instead reached down and grabbed the pistol, then tucked it in his new pair of tight sport shorts. Now that Flint had company, he felt ridiculous in his stolen outfit. He was about to send the kid away, but Dodong seemed so interested and innocent. He couldn't bring himself to cast the soaking boy back out into the rain. "Okay, you can help," Flint said reluctantly. "But don't be loud—I don't want the neighbors knowing we're here; not yet, at least. And no more jokes!"

He first headed up to the rooftop where Mao's ship had been. The heavy steel chamber was still there. Most everything was as it had been left. When the police had raided the mansion, they hadn't taken any of the heavy equipment; probably, Flint speculated, because it was too heavy and they might not know what to do with it, even if they did want it. Had Troy not shaken the world into a panic, the police might have been able to devote more resources to understanding what Shen Mao had placed in their own backyard. As it was, they probably had their hands full, taking care of their own people.

"How good of a mechanic are you?" Flint asked Dodong.

"I help my friend with a jeepney," he replied.

"That'll have to do," Flint said, shrugging his shoulders. He then pointed down into the yard. "Do you see that motor over there?"

Dodong nodded.

"That motor is important to this machine. It has something wrong with it. I need you to fix whatever is wrong with it." Flint scanned his companion for signs of understanding. Dodong looked nervous, and Flint doubted that the boy would be able to figure out what Dusty had done to sabotage the diesel pump nearly a week ago, but it was something for the boy to do while Flint worked on the ship. Dodong jumped at the chance to be helpful. He ran to where he'd entered the house, only to slow a bit before going back into the rain.

Flint started by examining the control for the vacuum chamber. He remembered that it had been damaged in the gunfight. He then looked inside the chamber at the ship before unwrapping the device that he'd stolen from Troy's base. The once spherical antique was now a mess of fiber optics, tape, and wire. The way everything was patched together, he hoped the mutilated device was tested and working. After all, Troy had used this to reverse engineer a new working part to move his ship through space. There were flat markings on the pieces, and Flint did his best to rest them on the corresponding metal nodes inside the cubby where he'd originally shot the device to pieces.

At first he couldn't get the pieces to stay, but a quick survey of the house landed him some strong tape. Then, fearing the device might still fall out, he taped over the cubby that housed it. It wasn't the best patch, but hopefully he wouldn't need it to last more than a few minutes. Having finished with that, he went back to the control panel and tore off the cover. Inside were a few wires, and Flint touched each together in varied order. None of them gave any response, and Flint decided to check on the power source.

The switches on the house still provided power, but he couldn't find any way of getting the electricity to the control panel on the vacuum chamber. His frustration was mounting when a small object caught his attention under the chamber itself. He wasn't surprised that the police had missed it; he would have missed it, too, had the touch-screen remote been turned the other way.

It was the battery indicator on the small remote that flashed, attracting Flint's attention while signifying that it was nearly depleted. Flint reached under and picked it up, finding just enough power to suffice for his current needs. He tapped the screen, and the lights around the deck blazed on. Another tap dismissed the low-battery window, and a third tap sent a few sparks leaping out of the control panel he'd just been working on. Satisfied that he'd routed the necessary power to the ship, he retested the wires to see if he could get any response.

The first few wires that he pressed together gave no reaction, but the fourth set that he tried made the pumps in the yard cough to life. Twisting the wires together to keep the pumps running, he ran to the ledge to see how Dodong was doing. Unfortunately, Dodong was staring at the wrong pump. The one that Dusty had sabotaged was next to him, and it was clearly beginning to struggle again. Dodong immediately realized his error, and moved to the faulty pump.

With no remaining caution pertaining to the neighbors, Flint called down, "Well, do you see what's wrong?"

Dodong craned his neck up to see Flint on the rooftop deck. "Yes!" he shouted. "It loose bolts!"

"Can you fix it?"

"Yes!" he shouted back, but then added, "I think."

Flint watched as Dodong tightened a few bolts back onto the machine. The boy then began to scramble about, as if he couldn't find something. Flint looked around on top of the deck. He remembered that after Dusty had sabotaged the machine, she had come up on the deck and thrown a wrench at a mercenary who was about to get the better of him. The spot where the incident had taken place was only a few paces away, but Flint couldn't see any sign of the wrench. He looked all over the floor, only to give up a minute later. He was about to run down and try to help Dodong when he spotted it in the center of the table that Mao had used for his presentation. *Why are the most obvious places the hardest spot to find anything?* Flint wondered as he grabbed the bulky wrench. Then, moving back toward the railing, he called after the boy.

Dodong reappeared with a few tools in his hands, and Flint tossed the wrench down. "Here, is this what you're looking for?"

Dodong studied the tool for a moment, then took it over to the pump. After thirty seconds of tightening bolts, the pump began to operate smoothly. Flint went back to Mao's ship and lowered himself in. The ship was much simpler than he expected. There was a touch-screen computer wired to a few marine batteries. Both the computer and the batteries were wired into another box, which Flint guessed ran to the device he had reinstalled.

With the tap of a button, the computer flickered to life. The operating system was generic, and the most prominent icon on the screen was labeled "Flight Control." Flint pressed his finger to it, and a program began that showed a three-dimensional outline of the cylindrical ship. Using some form of laser or sonar, it created a map of its surroundings. Flint realized that the front portal window was for seeing where he was going, and the sensor was for docking the ship inside the narrow magnetic vacuum chamber.

Already the vacuum pumps were creating a low pressure inside the ship, and Flint was worried that if he shut the chamber hatch before that of the ship, he might run out of air before finding Troy. Mao's ship had been built for demonstration purposes, not for extended travel. The lack of spare oxygen would be a handicap. At least Dodong was starting to prove useful. Flint only wished that he still had a little cash left to tip his young helper.

Getting out of the ship, Flint waited for the Filipino to join him on the deck. While waiting, he called Fran and asked for directions to Mars. When Dodong showed up, Flint felt that he had a good grasp on how to proceed, and he finished the call while the young man inspected the ship. Dodong was very curious about the contraption, especially when he looked in and noticed that it was floating inside the large metal chamber. "What is it?" he asked.

Flint hadn't cared to explain his mission earlier, and didn't feel particularly inclined to do so now, so he simply stated, "It's a time machine. I'm from the future, and to preserve the future, I can't tell you anything more about it. You've already seen too much." After all, why not? It was easier, and the kid would have an even more incredible story to tell his friends and family. Flint then added, "But as long as you're here, why don't you help me." He then explained what he wanted Dodong to do.

As he crawled into the ship, he reminded, "In ten minutes, be sure to turn off the pumps and open the hatch. If this doesn't work, I don't want to die in here. If it does work, and you open it up and I'm not here, well, thanks for everything."

With a smile of wonderment, Dodong saluted his time-traveling friend. Flint then shut his hatch and locked it down tight. He heard the chamber hatch slam shut. On the computer screen, he found a countdown timer and touched it. A five-minute launch timer began to tick away. During the countdown, as the chamber was vacuumed out, Flint manipulated the screen, and pointed the virtual ship into the air. There was a sidebar that indicated the speed level, and a launch icon that turned green at the end of the countdown. "Well, here goes nothing," Flint said as he pressed the button.

All at once the view outside his portal changed to a grainy look. Not only could he now see the metal chamber, but he almost thought he could see through it. He even thought he saw the faint silhouette of Dodong as he paced around on the deck. But not wanting to waste any time, he slid his finger across the speed bar, and the ship sprinted along the trajectory that he had initially input into the computer.

It took only a moment before he was above Earth's atmosphere, and knowing that he would never likely have this opportunity again, he pivoted the ship around to look at the planet. The grainy haze that came as a by-product of traveling inside the small pocket of space made his blue planet look very different from what he had seen in pictures. It almost sparkled, as if it were made of sand and glass. Flint wished he had a camera, because nothing he had ever seen could come close to describing the beauty of the Earth from this vantage point. Every color was more vibrant, and it sparkled with long stretching hues, as if he were squinting at a colored light. But again he turned the ship around, knowing that he only had maybe ten minutes of breathable air remaining.

He picked out the brightest speck of light in his current trajectory, which Fran told him would be Mars. Had Jupiter been in that window also, he might have been steered wrong, but Fran had settled that fear earlier, noting that Jupiter would be out of his approximate path. Flint made a slight adjustment to align the ship with Mars. Then, as he slid the bar up, the ship accelerated toward the red planet. Flint was surprised to find that within a minute, and not even at full speed, he had arrived at Mars. He hadn't needed to make more than a couple of minor adjustments to keep on course.

As he peered out the glass at the shining planet, the stale air inside the craft reminded him that he had perhaps only five minutes of air left. Creeping closer to the planet, he focused all his attention on finding Troy's ship. Several minutes passed without any sign of another ship, and Flint could feel himself becoming light-headed. He guessed that Troy would be in an orbit that would facilitate seeing Earth, but since he couldn't see any signs of the ship, he began to swing around the planet. Finding nothing on the back side, he continued to sweep back around. By this time, his vision was getting fuzzy, and he doubted his ability to find Troy. It seemed his only option was to head back to Earth before he lost consciousness. But for all Flint knew, he might have already crossed the point of no return. At the very least, Flint knew that he wouldn't have the capacity to dock back in Mao's vacuum chamber. That would require too much time and concentration. If Troy couldn't be found soon, there would be no second chances.

Chapter 38

Kore had left Lydia for a few minutes, with the promise of returning soon. In her absence Monk started to wake up, seemingly curious about the restraints he found himself in. He then looked at Lydia with a questioning glance.

"Sorry," Lydia said, as though this type of thing happened all the time. "It looks like we're going to die like a couple of caged dogs instead of going out in a blaze of glory."

Monk replied, "'A little more persistence, a little more effort, and what seemed hopeless failure may turn to glorious success.' Elbert Hubbard."

"I wish I could share your optimism," Lydia told him, and in fact she did still maintain hope. Only she had no idea yet as to how she would get out of this. With a deep exhale, she closed her eyes and worked on her breathing. It was a little trick she had learned to calm down and clear her mind. Ever since

Flint had come back into her life, not to mention the embarrassment of being so disgracefully manipulated by her brother, her self-confidence had melted away. When she hadn't been a mental captive of Flint's approval, she was a literal captive of Troy and his conniving hussy. She was now trying to pull herself back to that strong, logical, and determined leader she had been while leading GRIP's main combat arm. Granted, she'd been under the close supervision of Grisha, but she still knew that she wasn't the type to roll over and give up.

Roll over and give up . . . This thought made an impression on her mind. *Roll over and give up—or roll over and play dead.* She wasn't sure what to think of it, but she had learned to trust her impressions. She had never been a very religious person, and didn't believe in that magical mother's intuition, but occasionally she would have a thought enter her head that she couldn't explain, or account for. In those times she wondered if there was a God, and if He really did have some hand in her destiny. In any case, she was encouraged to ponder on the thought.

When Kore returned, she brought Grisha. Kore then tuned a mounted television screen into a delayed transmission from Earth. "I thought you might like to witness the fruits of our labors," Kore said, speaking to Lydia.

Lydia chose not to respond. In fact, she allowed her head and whole body to droop as though she was completely deprived of energy. After no reply, Kore said, "Ignoring me will do you no good." She then addressed Grisha, "I don't know who this Mexican thinks he is, but Troy tells me that he's extremely dangerous. Since I have no use for him, and because he's apparently so dangerous, I was hoping you might be able to dispose of him for me."

"You want for me to kill him?" Grisha asked, a little surprised at the reason Kore had brought him in. "I was busy, why you not do this yourself?"

"Because," Kore said impatiently, as if he should know. "I think Lydia needs to be taught a lesson, and if I kill him, she'll just turn away. I need to make her watch, so she'll understand that others get hurt when she disobeys."

Grisha was obviously annoyed. He was tough and could hold a good grudge, but he had nothing on Monk, other than he was a friend of Flint.

After a couple of years with Grisha as a copilot, Lydia knew that he also had a good sense of honor, even if his course was moving in the wrong direction. To kill a man who was bound, like Monk, would have been nothing shy of a cowardly murder in his eyes. Monk, on the other hand, simply stared at Lydia. With his penetrating eyes focused on her, Lydia knew it was only a matter of time before Grisha followed Monk's gaze and looked at his former comrade, so she resumed her ragged and beaten look.

She was purposely not focusing on anyone when Grisha took notice again of her and asked Kore, "What have you done to Lydia?"

"I haven't done anything to her, she's the same stubborn woman she's always been."

Lydia felt Grisha's powerful hands as he grabbed her head and lifted it. She made certain that all he saw was the whites of her eyes and her loose, gaping jaw. "She is not all right!" He accused Kore as he let go and Lydia's head fell limply to the side. She didn't want to let it fall straight down because it would be incongruent with the zero gravity. But since she let it float aimlessly from one side and then to the other, she knew that she presented a very disturbing image.

She also knew that you don't spend a lot of time with someone without understanding a little about them. Lydia always had suspected that Grisha still respected her, and she was beginning to believe that he might even have had other feelings for her, too; feelings that were made evident by his defending her from Kore. "You tell me what you did to her," he warned the woman who imagined herself to be some sort of goddess or demigod.

"Augh!" Kore grunted. "She is fine, just take care of this retarded Mexican, and I'll show you that she's okay." Kore then began to drift toward Lydia, but Grisha caught her by the neck with those same clamping hands that made him such a good boxer.

Kore gagged as he tightened his grip. She reached into her boot and pulled out a small dagger. Not wanting to kill Troy's number one guard, she stuck the point into his belly and cautioned him to release his grip. Grisha let go and they started to slowly drift apart. Then he reached out and grabbed her wrist that held the small knife and squeezed it until she released the blade. He pulled her near and reminded, "Troy may like you, but I know he would not like her harmed. I too would not like his sister harmed. You understand this?"

Lydia couldn't see the expression on Kore's face, because while they were having their own little moment of distraction, she had snapped out of her ruse and was using the dagger that had floated over to cut herself free. Once free, she held her position and flicked the small dagger over to Monk, who in turn began to free himself. Luckily Grisha's back was to them both, and Kore had been too distracted to notice this exchange. However, Kore did come to her senses enough to see Monk free his hands. "Grisha," she warned, her eyes pointing toward Monk.

Grisha caught the urgency in her voice and swung around to stop Monk from undoing the straps around his ankles. Lydia chose that moment to launch herself at Grisha. Learning from the mistake she had made when she accidently attacked Monk earlier, she tucked her legs against her chest and waited until she was next to Grisha then caught hold of Monk for stability and sprang her legs into the man who had moments ago defended her. This kept her from flying away uncontrollably, while Grisha started bouncing around the room.

Monk finished with his straps, right as Kore grabbed hold of Lydia. Monk casually allowed himself to float next to Kore and stuck his thumb and middle finger into her throat, pinching hold of her esophagus. She froze, partly from the pain and partly from fear of her throat being crushed or ripped. Monk then quoted, "1 Samuel 2:3. 'Talk no more so exceeding proudly; let not arrogancy come out of your mouth: for the Lord is a God of knowledge, and by him actions are weighed.'" He gave her a small shove as he let go of her, and he and Lydia managed to get out of the room and shut the door behind them.

Since the room had been Lydia's, it was made to lock from the outside. Lydia hoped shutting them in would buy her enough time to sabotage the ship. She would have much preferred to watch Kore suffer at her hand while she ensured that the killer received her well-deserved execution. But with more at stake than just her revenge, Lydia prioritized her actions, justifying them with the satisfaction that Kore would still die with the rest of them.

Chapter 39

Flint was examining the touch-screen, trying to retrace his path in an attempt to find his way back to Earth when he noticed an icon on his screen. It was small and flashing, so he tapped on it. Another window popped up and displayed a transmission that was being intercepted. The computer seemed to have an ability to locate transmissions, so that in case they overshot Earth, they could find their way back.

The idea behind it was easy enough for him, because when he had learned to pilot a plane, the first navigational lesson was how to use VORs to find the way. A VOR—or VHF omnidirectional range—station worked on the principle of having a central beacon that emitted a signal. A plane could tune its instrument to hone in on the beacon, making navigation possible. It was the next best thing to GPS; but since Mao didn't have anything like a GPS in space, he had equipped the ship with the ability to find and track signals emanating from Earth. The only thing was, the strongest signal it was picking up was not being sent from Earth.

Flint selected the signal, and began an intercept course. The signal didn't last long, but by the time it quit transmitting, Flint was already piloting his steel can in the right direction. Another minute passed, and Flint fought with a headache. The onset of involuntary hyperventilation scared him a little, but he exercised all his willpower to remain conscious. He was hoping that the signal came from Troy's ship, and not from something else like one of NASA's Mars rovers.

Since his approach had been on the shady side, Troy's dark ship against the empty black backdrop of space stayed hidden until he was less than a mile away. Were it not for a few lighted windows, Flint might have missed the ship completely.

Without losing a moment, Flint piloted his sad excuse for a ship into the hulking object that Troy had in orbit around Mars. The pocket of space that shrouded his moving metal coffin intruded on the matter that made up the hull of Troy's ship. The visual sensation of passing through the outer hull and then through subsequent rooms and people was dizzying. It was impossible for Flint to know if the bending objects he was seeing were due to the displacement of his ship, or if he himself was in the middle of passing out of consciousness from oxygen deprivation. He had to remind himself that he had already witnessed the phenomenon when he had passed through the vacuum chamber at Mao's mansion. But where there had just been one layer of metal to pass through then, now there were walls, rooms, and people. Flint was ill prepared for the illusion.

Once inside, Flint quickly found an empty room and placed his ship as close to the floor as he dared without actually touching it. He then disengaged the drive. Returning to normal space cause a loud boom as the air in Troy's ship was displaced at hypersonic speeds. This echoed through Flint's small ship, causing him to tighten every muscle, and he wondered if everyone on Troy's ship had heard it also. To his surprise there was no hard fall, and no sounding of alarms. The ship floated about three inches above the floor, drifting slowly down until it rested on a mesh floor.

Flint couldn't see how his intrusion wasn't loud enough to give his presence away, but of even more pressing concern was getting out of the ship to breathe some fresh air. Maybe as soon as he exited his suffocating enclosure, he would be surrounded by GRIP. He opened the hatch and took in a refreshing gasp of life again. Within seconds his mind began to clear, even though the headache remained, and he pulled himself free from the steel trap. The room he found himself in was on the lower deck, in what he could only describe as a cafeteria. If he was right, then he knew it wouldn't be long before he was discovered.

Wishing he had been able to fly Mao's ship through each of the rooms to get a better idea of the ship's layout, he tried swimming through the zero gravity, but found that he just bounced around. He assumed swimming in the weightless air would be similar to swimming underwater. Several bumps and bruises quickly appeared, proving his assumptions wrong. With a little more caution, he drifted out of the room to explore the craft. Holding his pistol, he found it odd that he hadn't seen any other person yet, but the whole ship breathed with noises that suggested people were in many of the rooms he was passing. Then, all at once, the ship was full of activity.

Several built-in speakers turned on and Flint recognized Troy's voice. "All available hands, the two prisoners have escaped. They are not armed, but are extremely dangerous. Find and detain them. Also, I need engineers to return to the lower deck and have a look at that closet area again. We've just received another report of a strange sound down there."

Flint breathed a sigh of relief, pleased that Lydia and Monk were still alive. The timing could have been better, though. Flint also wondered what the second half of Troy's announcement meant. The sound was obviously from Flint's ship, but Troy made it sound as if they were having issues with the integrity of the ship's structure. No time to dwell on that right now. For the moment, doors were flying open. Men and women with stun guns hurried out of their rooms, searching the ship for the fugitives. Flint found a closet and secluded himself inside, knowing all too well that it would likely get searched. But for the moment it was his only option to escape immediate detection. As he looked around the closet, he noticed that a few of the bolts that were supposed to hold the bent up shelving in place were missing. No wonder Troy was worried about his ship falling apart. It was obviously constructed poorly.

As he waited, he heard two people in the hallway. "Cover me while I check this closet."

Flint brought the gun up ready to fire when he heard one of their radios squawk alive. "We have them—they are heading down the hall from section two toward the port stern."

"That's where we are," one of the men said. "Come

on!"

Flint exhaled as they abandoned their search of his little closet. They hadn't seen Monk or Lydia yet in this hallway, but from what he understood, they would soon be here. He floated closer to the closet door and waited. He had no doubt that Monk and Lydia would cause enough of a racket to alert him of their arrival, and since the men trying to apprehend them were only armed with stunners, he wasn't too concerned about their safety.

As expected, he began to hear a commotion, which got louder as Lydia and Monk turned a corner and entered his portion of the hallway. Exiting the closet, he found much of what he was expecting. There were the two men who had nearly found him, and beyond them were Lydia and Monk, shooting toward them like arrows in the sky. Behind them were six more of GRIP's soldiers. His friends were making a valiant effort, but were hopelessly outnumbered.

Chapter 40

Lydia had not expected an alarm to sound so quickly. Kore or Grisha must have had a radio, because less than thirty seconds after they escaped the room, Troy had gotten on the ship's intercom system and started a manhunt. Since everybody on the ship was armed with stun guns, she knew she and Monk had to move quickly or else they would never get the chance to stop anything.

They barely had time to get down the first hall before they were discovered. With several people in pursuit, Lydia led the way toward the weapons room. If they could get inside without being caught, they might be able to lock themselves in. There was the chance that once inside they would get ambushed, the way they had the first time they attempted, but with no other choice sounding good, they made for it.

They had only one more corner to turn, then it

would be a straight shot to the weapons room. Upon making the turn, Lydia found two more men blocking her way, each holding a battery powered stun gun. She launched herself like a rocket toward them, blowing right past the first and hitting the second. There wasn't much of a struggle, as the man was unprepared to stop her momentum. He had been more concerned with zapping her than fighting. So with little effort, she made it past them.

Looking behind her as she drifted, albeit slower now, she noticed that Monk had also made it through, but the men who had been pursuing her were now very close. Lydia watched with trepidation as the first man raised his stun gun up, the metal nodes ready to shoot and paralyze her, but then a sharp crack thundered through the hallway. The pursuers' momentum was halted in midair as several bubbles of crimson went flying backward down the hall.

Five more times, the confines of the hallway amplified the all too familiar report of gunshots. Each time another approaching man was shocked from his momentum. Even when they understood the threat, the pursuers had no way of altering their course in time to avoid the hot lead in their way. Lydia was no stranger to death, as she herself had dealt it several times while working with GRIP, but she had never seen anything like this. One moment a man would be flying toward her, the next he would be stopped, as though somebody had paused time, or at least put it in slow motion. Each shot had been carefully placed, and for good reason. A stray bullet, or a shot that passed too quickly through a body might penetrate the hull, killing everyone on board. All that remained now was an almost surreal image of suspended bodies. Not one man was left tumbling toward her.

As for the two men she'd just passed, their backs were covered in the blood of their fellow crewmembers as they were retreating in the other direction. Lydia turned around to see who her savior was, but could scarcely believe who she was looking at. It was impossible, yet here he was. With his back against a doorjamb, so as to prevent the recoil of his pistol from pushing him down the hall, was none other than Flint.

Lydia's joy at finding him alive quickly turned into embarrassment as she tried unsuccessfully to swim through the air to reach him quicker. Flint chuckled as she flailed her arms and legs about. Regaining her composure somewhat, she countered, "Don't you dare laugh at me, have you seen yourself in the mirror?" referring to his tight workout pants and the T-shirt that hugged his chest and biceps. He really did look ridiculous. Both the shorts and the shirt were clearly meant for a smaller man, but even if he did look silly in the outfit, the fit accentuated his powerful albeit modest muscles. It made her want to laugh, but at the same time she found it highly attractive.

As she drifted closer, he snagged her arm and steadied her. Monk, the ever graceful one, seemed at ease in the air as simply as if he was grounded back on Earth. Lydia's excitement at seeing Flint was, however, short lived. The realization flooded back to her that she was undertaking a suicide mission.

Flint must have noticed the dread that she felt, since he commented, "You seemed so happy to see me just a moment ago, now you look like you wish I hadn't come."

"I'm sorry," Lydia confessed. "It's not that I'm disappointed to see you, it's just that I thought you were killed when we took off, but now that you're not, I wish you weren't here."

Flint was confused as he rebutted, "If I hadn't found my way on this ship, I bet you'd have just been captured."

"It's not that," Lydia said as she led the way to the weapons room. "But to stop Troy, we're going to have to set off one of his bombs and destroy the ship."

"Bombs?" Flint said. "What bombs?"

Lydia explained how Troy had been sending false videos and messages around the world to start a world war. She explained that the bombs had been, and would still be, used to destroy strategic targets to get the war moving. Flint in turn shared his perspective on the volatile situation back on Earth. He brought up a concern that Lydia knew in the back of her mind, but hadn't known how to attack. She was mostly concerned with stopping Troy, but Flint was now telling her that the war might already be imminent. Unless they could get word out to those back home, proving that GRIP was to blame, then destroying Troy's ship would do little to stop the impending destruction that the nations were ready to heap upon one another.

"I think that the only place we'll be able to send word from would be the helm," Lydia told him. "And that place is crawling with people."

"It's got to be done," Flint insisted.

"Maybe if you and Monk stormed it, you could take it," Lydia suggested, not at all confident in their ability to do so. "Then, while you're doing that, I could work on one of these bombs. Whether you can get a message out or not, I would still be able to blow this place."

"I think you might be onto something, but you

and Labeeb think too much alike," Flint started, surprising her by adding, "I don't like your kamikaze attitude. Let me offer one other suggestion."

Chapter 41

Bernard seemed pleased as he sent the last message that was meant to escalate tensions throughout the various nations. Troy had found the talented man only a year ago. Bernard had been making comical YouTube videos, substituting fake words in the mouths of various political and famous people. Troy had made up some garbage about the man having a Martian lineage, thought it wasn't true. But even though Troy felt the import of having everyone on GRIP's staff be able to trace their lineage to those early settlers, at the same time he couldn't ignore the talent possessed by Bernard Jublein.

The biggest threat was that Bernard, despite his talent, could use his knowledge to blackmail GRIP down the road. And since Troy had little desire to keep a pure-blooded Neanderthal, as he viewed the man, he knew that eventually he would have to kill him. In his mind, normal humans were inferior to their Martian counterparts. Troy truly believed that, had it not been for the enlightened thinking brought down by the last true Martians, men of Earth would still be chiseling wheels out of stone. Thus a man like Bernard could never have existed without Martian influence, and he was therefore indebted, even to laying down his life to further the advancements in civilization that Troy was compelled to deliver.

Troy didn't necessarily hate Bernard, merely differentiated the man from himself, in much the same way that he supposed a university college professor might look at a daycare teacher. He was therefore about to patronize Bernard with the customary congratulations on his good work when Kore came into the room and announced that Lydia and Monk had escaped capture in one of the lower hallways.

"My dear Persephone," Troy said, cutting her off before she had a chance to finish her explanation. He then ran a caressing finger across her cheek. "We're on a ship, in space. Where can they possibly go that we can't find them?"

"I was just about to get to that," Kore replied, a little frustrated. "They've managed to find a gun. Six of our men have been shot and killed. Their blood is still floating around in that lower deck."

This bit of news did alarm him, because he hadn't heard the gunshots. Even with each room being well insulated, he thought the sharp crack of a gunshot should carry. But he chalked it up as another triumph of Martian engineering. Still, he didn't think that Lydia would have resorted to violence. What could she hope to accomplish? Did she think she could take over the ship? Sure, she had seemed ill disposed toward Troy's mission; he couldn't blame her after the discovery of her manipulation, but it was nothing any rational person shouldn't be able to quickly get over. "Where did she find a gun?" Troy demanded to know. He'd had every gun locked up before they took off. Stun guns had been issued in place of guns in case of mutiny or in case Lydia tried anything like this, because a stray bullet could compromise the ship's hull. This was, after all, only a first-generation design of ships that Troy planned to eventually build. Future ships would be able to seal off damaged compartments, but this one could be crippled or destroyed with a single penetration anywhere on the ship.

"I don't know where she found a gun," Kore replied. "But if you will permit it, I will go after her myself and stop her."

Troy hesitated. He knew Lydia's strengths, and Kore's also. Lydia was smart and good in a fight, but Kore never played fair. She was much shrewder, and would undoubtedly hunt his sister down and kill her before she even suspected anything amiss. He'd hoped that Lydia would someday see the wisdom in his efforts, and though he wanted to stop Kore from going after her, something uncontrollable pressed him to swing a silent finger with an almost indistinguishable nod of his head, in affirmation to her will.

Kore understood and left before he could change his mind. Troy was left wondering if he had made the right decision. On one hand, he couldn't allow Lydia to compromise his mission. But on the other hand, she was still his sister, bound by the same noble lineage that he himself possessed. *No*, he thought, *I can't let her do it*. He called to Kore as she was almost out, "Wait. Stop!"

Kore grabbed onto a bar and paused, staring at her lover. Troy stammered. He could feel all eyes, especially those of his beautiful Persephone, as they pierced him with their judgments. He was their leader, and they all loved him. He couldn't let them think that he was weak. Giving in to the pressure of his mantle, he commanded, "Take Grisha with you. If Monk is still with her, you'll need him."

Kore nodded her approval and was gone. Troy remembered the words of Leo Tolstoy in the book *War and Peace*: "Why does an apple fall when it is ripe? Is it brought down by the force of gravity? Is it because its stalk withers? Because it is dried by the sun, because it grows too heavy, or because the boy standing under the tree wants to eat it? None of these is the cause.... Every action of theirs, that seems to them an act of their own freewill is in the historical sense not free at all but is bound up with the whole course of history and preordained from all eternity."

A single tear worked its way to the edge of his reddened eye. It hinted at either floating off into the room or dribbling down a cheek that had remained dry of tears for longer than he could remember. Though he felt the pang of guilt for having condemned his sister to death, he wondered if he'd ever had any choice in the matter at all. Tolstoy had mentioned that the more influence or power a man possessed, the less freedom he really had. Troy felt he was in that position now, and was a slave to the history of the past, and the history that was soon to be written. *The wise Tolstoy must have had some Martian blood in him*, Troy assumed as he pondered the great author's insight. The contemplation of the matter helped dry the wet eye before it fully manifest itself to his crew.

With this justification in mind, he pressed a button on his console and informed the weapons room to prepare a nuclear warhead for launch. Everybody's eyes were still fixed on him, waiting to see his next move or reaction, when Troy announced, "Brothers and sisters, it is time to destroy, so that we may create. Some have said that the god of this world is the same as the god of our world. If that were true, then why would he have allowed ours to be destroyed? If you ask me, I don't believe in him, but if he were to exist, then the destruction of our world would have been so that we could someday civilize those men on Earth. That day is today. And if you do believe in that same god, then now would be a good time to pray for a speedy conclusion to the work that must be done. Many will suffer because of what we do here today. But after the darkness, the light will shine, and we will have been the means of saving the world from itself. Let our hearts go out to those who will not make it through this cleansing transition, but let us not forget to hope for that day when peace will be global, and eventually universal."

Everyone in that command room bowed their heads in solemn respect and prayer. With Bernard monitoring the airwaves from Earth, Troy took leave to oversee the launch of his first nuclear strike. Throughout the night, he had used some of his smaller bombs to disrupt repairs on oil pipelines, but this one would be on U.S. soil, made to look as though it had come from Russia. By targeting the oil-rich Alaskan state, he hoped that the bomb would tie together all the convoluted theories of nations attacking one another to become energy leaders. Not every piece of the puzzle would be explained by this, but with all the finger-pointing already taking place down there, he hoped the one launch would be enough to get the world war started. If not, he still had nineteen more nuclear bombs, more than enough by his estimation to start and stop the war.

Not all instances would require nuclear strikes, either. The smaller bombs could be used for assassinations, and to take out smaller strategic targets when the time came.

As he exited the helm, he thought he heard something or somebody moving in the hydroponics park. Grabbing his stun gun, he silently drifted into the greenhouse portion of the ship. If it was Lydia, then he might still be able to stop her while preserving her life. He doubted she would shoot to kill him. If it was Monk, then a close hand-to-hand fight might be the Hispanic man's preference, in which case Troy felt confident that the stun gun would prevail.

Chapter 42

Flint and Monk had left Lydia alone to get a bomb rigged to blow. Flint didn't intend to use it, but he wanted the leverage in case he was captured while trying to get a message back to Earth. Inside the weapons room, two men were busy trying to guide one of the larger bombs over to the bigger vacuum chamber. On Earth these heavy bombs would have required a hand truck or dolly to move, but here they were able to just float them into place. Lydia crept around the room and hid behind a stack of smaller bombs that were held in place by net and anchors.

To her, Flint's plan was possible but risky. But what could be more risky than dying, anyway? Flint had no intention of dying and going down with the ship. But Lydia wasn't willing to risk a simple bluff. To her, the stakes were higher. They compromised: If his plan failed, she fully intended to destroy the ship. A war might still happen, but at least Troy wouldn't be there to escalate it.

As Lydia worked on one of the straps to free a small bomb, she overheard the men talking.

"Why does Troy want us to target Alaska? Wouldn't a more obvious place like the White House be better?"

"It has to believably come from Russia."

"Still, a submarine could hit the capitol, couldn't it?"

"I don't know. He's got everything all planned out."

"Well, do we set the bomb off in the air, on the ground, or below ground?"

"A typical Russian nuke would go off above ground. I don't know how far above, but we could try for one hundred feet."

Lydia listened as she carefully worked on freeing a bomb from its hold-down. As soon as she had one of the straps undone, she tugged at the closest unit. It came free, but not without shifting a few of the others. Lydia winced at the sound, certain that it would give her position away. For a few tense seconds she waited, holding her breath. The two men had gone silent, and she was positive they could find her by following the sound of her thumping heart. Almost sure of her inevitable capture, she prepared herself mentally to spring out in a surprise attack against her stalkers.

But before she was able to maneuver herself to a good angle, one of them spoke up. "Troy, we didn't expect you to come down here for this."

"I wasn't going to," her brother's familiar voice sounded. "But with Lydia and her friend on the loose, I wanted to make sure everything went smoothly."

"Any idea where they might be?"

"Well, when I left the helm, I could have sworn

that I heard them in the nature room, but if they are there, I couldn't find them. But to be safe, I dispatched several men to search the area."

Lydia started breathing a little easier, knowing that she was temporarily safe from detection. She then began to study the bomb she'd freed. The outer shell was about the size of a small beach ball, with little more than a foot and a half diameter. The outer metal jacket was held together by four metal screws. On one spot, a hinged panel, not unlike the cover of a gas cap on a car, waited for her prying fingers.

Upon opening the panel, she found a small touch-screen tablet that was the same size as a smartphone. As far as Lydia knew, it might even be a smartphone. There was, however, only one app on the home screen. The app was a targeting program, meant to deliver the bomb to a certain location on Earth. Once the target destination was entered, a countdown timer would begin. This would give the crew enough time to place the bomb inside one of the vacuum chambers and get the air sucked out before it actually launched itself.

All Lydia had to do was to set the target for anywhere but Earth, and let the countdown timer reach zero. Since the bomb worked on the same principle as the ship's propulsion drive, when it eventually created the pocket of space around it, the air particles that would split should cause a chain reaction and destroy Troy's ship, just like Mars had been destroyed thousands of years earlier.

Lydia fiddled with the small touch screen, only to find that it was firmly set to target locations on or around Earth. She guessed this was the case because of all the careful calculations required to hit an exact target there. It likely took all the device's computing power and memory just to perform that function. There was no reason the crew would have cared to program any targets away from Earth. She didn't want to let the bomb get there, because if she did set it off, she wouldn't be using a vacuum for the launch. So if it did manage to get all the way to Earth without destroying itself, then it might destroy Earth's atmosphere also when the burning portion inside of the bubble reentered. She recalled that Troy did hit a Russian satellite, so she could try for the upper atmosphere; but still, she didn't dare risk it.

The only option she seemed to have was to find the outer wall of the ship and remove the propulsion device. Thus the bomb would never leave the ship, but would only think that it did. When it detonated, if placed well, it should have enough punch to blow a hole in the side of the ship.

Currently there was another problem. Troy and the other two men were about to launch one of the nuclear bombs. The time for Flint's plan was running thin. She had to act now to buy him a couple more minutes, then, if necessary, destroy the ship anyway.

She set the countdown and it started ticking away, from sixty seconds. Then, pushing the tablet out of the way, she attempted to remove the spherical propulsion device. She couldn't pull it out, but she was able to bend some of the nodes that were around it so they were no longer touching the piece of hardware. Then, with only five seconds left on the countdown, she threw the bomb against a wall and let it bounce into the middle of the room where Troy and the other two were floating. There was a delay between the time when the bomb should have activated and when it was supposed to blow up. This was meant to be reserved for travel time. In these precious few seconds, Lydia freed another bomb and pushed off in the direction of the doorway.

Letting her next bomb float ahead of her, she tightly placed the palms of her hands over her ears as she drifted out of the room. The concussion of the bomb behind her was still louder than anything that she had ever heard before, mostly due to the confined space, and her whole body felt crushed when it exploded. She did notice, however, that not only was she still in one piece, but the bomb had not destroyed the ship, either. In fact, she doubted the small bomb had even hurt Troy or anything in the weapons room. It was mostly used for precision targets, and would need to be perfectly placed for any effectual damage to be inflicted. But the fact it had detonated would definitely create a commotion and delay.

Happy to be alive, she scrambled to find a safe place to work on and place the second bomb. She hoped that her little stunt had at least bought her time enough for Flint to send a message before Troy could recover and launch the nuke. Besides, if Flint's plan worked, she might still live beyond this day.

Chapter 43

Flint had found his way to the upper deck and hid inside the spacious greenhouse, where he planned to survey the control room. Spinning upside down, he'd positioned himself above the entrance of the room so he could float down a little and drift back up again to spy across the hallway into the brains of the ship.

He had just gotten into position when he overheard the end of Troy's speech. He managed to hide above the door seconds before Troy exited the helm. Flint was glad that Troy was still thinking in the same two-dimensional perspectives that had bound him when there was gravity. He entered the green room with his stunner at the ready, took a good slow look around the room, but neglected to look directly above his head where Flint and Monk were silently positioned.

Clicking on his portable radio, Troy ordered Grisha and Kore to bring four men to the hydropon-ics room. "This is my ship, Lydia!" he yelled into the room. "What do you really hope to accomplish? Show yourself now, or I can't guarantee your safety!"

Troy paused for a few seconds, then called out, "Fine! Have it your way!" He then left, crawling his way to the weapons room.

"Come on," Flint said to Monk. "This place is about to get a little crowded." He had no idea where Grisha or Kore were, but he didn't want to be trapped inside when they arrived. Flint wasn't a moment too quick, either, because right as he got back into the hallway, he heard voices coming from the lower deck. In sec-onds Grisha would be upon them, and Flint was all too aware of the Russian's temperament.

Once Flint and Monk were inside the luxurious control room, Flint shut and locked the only door. Pulling out his pistol, he quickly convinced the star-tled officers to surrender their stun guns. Flint found the intercom console and announced to those pres-ent, "My name is Flint, and this is Monk. You might as well know that I have complete control of this ship. If any one of you opposes me, we will not hes-itate to kill you. As added insurance, Lydia, Troy's sister, has secured one of your bombs, and either at my command, or if she doesn't hear from me soon, she will detonate it and destroy this ship."

"You're too late to stop anything," one man com-mented.

"What's your name?" Flint asked.

"Jublein, Bernard Jublein."

"Well, Jublein Bernard Jublein," Flint added, "if I really am too late to stop anything, then you shouldn't mind taking my orders, since nothing I do could hurt your plans, right?"

The gawky technician muttered something under

his breath, but found no words to combat with. Flint then gave his first order. "To start with, I want all power cut to the weapons room. Nothing further is to leave this ship."

Everybody remained motionless. "Well, what's the problem?" he asked.

Again Bernard was the one to reply. "This isn't the starship *Enterprise*. We don't have the ability to reroute or cut power to certain parts of the ship at will. This is more like a boardroom in a large corporate building. We have navigation control here, but other than that, we just issue orders to the other parts of the ship."

Flint wasn't sure if he believed the snooty nerd, so he decided to test his resolve. Flint pushed off the main chair and floated over to Bernard, who was strapped into a chair of his own. Then, putting him in a headlock, he jammed the pistol into his temple. "From what I know of Troy, he's far too controlling to let an arrangement like that slide. Now if you value your life, you will shut down the weapons room."

The techie had clearly never had his life threatened, and he began to shiver with fear. He pleaded with Flint to believe him. Either the man was being honest or he was an amazing actor, but Flint was compelled to release him, but not before giving him a brutal pistol whipping as an example that he was serious.

"Which one of you controls communications to Earth?" Flint asked the crew. Someone pointed to Bernard who was barely conscious, trying to nurse the wound.

Great, Flint thought. "Monk, watch my back. I'm going to try and get a message out to Fran."

Monk took hold of Troy's pilot chair and braced himself at the ready to spring on anyone who dared oppose them. Flint whispered in Bernard's ear, "Try anything, and either Monk or I will kill you." He then began to familiarize himself with Bernard's console. A simple phone call would be difficult, since it would take anywhere from five to fifteen minutes for a signal to pass back and forth. Bernard, however, was also set up to send e-mails or text messages, so Flint wrote an abbreviated message and sent it to Fran's phone. He mentioned that the threats and videos that were fueling the war talks were from GRIP. With any luck, Fran could use that information, and show the powers-that-be just who was really manipulating them.

No sooner had Flint sent the message than a pounding came at the door. "Well, Monk," Flint asked, "how likely do you think it is that Lydia would be pounding on that door?"

Monk replied, "Titus 1:12. 'One of themselves, even a prophet of their own . . . evil beasts.'"

"I figured as much," Flint replied. He braced himself against a console and waited as the door was slowly pried open, and caught sight of Grisha, his face red from the strain of opening the locked door. A few pops were heard as the door finally gave way to his brute strength. Then the reddened face turned another shade darker from hate and fury as he met gazes with Flint. His wicked grimace etched what Flint knew would be a permanent scar on his memory.

As Grisha and the others with him forced their way into the room, Monk quietly quoted, "Luke 11:4. 'And forgive us our sins; for we also forgive every one that is indebted to us. And lead us not into temptation; but deliver us from evil.'"

Then, as if heralded in by divine providence, the whole ship shook with thunder as if an explosion

marked the beginning of what could be Flint's last
fight.

Chapter 44

Flint tucked his gun into his shorts. Normally basketball shorts wouldn't hold a gun, but these were a little too tight and served well enough as a holster. Then, with an acrobatic kick off a computer console, he contorted his body and managed to flip so that he was flying feet first toward Grisha. Grisha seemed pleased at the prospect of a rematch. He even tucked away his stun gun and pushed off to meet Flint halfway.

However, just before they met, Monk surprised them both by intercepting Grisha with a powerful kick. Where Monk's shoe made contact, a hidden tear of skin under the Russian's shirt darkened the garment with blood as the boxer drifted off course. With him out of the way, Flint was able to refocus his attack on Kore and the others who were pushing and pulling themselves through the opened door. This all happened so suddenly that they didn't have time to draw their stun guns before Flint slammed into them like a 165-pound bowling ball.

From there things turned really interesting. The crew that had previously been strapped into their consoles were now joining the fight. Punches were almost ineffective, as they would throw off all control in the weightless environment. Even though there were now close to a dozen men attacking Monk and Flint, the result was more in Flint's favor. Monk and Kore seemed to be the best at maneuvering through the zero gravity room, and Flint was fair. But everyone else kept getting in their way. One person would be about ready to grab Flint, and another would bump into him or her, completely throwing off their advantage. Even the proud Grisha was struggling to lay hold of Flint.

One of the crew realized that they were getting nowhere, and she tried to hit Flint with her stun gun. Her first shot stunned a fellow crewman who drifted in the way at the last second, but it inspired someone else to attempt the same. Flint was able to see the man level a stun gun on him. Though it seemed unsportsmanlike, and ungentlemanly, Flint punched Kore in the back as she sailed above his head, causing himself to float in the opposite direction just as the wire prongs from the stunner raced over his shoulder and into the navigation console.

Sparks flew everywhere, and Flint thought he heard someone mention that the flight controls were damaged. Flint wasn't sure if that meant that he would no longer be able to pilot the ship back home, but it gave him another idea. "Monk, get me a stunner if you come across one!" he shouted to his friend, who was systematically grabbing people and using them as a shield while he put them in a sleeper hold.

Monk obliged by taking his current victim's stunner and threw it to Flint. Flint caught it, and jammed it into the closest light, sending a surge of electricity into the circuit, shorting out the lights for the whole room. With the lights out, Flint made for the door. One crewman followed but was bumped out of the way by Monk, causing the man to run headfirst into the wall next to the doorway.

Once Monk was out, Flint motioned for him to head to the lower level. Flint then repeated the process of shorting out the lights. This time every hallway light went out. Flint then reached into his pocket and pulled out the two stones he'd held on to from the cave where he had discovered the Martian moss. The stones gave a dim glow, enough to at least guide their way through the darkened hallways. Tossing one to Monk, and keeping one for himself, they made for the weapons room.

He figured that Grisha and Kore would be close behind him, but with his head start and the pitch-black hallways, Flint was sure they would be moving more cautiously. Flint and Monk only revealed the stones enough to see where they were and what was ahead. They didn't want to use them the whole time, lest the glow give their position away.

Flint only had to short out the lights in one other hallway before the whole ship was dark. The wiring in the ship was so poorly designed that even the rooms next to each hallway were darkened by the occasional shock to the hallway lighting. This temporarily gave Flint and Monk the full advantage, at least until the crew either reset a breaker somewhere or found flashlights. Flint wondered if something like this was in GRIP's contingency plan. With Troy's gaudy self-confidence, Flint doubted that the aspiring tyrant had ever imagined anything going wrong with his ship.

It wasn't long before Flint heard the sound of metal thudding against the moss-covered walls. He risked revealing his position by pulling out the light again. It showed him Lydia, and she seemed alarmed to have been found. She tried to move in the opposite direction, but Flint called out to her. With her weightless drift already set in motion, Lydia had to wait until she reached another wall before she could stop her flight.

Once they were together, Flint asked, "I heard an explosion earlier. You didn't have anything to do with that, did you?"

Lydia explained what had happened, and Flint updated her with his news.

"I was afraid we wouldn't make it out of here alive," Lydia admitted.

Flint wrinkled his brow and forehead in a quizzical expression. "When have you ever known me to give up? But just so you know, we can't pilot this ship back to Earth, the controls were damaged. Even still, that doesn't mean that we're done for. I think I have one more idea."

"From what I've seen," Lydia explained, "Troy doesn't have escape pods. If this ship's navigational ability is damaged—how do you expect us to get back home alive?"

"Oh ye of little faith," Flint assured. "It'll be easy. After all, I've gotten out of some tough ones before. I came here in a ship, so why not just leave in that same ship?" Without waiting for an answer, he sprang out toward the cafeteria. "Let's hurry before they catch up to us."

Lydia left her bomb floating there and followed. "But if your ship works the same as this one, won't it kill us all when you start it up?"

"I didn't say it was without risks. But it's our only chance. After all, your Martian ancestors made it to Earth after having fried their planet. We could make it," Flint offered.

Lydia replied, "If it does work, which it may not, the only way I see it happening is if we take off and immediately disengage the bubble once we're outside the ship. This will have to happen in a split second to release the heat into space before it has a chance to destroy us."

"That's thinking," Flint said with a smile, knowing full well that she had little confidence in the success of it. They then listened as the ship's intercom, which apparently wasn't affected by the shorted lights, came to life. An unfamiliar voice was urging all crew to find and kill them. This spurred all three of them on to reach Mao's ship even faster.

The three swam as quickly as possible through the weightless environment. Speed was a tricky thing to master in zero gravity. Too slow, and not only would GRIP catch up, but they might find themselves trapped, slowly drifting but with nothing in arms reach to propel them along or to help them maneuver. On the other hand, if they went too fast, then impact against a perpendicular wall, or evens scraping against a parallel wall could really hurt, possibly causing an injury that might hold them all up. Flint hoped as they flew down the corridors that Mao's ship hadn't been discovered by anyone else yet. Eventually someone had to pass the cafeteria and notice it.

There was one other big problem that Flint chose not to tell Lydia at that moment. He was sure that Mao's ship would be too small for all of them to fit in. He had already decided that Lydia and Monk were to go, and he would stay. Once inside the cafeteria,

Lydia took a good hard look at the ship, and turned to face Flint. "We can't all fit inside that thing!" she pointed out.

"Are you kidding?" Flint said with skepticism. "Take another look."

Lydia turned around to reexamine the ship, and Flint took out his gun. Then, grabbing her from behind, he brought the butt of the gun down hard against her skull, knocking her unconscious.

"Whew," Flint exhaled. "I'm glad that worked. Monk, she was right; there is only room for two on Mao's ship. I need you to get her home."

Monk understood but began to protest. Flint cut him off. "It's already decided. Monk, you're the best friend a guy like me could have. Please take care of her."

Flint, having only ever guessed about Monk's feelings, had no doubt now as to his emotional state. He'd only ever seen Monk show emotion once before, but now found his good friend with a tear descending from those deep dark eyes. Flint embraced Monk, and Monk for the first and last time returned the gesture. He then quoted, "John 15:13. 'Greater love hath no man than this, that a man lay down his life for his friends.'"

Collecting himself, Flint briefly explained how to operate Mao's ship, and even though Monk had a perfect memory, Flint reminded him about Lydia's suggestion to disengage the drive system immediately upon clearing the ship. Then, with a little effort, they placed Lydia inside, followed by Monk. Flint shut the hatch and drifted back a few feet. A thought entered his head that he quickly forced out. Yes, he did want to be in there with Lydia, and to see if they could restart their life together. But it was unthinkable to choose himself over Monk. Instead he waited to see them off, knowing full well that as soon as Monk launched the small craft, he would likely be incinerated. But at least it would be quick, and he would die having no regrets.

Chapter 45

Troy was just regaining consciousness from the explosion a few minutes earlier. He grabbed his head in an attempt to stop the throbbing pain. As the haze in his mind cleared, the memory returned of seeing one of his own bombs bouncing off a wall and flying toward him. The other two men in the room took the brunt of the explosion and looked dead. Upon self-examination, Troy discovered a piece of shrapnel in his own leg and pulled out the twisted, muscle-grabbing metal. The pain was excruciating as it came out, pulling a strip of muscle and throwing a slow-moving, beady stream of blood across the room. The pain almost caused him to fall unconscious again. In fact, his whole vision went dark, only the agony didn't stop.

He blinked a few times, trying to recover his vision, not willing to believe that he was hurt badly enough to go blind. A small panic started to rise in his gut, the type that causes one to feel nauseous and helpless. *It can't be*, he told himself. *Not me!* Troy's eyes were wide open but everything was pitch-black. Then he noticed something that suddenly relieved his terror: a small green LED from inside the weapons launch panel. A minute later his eyes began to adjust to what he now realized was a light failure. The computers were still working, and he activated one, using the dim screen to supply the illumination needed for him to safely start moving about the room.

The nuke was now a lower priority. He could hardly believe that anyone, especially his own sister, would be willing to sacrifice her life by destroying the ship. But now that he suspected her intentions, he needed to find and stop her before she succeeded in killing them all. Reaching for his radio, he called out, "Kore, Grisha—I just ran into Lydia down here in the weapons room. She set off a bomb, and I think she plans to do it again. She needs to be stopped before she blows a hole in the ship."

Grisha came back on the radio, "She's not only one we have to worry about. We just had fun little run-in with Flint and his retard sidekick."

"Flint!" Troy exclaimed. "How did he get on-board?"

"I do not know!" Grisha replied. "But navigation is broken, and he has shorted our lights. Do you still have lights in weapons room?"

"No," Troy replied, his frustration boiling by now. "Find them, and when you do, kill them this time!"

"Don't worry," Kore's voice came through. "They are as good as dead."

"Hurry up," Troy ordered. "Pull every man and woman from their post if you have to. Remember, Lydia has a bomb, and might use it at any minute."

Within seconds the ship's intercom came on, and a groggy-sounding Bernard was calling all hands to search for and kill the intruders. Troy began searching the room for anything that could be used as a light and a weapon. His stun gun had floated away somewhere, and since the hallways had no windows, they would be pitch-black. At last he found a tool kit, which contained an eighteen-volt battery-operated light. A little more searching revealed a screwdriver, which he armed himself with.

The maintenance room wasn't far away. It was near an exterior wall, and he knew that if he didn't find Lydia there, he would at least find the breaker box for the ship. With a little light, his crew should be better able to find the fugitives. Already there were members of the crew floating down the hallways in search of them. Some had cell phones to light the way, which was their only practical use on the ship. Others were blindly feeling their way through the ship.

Upon reaching the maintenance room, Troy found one of his bombs floating in the hallway just outside the room. It had to be the one that Lydia stole, and he opened the panel to inspect it. To his surprise, it had not yet been tampered with. It was not activated, and therefore, posed no risk. But why would she have brought the bomb out here, just to abandon it? Maybe she had come to her senses and realized she was making a mistake. Or could it be that one of his crew had already caught her before she could detonate it? Whatever the case might be, he carefully entered the maintenance room. Upon finding it empty, he went to the breaker box, pulling the breaker panel door open, whereupon he pointed his flashlight in. The ship's electrical system was very simple, more simple than some people's homes.

Within seconds, he found the tripped breakers and reached in to flip them back on.

Chapter 46

Less than a minute after Flint had sealed Monk and Lydia into Mao's demo ship, he heard a sizzling coming from the compartment that held the propulsion drive. His heart sank, and he knew that the damaged propulsion device had likely burned out after his last flight. Monk then emerged from within, and they opened the compartment to find the part smoking. It was clearly beyond their ability to repair this time.

Monk looked at Flint and asked in his own unique way: "'And I turned myself to behold wisdom, and madness, and folly: for what can the man do that cometh after the king? Even that which hath been already done.' Ecclesiastes 2:12."

"Monk, I really do admire your commitment to the faith," Flint commented. He then suggested, "This was the device that Troy used to reverse engineer the propulsion technology from. He has one of these that works on every bomb in the ship. All we have to do is find the bomb that Lydia was working with and swap parts.”

Leading the way, Flint raced back out of the cafeteria and toward the area where they had met back up with Lydia a few minutes ago. There were men and women all over the ship, looking for them, but in the darkness they were able slip past most of them, pretending to be fellow crewmen. They were just about to reach that point where the bomb should have been when the lights flickered back on.

Voices and shouting started from everywhere, and Flint followed Monk into the first open door that they found. Inside they saw the bomb, and Monk went to work trying to open it up. Flint was almost caught off guard when a shadow came over him. Instinctively he flipped his body around just as Troy drove a screwdriver down onto him.

Had he not acted so quickly, the dull shaft of the tool would have gone directly into his back, undoubtedly puncturing his vital organs. But as it was, the muscle of his lean shoulder caught the tool and ripped it out of Troy’s hand instead. Flint flinched back in pain, but didn’t have enough time to pull it out before Troy was bearing down on him again.

Monk almost left his bomb to help, but Flint called out, “I got him—you take care of the bomb!” Flint then continued to struggle with Troy; his useless shoulder gave him quite the disadvantage, especially each time the handle was bumped, sending jolts of pain like he had never felt before.

Flint fumbled for the stun gun that he’d seized earlier and used on the lights, but he couldn’t find it. He did still have his empty Chinese pistol, and it gave him an idea.

His strength was fading, and he knew that Troy’s

confidence was increasing, but he had to give Monk enough time to finish. Flint also knew that at any moment the room would be flooded with more crewmen, so he kicked off of Troy and flew toward the doorway, locking it just as somebody on the other side was trying to get in. Next to the door was a waste bin with a spring lid. The lid was jammed half open by a used aerosol can of what had been black spraypaint. Flint guessed that it had been used when they were back on Earth, but hadn't gotten removed before their accelerated takeoff.

Discreetly pulling the can from the jaws of the waste bin, Flint simultaneously made no attempt to hide the gun that he was pulling from his waist. He knew that Troy would soon come to him again, and come he did. He flew at Flint feet first, making sure to land one good foot on Flint's already stabbed shoulder.

Flint tried to spin in order to soften the blow on the tender nerves, and in so doing, he felt the gun get torn from his hand. When his spin was completed, he found himself staring into the barrel of his own pistol, with Troy on the smart end.

"This has been fun, Flint," he said. "But it ends here." Troy then pulled the trigger on the pistol.

Flint brought the spray can up as the hammer struck, and to Troy's surprise, nothing happened. Troy looked at Flint, confused by the gun's refusal to fire. Flint just pressed on the aerosol's spray nozzle. The paint can was empty, just like Flint's gun, but even without any paint, some of the aerosol and thinner remained. The stinging chemical burned Troy's eyes and caused him to retreat in blinding pain.

During the commotion, Monk was able to remove the part from the bomb that was needed, and unlocked the door to the hallway. Monk was first out the door, and his agility allowed him to slip past every other person in the corridor. They didn't even notice Flint as they all gave pursuit to Monk. But since Monk would need a free minute to insert the device into Mao's ship, Flint decided to buy his friend as much time as possible.

Exhausted, he still grabbed the bomb and carried it out of the room, making sure to bang it against the doorway on his way out. As he had hoped would happen, someone turned and noticed him. "He's got the bomb—stop him!"

Monk was ignored as everyone turned and pursued Flint instead. Flint went as quickly as he could down the hallway until he reached another open doorway. Ducking inside he shut and locked the door. He remembered that Grisha had forced open the door to the control room earlier, and he guessed there were only a couple of minutes before these men did the same here.

Looking around the room, he discovered several other bombs strapped down. He had inadvertently barricaded himself inside the weapons room. Two dead men were floating awkwardly around the room. A third man, who must have been there trying to secure the room, showed his face as he fired his stun gun at Flint.

Flint deflected the prongs with the metal orb he was still holding, and then warned the man to lose his stun gun or he would activate the bomb. He was bluffing, since it would take a minute to figure out how to even activate the thing, but his adversary didn't know that it wasn't ready to blow.

The man relented, letting the stun gun drift away. Flint approached the man, and right as he floated up against a wall, Flint jammed the bomb into his face, causing the man's head to not only hit the metallic shell of the bomb, but also hit the hard wall behind. The man drifted away unconscious, and Flint allowed himself to relax for a moment.

Soon everyone would barge through that door, and he would likely be killed. Flint only hoped that Monk would be able to launch Mao's ship before that happened. He much preferred to die by having the ship blow up than by having Troy's men beat him to death.

Chapter 47

Monk was flying down the hallway. He felt like an arrow shooting straight and deadly. Since making his way past the first crowd, he had been met twice by somebody trying to stop him. But since he was going to kill everyone on the ship by launching Mao's craft, anyway, he didn't hesitate to kill the couple of men who tried to bar his way. He was swift about it, and they didn't even know what happened to them.

Behind him, the crowd that began pursuit had changed targets and proceeded in the opposite direction. His dear friend Flint had managed to distract them, and Monk knew that it was to allow him time to fix Mao's ship, and escape with Lydia. Already he missed his only real friend, and he wondered why Flint had chosen to stay behind when he himself would have been a better candidate. Flint always had a good reason, though, and Monk knew better than to question his judgment.

Once in the cafeteria, he found two more crewmen. One he recognized as Grisha, the other was the mean-looking woman that he knew to be Kore. Grisha was in the process of looking inside the hatch of Mao's ship when Kore warned him of Monk's presence.

The boxer was well aware of Monk's reputation, and left the hatch to subdue his only conscious opponent. Kore also moved in to provide backup in case Grisha couldn't handle him. Both of them shot their stun guns at Monk, but he was moving so fast through the air that they couldn't help but miss. Upon reaching one end of the room, he let go of the propulsion devise while he dealt with these two.

He found the fight to be mostly even, even though he was outnumbered. Kore was able to match his agility, while Grisha was able to match some of his martial prowess, thus making the fight interesting. Monk would have easily been able to take on either one individually, but combined they proved to be challenging.

Adding to the difficulty, Monk's mind was still somewhat split, as he was also contemplating Flint's inevitable death. Sure, he was giving his life for Monk and Lydia to live, but it was also unlike him to abandon all hope of survival.

Monk dodged a blow from Kore, just as Grisha came down hard from the other end. Monk didn't mind the pain, as it was manageable. He instinctively bent his body to absorb some of the impact, resulting in a spin that allowed him to counter the attack. He was fighting on pure instinct, letting his mind dwell on Flint.

He recalled that when Flint had distracted the crew, he was heading in the direction of the weapons room. In fact, before entering the cafeteria, Monk saw him duck into a room at the far end of the hallway, which could very well have been the armory. Monk contemplated for a moment, dodged a kick from Grisha, and wondered if there was any way Flint could use that room to his advantage. A thought did pop into his mind, and he hoped it was possible.

The idea was so simple and he was sure that if anyone else could think of it, Flint could. Monk gave silent thanks to God for this fight, and the delay that it was causing to his launch. He knew that he would eventually have to put all of his energy into the fight, and finish it before more help arrived to stop him. He only hoped that Flint could manage things on his end in the few minutes before Monk ended this skirmish and fixed the ship.

Monk dragged the fight out for another two minutes before he dealt a critical blow to Kore, leaving only Grisha to contend with. Grisha, however, surprised him by managing to get him into a submission hold. Monk knew better than to have allowed it, but Grisha had feigned one attack then fallen into a completely different one, taking him completely off guard.

Monk realized that he had two options. The first would require him to dislodge his shoulder in an attempt to escape, and the other was to allow Grisha to snap his neck. So really he had only one choice. With a twisting jerk, he popped his shoulder out of its socket; something he had never done before. The sensation was torturous, but it gave him the slip.

With one arm still being held on to by Grisha, Monk noticed that the crippled Kore was leveling her stun gun at him. Monk decided that the best way to reset his shoulder and avoid Kore's stunner was to fold himself back into Grisha's arms.

Monk watched Kore for the perfect moment, that

instant when her hate intercepted with her aim. Monk had seen it before in people's eyes—that fateful flash that passed across one's face when they made the decision to act, or in her case pull the trigger. As soon as he saw it, he pulled Grisha in. Grisha attempted to renew his hold, but Monk used the opportunity to pop his shoulder back into place. It was as painful a task as dislocating it had been, but it also allowed him to use Grisha as a shield. The prongs from Kore's weapon flew true, right into Grisha's back, causing the boxer to spasm into unconsciousness.

Monk forced a smile and bowed a thank you to Kore, which made the suffering woman even angrier. She began to shriek like a blood gurgling banshee, her injuries preventing her from any significant movement as Monk casually made the necessary repairs to Mao's ship.

Chapter 48

At first Flint resigned himself to whichever demise happened first. There were the men on the other side of the door, or there was Monk's launch of Mao's ship. He glanced at the bomb he had been holding, and noticed that with exception of the explosive material, the shell was mostly empty inside. A thought then occurred to him; he still had a chance.

The small bomb wouldn't work, but the larger nukes just might. He looked around and saw that there was already one nuke loaded into the vacuum chamber. He painfully made his way over, and noticed the small tablet computer was all set to launch. He had no idea where it would send him, but he decided that it was his ticket out.

There was a large access panel on the side of the shell, and Flint grabbed the screwdriver that was still lodged in his shoulder. Clenching his teeth together, he yanked the tool from his flesh. He opened his mouth to shout, but the pain was so intense that not a sound escaped. His breath came in short labored gasps as he fought to stay conscious. His head was spinning and he ignored the door that was starting to get forced open.

As quickly as he could, he unscrewed the panel on the side of the bomb, leaving one screw loosely connected so that the panel could fall back into place when it was let go. Pivoting the panel up, he looked inside. The payload of the shell was an ominous nuclear bomb, with a simple plumbing strap to hold it in place. It only took a few twists of a screw to loosen it enough to free the actual bomb portion. On Earth this task would have taken at least two men to pull the nuke from its outer casing, but here all Flint had to do was guide it as it floated out and away from its steel shell.

Flint then memorized the control panels to the vacuum chamber before he climbed into the hollow bomb. Once inside, he reached up and pressed the launch icon on the tablet computer that was attached to the bomb casing. This started a two-minute countdown. He then fumbled outside the vacuum chamber till he found the launch button on the vacuum chamber. It had a one-and-a-half-minute countdown.

As soon as he pressed it, he withdrew his arm into the bomb shell, and let the access panel swing back down to seal him in. He parted the panel slightly to watch the door of the vacuum chamber close, the whole time being nervous with the anticipation of having no air to breathe once the vacuum started. As the door was closing, he saw beyond it to the weapons room door. Troy's face had become visible. His eyes were red with rage and chemical burn. He was trying so hard to force his way inside the room that he was actually getting in the way of his crew who were working on the door. Flint knew that he would be in the room before the countdown to his launch finished. But that was the least of his concerns.

Monk was already overdue to launch Mao's ship. Flint wouldn't be surprised if Monk's launch came before the countdown to his own makeshift escape pod had a chance to launch. Right before the vacuum chamber door sealed, Flint sucked in a deep breath of air. If he could survive holding his breath in the Egyptian well, then he was sure he could manage holding it long enough here. With one hand pressed tightly to his stab wound, Flint waited for the next minute as the vacuum chamber depressurized.

Only after the door was sealed did he realize the unanticipated difficulty of holding his breath in a vacuum, but as the chamber began to suck the air out, he remembered his scuba-diving training. If he did continue to hold his breath, then his lungs would explode from the negative pressure outside his body. When scuba diving, one had to breathe continuously while ascending from the depths of the high-pressure environment of the sea to the lower pressures above. So to avoid bursting his lungs, he began to softly hum, a trick used by scuba divers in an emergency ascent.

Humming gave the lungs a steady pressure release. Since the air in his lungs was expanding as the pressure inside the bomb decreased, this little trick did not leave Flint wanting for air. But he was just beginning to realize the other problems associated with being inside a vacuum. With the air pressure rapidly going out, he would undoubtedly fall unconscious until the bomb reentered normal space.

He almost welcomed the fog of unconsciousness.

His whole body burned with pain. His skin felt like each cell was bursting, his eyes felt like they were being sucked from their sockets, and his tongue felt like it was dipped in a boiling pot of oil. On top of all that, the wound he was nursing in his shoulder surged with renewed pain as if a paddle bit drill was reaming out his puncture wound. He had been counting down from two minutes, and was at thirty seconds till launch when he lost consciousness.

Chapter 49

Fran's first several pleas were met with skepticism and ridicule. Flint had indeed made his way onboard the GRIP ship orbiting Mars. Fran had little doubt that Flint would manage to get there, but what he hadn't expected was the e-mail that the maverick had sent him. It did explain a lot, however. All the recent tension between Russia and the U.S. and several other countries had been forgeries, not from neighboring countries, but from GRIP.

Fran had contacts in several government entities, on all sides of the world. At first they had all refused to believe this was an elaborate coup from a terrorist organization. Fran had to pull every string and favor he'd ever saved up to get anybody to follow up on his story. All he was asking was that they confirm his outrageously science fiction tale by consulting their observatories, which Fran had already been using to search for the ship. The Americans were the first to confirm the ship, with the Chinese backing them up.

Fran was on the telephone with the Russian ambassador as they were repositioning their own satellite to view Mars. "You know, if this is a hoax on your part, war will ensue?" he mentioned as he was observing a video feed from their orbiting telescope.

"I'll defect, and personally lead the nuclear assault on America, if you can't see the ship," Fran assured.

"Let's hope for both our sakes that you are correct," the politician replied.

Fran waited patiently as the ambassador talked him through everything that he was witnessing on his computer monitor.

"We see Mars now, but no ship yet. We are zooming in on the quadrant you say they can be seen. There is something, but I can't make it out yet."

Fran was on the edge of his seat. If they confirmed the ship, the world war that was threatening might not happen. Fran was, however, startled when the ambassador asked, "What just happened?"

"What do you mean, what just happened?" Fran countered.

"One minute we see something, next second we see explosion. Now we see nothing."

Fran quickly refreshed his own computer to see what the American telescopes had picked up. It took thirty seconds for the download to complete, and he watched as the GRIP ship not only exploded but blew up with the force of a nuclear blast. "That, my dear ambassador," Fran said soberly, "was our operative laying down his life to save the world from the worst terrorist we have ever known."

"If this is true, my condolences," he replied. "We will be analyzing our images to confirm. Please make sure that the U.S. also sends us their information."

"I'll put in a call," Fran replied. "And I don't know how much the Chinese are going to want to share, but they recently stormed the headquarters of this terrorist group. They might be willing to confirm what I've told you."

They exchanged a few formalities before hanging up. Fran ran his hands across his balding head. This had been too close for comfort, and though it would likely result in more-peaceable relations, there were already some international bridges that needed mending. He swiveled around in his chair to see a teary-eyed Dusty staring at the screen that had just shown Troy's ship being destroyed.

"I'm sorry you had to see that," Fran tried to comfort as he stood up to hold her. She said nothing, only letting her tears wet his shirt.

After a few minutes, her sobs began to ease. She attempted to change the subject, but the shake in her voice gave her away as she asked, "Without GRIP, do we really need to keep passing out this moss?"

Fran knew that she cared little for the moss at this point, but just as one made conversation with an old acquaintance they'd accidentally run back into, he struggled forward with his best explanation, even though it would likely fall on distracted ears. "The moss was supposed to give the world hope. Flint may have stopped the war, but oil is still a couple of years from making a full recovery. The world is still going to pass through a depression because of the shock, so more than ever, we need to give everyone something to work toward and believe in. I can't think of anything better than a fully renewable energy source such as the moss."

Another tear slid down Dusty's face. "Flint saved the world from war, but without him, we would never have even found this moss. I hope the world remembers him."

Fran reflected, "Often the best heroes come from the most ordinary of men."

Chapter 50

August 13th

Slowly, fuzzy eyes blinked. Blurred shapes came into focus as his eyes adjusted. Daylight shone through a small window, gracing the spot where his feet were covered. He shifted on the comfortable mattress. Nothing made any sense. The last thing he remembered was seeing the angry face of Troy. Flint was aware that death had not come yet, because he hurt far worse than any dead man should. He took a good look around him, but his mind was still not fully awake, so he closed his eyes and tried to concentrate on clearing his head.

A faint memory came back to him like a dream. He recalled gasping the fresh air as he was experiencing a sensation like being trapped inside a falling elevator. He remembered crashing into some frigid water, and scrambling to escape the metal coffin that he had just traversed in. The cold water had zero visibility, and his weakened lungs struggled to give him the strength he needed to swim to the surface of the water. When he did manage to reach the surface, his memory faded again. He remembered seeing a man's face, but then nothing.

Now he was inside what appeared to be a log cabin. He tried to sit up in the bed, but groaned as he succumbed to a wave of dizziness. A tender voice called to him, "Easy there, friend, you've lost a lot of blood. But I'm glad to see you returning to the land of the living."

Flint let his head fall toward the direction of the voice. He made out a short, beautiful woman wearing an apron. She looked as though she had been cooking something. Her sweet smile and caring eyes set him at ease. "Where am I?" Flint asked.

"Just wait one moment, dear," she replied. "I'll go let the others know that you're awake."

Flint looked up at the ceiling, trying to make sense of everything. Not more than five minutes passed when his caregiver returned with her husband and two others. Flint squinted, then said with surprise, "Lydia? Monk? What? How?"

Lydia rushed up to Flint and kissed him gently on the lips. Tears were rushing down her cheeks. Then the husband of the sweet short-haired woman spoke up. "We weren't sure if you were going to make it for a while there, buddy."

"Forgive me if I should already know," Flint apologized. "But who are you?"

"My name is Brent Lindstrom, and this is my wife, Colette. We have a small patch of land here in Alaska, mostly for recreation. When the oil crisis hit, oil prices went sky high. Well, we figured that we should try to cash in on the boom, so we moved up here. Unfortunately for our get-rich-quick plan, but very fortunate for you, I found that I liked fishing much more than I enjoyed digging for oil.

"I was out fishing three days ago when I heard a loud thunder. The storm that just blew through here wasn't due for several more hours, so I found it odd that it would be thundering already. I looked up in the sky to see a large metal container falling about one hundred feet through the air. You landed in the water only twenty feet away from my boat. My curiosity was piqued, but imagine my surprise when I saw you swim to the surface. I don't know how you did it, because that water is cold enough to cause hypothermia within only a minute or two of exposure.

"Well, I fished you out; you were unconscious by the time I got you onboard. Then I brought you home, where my wife watched over you. We had to wait out the storm, but when the weather settled down, we were just about to put you back on the boat and take you to town when your two friends showed up here looking for you."

Lydia continued the story. "I came to, right when Monk was launching Mao's ship. He explained that you might try something like escaping in a bombshell. I remembered overhearing that GRIP was targeting this part of Alaska, so I had Monk bring us here. It took a couple of days to find you, but Brent had radioed into town that he had an injured and unknown man here. We hired a floatplane and had them drop us off as close as they could to this place. You wouldn't believe how expensive fuel is around here. Anyhow, the sea was still pretty choppy, so he didn't stick around, but we found our way here all the same. I'm just so glad that you're alive!"

Flint smiled but, noticing himself slipping again, he said, "I think I'm going to take another nap now.

But please, don't worry about rushing me to a hospital just yet."

One week later Flint and Lydia walked out onto the back of Brent's fishing trawler. With fuel so scarce and expensive, Flint guessed that Brent was barely able to pay for his fuel with the catch he would bring to market. But that didn't seem to bother the man. Brent was just happy that his proximity to such an oil rich area allowed him the chance to support his passion for fishing. This was the first full day Flint had been able to get around, and he took Brent up on an offer to go fishing. Toward the end of the day, they set out a long line on the edge of an underwater shelf, keeping it to the more shallow side. The shallow side was about fifty fathoms deep, while the other was close to two hundred, too deep for a long line. Brent promised that they would catch some mighty good halibut along this stretch of water.

They set the lines right before dark, and had planned to pull them up in the morning. But as they finished dinner, Flint decided to step out with Lydia and bask in the magnificent northern lights as they played across the sky. Monk was inside the boat listening to another one of Brent's fantastic stories. That man had either lived an adventurous life or he had quite the imagination, but he could really spin a good yarn.

Flint leaned against the rail and reminisced, "You know, it was just a few nights ago when I was sitting on a Filipino beach, thinking about the Aurora Borealis. Now I'm enjoying it for real with the one person on Earth who I really wanted to share it with."

Flint rested his arm around his wife, but she teased and pulled away, saying, "By the way, I'm still mad at you."

"Mad at me?" Flint wondered. "I thought I was your hero."

"Yeah, but remember, you pistol-whipped me on Troy's ship. You could have just said that you were going to strap yourself to a nuke and ride it down to Earth like some cartoon cowboy."

"In my defense," Flint countered, "I fully intended on dying up there to save you."

Lydia snuggled closer and kissed him. "Yeah, I know." She smiled mischievously. Then, changing the mood, she warmly added, "By the way, I got you a present."

"Oh?" Flint prodded, happy to find himself rekindling their relationship.

Lydia ran into the galley, then quickly emerged with a round object. Flint instantly recognized the black sphere as the replacement propulsion device from Mao's ship. "I thought you might like the souvenir," she said.

Flint suppressed his honest reaction and gave her a hug and a kiss. "I've really missed you, Lydia."

Lydia smiled, "You know, it's funny, but from the reports I've heard over the radio in the last couple of days, nothing is mentioned about GRIP having a spaceship. They are labeling the last week's events as an elaborate terrorist hoax. Somebody has really done a good job of covering up what really happened."

"Changing the subject?" Flint inquired jokingly.

Lydia was about to reply when she noticed a small boat motoring toward them. "Who could that be out here?" she asked. "They're coming straight for us."

Flint tried to make out the driver of the little fifteen-foot skiff. He knew it wasn't unusual to see some of these this far away from land. Most of the ocean here was landlocked between islands and mountains. What did catch his attention was the person driving the little boat. She was Chinese, and looked very familiar. Once she arrived, she threw Flint a rope, and with the agility of a sailor, found her way onto the larger trawler.

"Mr. and Mrs. Krieger, I have been looking for you," she hailed. "Flint, do you remember me?"

"Your face is familiar," Flint admitted, "but I can't place you."

"I was there when you stopped Shen Mao," she introduced. "My name is not important to you at this time, but I have two questions that are important. First off, I see that you have the engine component from the ship. Our organization will keep that from falling into malicious hands. May I take it with me?"

Flint held up the orb, then eyed the woman suspiciously. "I don't know anything about you or your organization, and I've seen firsthand what this thing is capable of doing and inspiring. As far as I'm concerned, there's only one real safe place for it." He used his good arm to send it sailing over the edge of the boat. He wasn't as strong in his left arm, but he was sure that the orb splashed far enough away to sink to the deep side of the underwater shelf.

"Fran told me to expect something like that," the woman commented. "Honestly, you are right, and I thank you for saving me the trouble."

"So you work for Fran?" Flint digested out loud.

Lydia broke in, "Wait, so are you and Fran part of the real group of Martians that my dad belonged to?"

The woman gave a slight bow of her head, and Lydia stood back trying to piece everything together. Flint spoke next. "You said you had two questions?"

"Yes. Fran was very impressed by your commitment and ability to stop both Shen Mao and Troy.

He is offering a hand of fellowship into the Nephilim Society, to which we belong, if you are willing to accept?"

"I thought you had to be part Martian to get accepted into that," Flint said. "And last I checked, I was pure human."

"Do I look like I could be a descendant of giants, Mr. Krieger? You're still thinking of GRIP. We don't actually care where your bloodline came from, whether it is from Earth, Mars, or . . ." She paused, as if she almost said too much. "We are more interested in men and women who act with wisdom and diligence," she finished.

"Please don't take this the wrong way, but I hope I never see Fran or you ever again," Flint submitted.

The woman bowed again and replied, "Fran also thought that you would say as much. Since that concludes my business here, I shall now leave you. Thank you again."

As the woman started back toward her skiff, Flint called after her, "By the way, your group is aware that the Chinese government raided GRIP's compound, right? You might have a hard time getting them to give up what they have likely found there."

"That will not be a problem," she replied. "A friend of yours, and a new recruit of ours, a man by the name of Labeeb, has made sure that they will find nothing of any significance. By the way, he sends his best wishes to you both."

Flint laughed, happy to know that Labeeb had survived. Then, as the woman started leaving, he called out one last time. "By the way, how did you find me? Do you have some other crazy secret technology that I don't already know about?"

"Yes," she smiled. "It's called a satellite phone. The one Fran gave you, I tracked you here using it."

"I thought that would have been damaged when I fell into the water," Flint said as she fired up her motor and drove away. But he had not actually looked at it since he had been back on Earth. "Remind me to destroy that phone later," Flint told Lydia.

She questioned, "Wouldn't you like to use it to call your friend Philip—let him know that you're okay?"

Flint pulled Lydia closer, "As far as Philip knows, I'm still island-hopping across the Philippines, enjoying the last of my vacation. I don't much care what he thinks for at least another week."

"Yes," Lydia remembered. "Now tell me more about you and this Dusty girl you were island-hopping with."

Flint just smiled and gave Lydia a gentle squeeze. "Dusty?" he asked inquisitively. "Who's that?"

A Word From The Author

Hello again, and thank you for reading this third and final book in my Nephilim Series. That's right, I don't have any plans to write any more in this series. Granted I'm not discounting the idea all together, I just have too many other stories that I want to tell.

As I've been releasing these first three books, it's been very interesting to see what people are starting to say about it. To a seasoned writer, this is probably common sense, but for me, it's all new. I really like learning how other people interpret the characters in my stories. Monk is a prime example. I never would have guessed it, but this has been one of the series favorite characters. The interest in Monk has almost convinced me to write his back story—*almost*. Like I said, I don't have any plans to revisit this series or any spin-offs of it in the near future.

Like Monk, many of my characters just popped into being. I've been asked how I came up with him, and I just really don't know. I had my outline for the story, but this never included him. Then, somehow, Monk appeared. You could say that the story took on a life of its own. This series would have been nothing without him. I'm very glad that he auditioned for the part.

Another character that I had envisioned one way, but found to be perceived in a completely different way was Philip Noon, the mentor/boss/father figure for Flint. Nowhere was this made more apparent to me than by Gordon Lindstrom, the talent behind the audio version of my 1st book, (and hopefully all three). The voices he came up with were great, but nothing like what I'd imagined as I'd originally put them on paper.

This whole experience, writing and subsequently publishing these books, has been such a great learning experience for me. I've always believed that the best way to learn anything is to dive in, head first, and paddle your way to the top. My biggest lesson in writing these books has been the acceptance that I am not yet where I someday hope to be. If you liked these first three books, thank you. I mean that. But I fully expect my next books to each be better than the one before.

As you may or may not know, I am only a part time writer. I wake up at 5:30 every morning and write for an hour before going off to work. I'm a general contractor, building wonderful communities in Utah. During my lunch breaks at work, I usually spend a few minutes on my blogs and website. Come evening, if I'm not doing anything with my family, then I might spend another half hour to an hour working on my books again.

At this rate, I can only complete about one book per year, or so I estimate. So if you've finished this book before my next one is released, by all means, please look me up occasionally to see when my next book is due to be released. I've said it before, but if you've read one of my books, you haven't read them all. Some author's books are so similar to each other, that you can easily predict what is about to happen next. With me, I write about those things that fascinate me at that given time. The Nephilim Series was an attempt to write an action series that tied in some biblical mysteries, my next book that I'm working on now is more of a journey type novel. It is a stand-a-lone book that follows the early life of a young man in South-East Asia. It's not a dystopian novel, but those who like dystopian books might find this one interesting. I'm very excited about it, and I think you'll really enjoy it.

As always, I try to write my books with an adult audience in mind, but since I might cross traditional genre boundaries, I suppose that I might label myself in a genre of my own. I would call this genre: Clean Adult Fiction.

Why write clean adult fiction? Well, it all started with my wife. She is a wonderful woman, who strives to keep her mind clean of all the worldly smut that seems to pollute the media today. Many in the media, whether it be movies, TV, radio, books, etc., seem to think that an unhealthy dose of sex, profanity, and violence are necessary to captivate an audience. As you may already know, I do have a little violence in my books, but I try to limit the sex and profanity to the slimmest of margins. I am a firm believer in God. I want to write my fiction so that I wouldn't cower away if Christ himself were to pick up a copy and flip through it.

Likewise, I wouldn't want my books to contain anything that would obligate you to hide my novels from your children.

Thanks again for reading.

Sincerely,
B.C. Crow

Don't forget to write a review!

There's a whole bunch of places you can leave feedback on:
Amazon, Barnes & Noble, Goodreads, Facebook, etc.
Please don't forget to do this. For a new author, your reviews are what makes a successful author.
Thank you.

Blue House Publishing

Is a Utah company

We are very proud of our heritage and where we live.
But B.C. Crow is not the only author we know who calls Utah home.

We've been collecting names of other authors who've also called Utah home. The list is long and growing.

Come visit our website at:

www.BlueHPublishing.com

Even though we don't represent them all, we want to help you discover them.

You'll find many authors you recognize, and you'll find several you've never heard of before.
Come check us out today!

Blue House Publishing would like to share a piece of Utah with you. Check out all the Utah author's we've been finding at:

www.BlueHPublishing.com

9 781943 239047